The Harrowing

Robert Dinsdale was born in North Yorkshire in 1982 and studied in Leeds. He now lives and works in London.

THE HARROWING

Robert Dinsdale

faber and faber

First published in 2009
by Faber and Faber Ltd
Bloomsbury House
74–77 Great Russell Street
London WC1B 3DA

Typeset by RefineCatch Limited, Bungay, Suffolk
Printed in the UK by CPI Mackays, Chatham

A CIP record for this book
is available from the British Library

ISBN 978–0–571–23825–5

2 4 6 8 10 9 7 5 3 1

IAGO: He hath a daily beauty in his life and it makes me ugly.

Othello

Prologue

They walk in the shadows of their redbrick haunts. It is what they have always done, these two brothers, side by side since the elder led the younger on his first faltering steps along the terrace. They know each alley and gutter, each doorstep and old man who sits upon it. This is all they have ever known, their whole lives bordered by the railway to the north and the moorland to the south: a labyrinth of red brick and grey slate and chimney-stacks that, it is said, they will soon have to leave. And so – though they know it will not be the last time, though they know they will surely have the chance again – they wander the streets in which they have been raised and visit each secret place in turn.

William and Samuel, they are called: the names of their grandfathers, now long gone and given to the ground. William, the elder, is leaner than his brother Samuel, but they share a look – sad, opaque eyes and high, crested cheeks, the traits that have been worn in their family since a time no living soul can recall. They have the same black hair on their heads, and the same widow's peak curled in a tuft. They have shared friends, and they have shared girls.

One after the other, they emerge from the yards at the brewery's edge and follow snickets deep into the sprawl. They have stolen drinks together this afternoon – though, as ever, it has been Samuel who has stooped to do the stealing, spiriting tankards from the back rooms of an inn while his brother stands angelically by. They have decided to share this day, for it may be the last that they share; the seasons might have pushed them apart these last years, but there is still something draws them back together. They have spent the afternoon telling stories; it has been a strange realisation that, though they recollect the same days, the stories that they spin are never quite the same.

Samuel picks a rock from the gutter and pitches it up the street. They are climbing a hill now, bordered on each side by the crooked terrace, and the stone disappears into one of the thin, neglected yards. It seems, after all these years, that Samuel is at last the bigger of the two. In the last months he has grown and swollen so that, now, he can look down upon his brother where once he had to crane his neck.

'You'll break a window again,' says William. He is trying to laugh, but the laughter does not suit him today; he cannot say whether this is because of the places he will be sent tomorrow or whether it is something else that troubles him.

'It doesn't matter,' answers Samuel, refusing to turn and face his brother. 'I never did get found out.'

He is remembering, now, a treasured memory of childhood, before all this began, before the streets dredged of young men to go and grapple in the Flanders mud. He might have been nine years old, or he might have been ten. They were pitching stones with some other boys. They had set up a range along one of the alleys and lined up tin cans spirited from the kitchens of their homes. The competition began in earnest, and soon there was a leader, a rotund boy from the houses on the other side of the scrub. Samuel grins as he remembers how much he had wanted to defeat that boy, how much he had wanted the rest to look at him as they now looked at that piece of gristle and bone. He can still remember the arc his final stone took as it curled over the tin cans and shattered the window of one of the neighbouring houses. He cannot remember the lashing William took as punishment in his stead – because William has never cared to tell him.

'You really want to go?' asks Samuel. It seems an incredible

thing to Samuel, that boys might truly want to go out there and die in the name of this blasted island. He has seen the looks these brave boys get, and still he wants no part in it.

'There are trains leaving in the morning. I'll be aboard, like all the rest. But I do want it, Samuel. I want to help.' William pauses, trying to read the inscrutable look on his brother's face; it is a look he has seen countless times before, his brother retreating to a place where no other soul has ever been permitted. Vaguely, William can still recall the day of his brother's birth, the moment he was handed the swaddled bundle and looked into those new, unknowable eyes. 'There are places I'll have to go first,' he continues. 'They'll send me to Catterick.'

William knows of Catterick, that little town over the hills. At the garrison there he will learn how to fasten a gas mask and wield a bayonet. Some of the boys, they had a good time at Catterick. Perhaps it will be the same for William. Perhaps it will be the making of him. Samuel, too, has heard stories of the place: a prison of shacks squatting on a hillside where, one day, he will be thrown together with boys who have never cared if he lived or he died. No doubt the captains will remember William when the time comes for Samuel to take up a gun. No doubt they will be expecting another William to stride gallantly through those doors. Already, Samuel can feel that shadow falling upon him.

'And there's nothing to be done?' he asks.

'They tried. I didn't ask them to, but they tried.'

'Yes,' says Samuel. His eyes are narrowing, now, thinking of the things his parents have done in the name of his brother. His voice, once flat and without emotion, is wavering at last. 'You didn't ask them to do a thing,' he utters, 'and still they tried.'

Their father visited an old friend at the Conscription Board only last week, but his pleas fell on deaf ears; it is a matter of some regret in the Redmond household that their eldest son will soon be going to war. It was only this morning Samuel had awoken to hear those familiar conversations stirring in the chambers beneath: his mother, distraught at William's conscription, comforted only by the words that William would still be with them for another day. Samuel had dropped silently down the stairs, then, pushed through the scullery door to see his mother entwined in the arms of his father. He had tried to speak, begun to say that he would still be there, that he would look after her – but his father's eyes had flared, there had been a hissed command, and Samuel had beaten a retreat from the room, leaving his parents to comfort each other. He has stalked the streets ever since.

'It will be over by the time the Board calls for you,' says William. Samuel is studying him, but with what intent William cannot be certain. It has been spoken of for many long months along the terrace, how William, who was bound for greater things, who might even have grown to wield a fountain pen instead of a pick, will soon be taking up a gun. Since a time immemorial, Samuel has heard it said that his brother was marked from birth to lead a better life. It is a fable that has never been told about himself.

Softly, William tries to lay a hand on his brother's shoulder. 'They wouldn't have it any other way,' he says. 'It won't come for you. It wouldn't be right.'

Samuel's silence persists. In spite of the mock kindnesses his brother professes, he has long known the way it would go. He remembers the first boys who left. He remembers knowing, even then, as the town gathered to cheer at the transports that took them away, that one day he too would be shepherded into the back of one of those wagons, that he would be unnoticed and unremarked upon as they dressed him in a soldier's garb and took him from everything he had ever known.

'Samuel?' ventures William, hoping to tease something from his brother.

'It will be over by Christmas,' mocks Samuel.

Both boys rise, then, and come to the crest of the street. The grassland is before them, lined with trees and the rags of allotments where old men and their grandchildren tend to the ditches. The streets have been devoid of young men for many months now, so that everywhere it is the same odd tableau: the very old and the very young walking together, half only just come to this grey earth, half hurrying to depart it. William stops and watches a grandmother help a child from the crumbled kerb. Many of the streets are fallen like this now; there are no longer any hands to tend them.

Samuel is the first over the road, and onto the grassland. It is called Woodhouse Moor, and for many years it was a land to which they were not permitted passage. A glowering stretch of scrub, the little townships of Leeds gather about it as if it is some prehistoric monument, or some borderland between the vales never to be claimed by any one town. William hesitates, watching his brother stride boldly over the reeds. He remembers the times when it was he who would lead Samuel along the redbrick rows. Lately, it has been different. Lately, both his brother and the world have changed. Their father, invalided from some war already forgotten in the shadow of this one, tells them the same thing every night, his words intoned like some grave sermon: we can come through this, but we will not be the same men who wandered unknowingly in.

'Samuel!' William calls. 'It's going to rain.'

He follows his brother over the road and onto the Moor. The path is lined with trees here. Nobody can recall a time before those trees. They follow, one after the other, the trail that climbs the escarpment until they reach the highest tract, a stretch of flat grass and scrub from which they can see for miles around: the tumbledown terraces and the clock tower, the spires of an abbey that neither of them have cared to visit. From here they look down upon each of the towns and ribbons of redbrick that have sprouted from the bedrock and grown against each other to make up this city. Samuel has stopped by a withered elm, gazing upon the banks of slate roofs that make up Little London, when William catches him.

'We should think about going back,' says William.

'I'll think about it,' scoffs Samuel.

They stand together for a while. Above them, the sky threatens rain. There are gusts flecked with the first droplets, and William wishes they had brought their overcoats. It was the last thing their mother shrieked at them as they left their home: they must wrap up warm. It might be the start of a new year, but spring is still a lifetime away.

'What will it be like, William?'

For the first time, William senses that there is fear too on his brother's face. Fleetingly, he allows himself to think that it is fear for what William will find on the other side of the water. It does not strike him as a vain thought.

'I don't know,' he breathes. 'I'll write. I'll write and tell you all.'

'And Lucy?' Samuel's eyes dart at his brother, as if tempting a secret.

'I'll write to her as well.'

'Write to us together,' Samuel insists. There is a warning in the way that he speaks. Since the day he first kissed her, there has been a warning written on him every time William mentions her name. He pushes on a little, to where the scrubland narrows. Through the wraithlike branches, the city sprawls. 'Dear Samuel,' he intones. 'Dear Lucy . . .' he goes on.

For a while: silence.

'Samuel,' William ventures. 'If it does come for you, I'll be waiting. They'll send you to my battalion. I'll find you there. With everything the School Board said, I might not be carrying a

6

rifle by then. I might have earned my spurs. Risen through the ranks. I won't forget you.'

Is that supposed to be a glorious thought? Samuel at William's command, as together they claw at the scaling ladders and roll over the top? Samuel might even smile at that one. William the Captain and Samuel the Private. So shall it be. So has it always been.

'You want to lead me, William? Put me at the head of the phalanx and watch them cut me down?' A thousand different memories are hurtling unchecked through Samuel's thoughts. A thousand different times, but all of them the same. 'They'd congratulate you,' he says, 'even for that.' He wants to say more, but he chokes on the thought. Valiant William Redmond, championed for the brave decisions he has made; his unknown sibling basking in an unmarked grave somewhere under the sod.

William does not know what happens next. He only knows that the rock is in his brother's hand.

Part One

WILLIAM

I

When first he opened his eyes he was alone. He could not move. It was like the night terrors he and Samuel had had when they were children, and some ancient instinct held him from panic. He lay there and breathed, and slowly he came to know that he could move again. He twitched involuntarily and his eyelids, sticky with some ugly residue, seared as they came apart.

Slowly, the room fell into focus. At first he saw everything in double, ghostly images of curtains and lanterns hovering, one on top of the other, until at last they settled. He closed his eyes and opened them again, pressed his lips together until they felt less scabrous and he could breathe without the soreness in the back of his throat. He tried to turn, but his body was in revolt, his arms and his legs as light and useless as flags flying in a gale.

He swung his legs from the bedstead.

It took a long time, but somehow he found his balance. He stood there, braced between bed and wall, and took tentative steps until, like an infant full of courage, he set out on his own. The floor was cold stone, and he felt for the first time that he was wearing no shoes. Instinctively, he lifted his hand to the back of his head; there was no hair there, only a sprawl of thin fur where it had been cut away and started to grow back.

His fingers lit upon the wire stitches in his scalp, and a twisted picture of trees roaring forced itself upon him. He was immeasurably cold.

It was a small room in which he had awoken, and he soon chanced upon a door that opened onto a long, silent passage. He stepped out, looked up and down, rested for a moment against the wall. The world was still, and each step that he took echoed loudly along the corridor. He started to walk, listening to his footfalls as they rebounded off ceilings and doors. He thought that he was the only man left.

He went past banks of windows and peered through each one. Beyond them, men lay in strange attitudes, bound in cloths or with legs set in splints. Others lay with their eyes wide open, staring glassily and unmoving at something nobody else could see. From one room to the next, William moved – and still the world was silent. He groped around a corner in the passage and saw, then, that the rooms went ever on: on each wall a window, and in each window another man lying, alive and yet dead, like the knights and maidens he had read about in stories when he was young. He stopped to get his bearings.

He did not know how far he had come. He pressed his face to a pane of glass and saw, beyond it, a man no older than he was. The man was awake, and intermittently, his body twitched and wrenched as in spasms of pain. William saw, now, that the man's face was not there, that somehow it was crumpled and sunken in against itself. He looked to the door. 'Private Hatherley,' it read, in somebody's crude scrawl. There was another word scratched in chalk beneath that. 'Gas,' it read, as if in explanation or sentence or judgement. 'Gas,' it read. 'Gas,' it ordered. William stumbled back, and tried to retrace his steps.

They bore down upon him now: men on each side, every one of them in his cell, names and afflictions daubed upon the doors. As he walked, he thought that the passageways narrowed. He thought that he was walking down some trick-some alley that would soon ensnare him, an unsuspecting insect walking headlong into a web of silk. Each row looked the same. Each corner he turned only led to another row of windows and doors and afflictions and names. Each lantern cast the same jagged shadows. Each footfall: the same dull, reverberating sound.

At last he came to the crux of two passages and saw, there, that the shadows were different. He stopped. He walked more slowly. From one of the doors, the light spilled more eagerly, refracted differently through the glass in the walls and the wood. Three doors away, he stopped and, pressing himself against the stone, craned his neck to spy upon the strange, new room. The scar at the back of his head burned suddenly hot, and when he lifted his hand he felt that it was sticky and his hair was matted. He pressed his fingers to his lips and tasted tin.

Slowly, he went to the room.

The door was ajar, and light from beyond fell into the corridor. He walked warily upon it. Yes, this had been it. This had been the room in which he first stirred. As he approached, he saw his own face looking back from the glass. It was a strange thing to see, this spectral image of himself. He was old, and there were shadows underneath his eyes. He lifted a hand, as if he might be able to touch that image and feel what was wrong.

There was another face in the glass.

'William?' somebody ventured. 'William, is that you?'

She was sitting in the room when he pushed through the doors, perched on the edge of a wooden railing, her dark eyes aglow. She was tall and she was thin, and her light hair was scraped back into a bun. William felt certain that he knew who she was. He squinted at her, and waited for something to rekindle the memory – but all that he could see, scorched on to the back of his eyes, were the trees and the scrub on

13

Woodhouse Moor, and the flurries of snow that had lashed at his face.

'Mother?' William asked.

'William?' the woman repeated, as if she had seen some spectre stalking the room, an ugly wight with the features of her child.

'Yes, Mother?'

'William?' she sobbed, and took him in her arms.

There was something different in William when he woke. That was what the people said as they drifted through the infirmary, bringing with them the foodstuffs and gifts that they offered up to him like sacrifices at an altar. They said it was in his eyes. They asked him how it felt to come from that kind of a sleep. What sort of visions had he seen while he was flailing, down there in the inky brine? There were a thousand things that William wanted to say to the nurses and the well-wishers who floated through, but of them all he said only one: that he had lived again the day of his brother's birth, and heard again each of his mother's groans as Samuel tore the caul and came, at last, into the world. He asked each of them when he might see his brother, and each of them bowed their head respectfully and uttered not a word. For days, it went on like that, until one night William's mother and father came to him and he dared not ask the question. William supposed that they must have sensed a change in him, then, because they asked him every hour if he was well. And each time, William mouthed the same words. 'No,' he would say, listening to the dull cries that echoed in the infirmary halls. 'No, Mother, I am not.'

For William felt it, too. It was not only the dull, insistent ache at the back of his head. It was not only the images seared onto him of the grove of thorns up on the Moor. He felt it each time he woke, that there was something different now. Was it that something was missing? He grew in strength with the passing of each day, and he got to asking his mother and his father and his old schoolteachers and his family's friends what it might have been. Did he look different? he asked. Was it there in the way that he spoke? Was there something that had happened to him that nobody dared tell? It must have seemed to his mother and his father, then, that his memory was shattered and he knew nothing of that day when he had fallen, but he told them what little he could remember – that they had been walking on the Moor, that the rock had been in Samuel's hand – and they in turn told him that it was over, finished with now, that he need never have to think of those times again. This is a new world, they said to him; the old one is gone.

It was his uncle who told him what had happened, late at night when his parents had gone back to the terraces. He made a gift to the nurses so that he might steal within and not have to see his brother and his brother's wife – and, crouched there at the bedside, smelling of stale tobacco, he spun the story of William's slumber. Even to William, sweating into those sheets with the war wounded wailing around him, it sounded more like some story plucked from a fairybook than his own history. Because he was not a gallant knight, nor a woodsman with a true heart and a true axe; he was only a boy, dragged up on the streets, and certainly such fanciful things did not happen to him.

'The doctors don't want you to know it,' he began, looking furtively at the curtains and the passageway beyond. 'They've said it to your mother and they've said it to your father too – that silence is best. There's never a good thing come from a man knowing such things about himself – that's what they all say. But you died, William. You were lying here, in this infirmary bed, and they thought you were going to come from it, they thought there were good signs, and maybe it had been one week or maybe it had been two – but then your body began seizing up, and it was a horror to behold, the way your arms tensed and the muscles in your legs all flexed. And then: the way it all stopped. The way the nurses looked from one to the other, before the cry went up. Because your heart wasn't beating, and your chest was still – and there was snow falling outside, little flakes, thin snow like it is tonight, and it really was a beautiful sight, William. It was still and it was silent. And then, one of the doctors was hunching over you – and then there was another spasm, and you breathed deep and ugly, and then you were back. And they kept a nurse with you for three days and three nights afterwards, just to be there with you, in case it happened again. But you settled after that, and then you woke, and maybe if it wasn't for that mark on the back of your head nobody would know what happened to you, up on the Moor.'

'Uncle?' William asked, propping himself awkwardly in the bed. 'You didn't tell him, did you? You didn't tell Samuel that he killed me?'

Joshua smiled and pressed an aged hand to William's brow.

'No, son,' he said. 'Why would I tell the boy a monstrous thing like that?'

They readied him to leave. Days passed, and William was stronger. He no longer spent his days lying in bed, searching for constellations in the ceiling tiles. He helped the nurses with their rounds up and down the wards, tending to the men brought back from Belgium and France. He sat and he listened to their stories – and, always, they asked him for his. More than once, he tried to tell it. And each time he faltered. Because didn't good things happen to good people? Wasn't such punishment reserved for those with the blackest hearts? How could he ever spin such a fable? He told them, instead, that there had been an accident, and that he had been asleep, but that he was regaining his vigour with each passing day, and soon he too would put his name to the paper at the Boards and hold his first issue gas mask and wield his first bayonet. Some of the men would smile at him, then, and tell him of England and of what acts of courage an Englishman was capable. Others would breathe oddly and clasp his hand and leer at the wound that still bulged on the back of his head. 'You don't have to go,' they would whisper. 'With a blow like that, you might never have to go.'

He grew to like those hours that he spent with the fallen soldiers. He thought that they were growing to like him. He thought that they were the same. One of the nurses said it to him as she brought his food on the final day of his recuperation: that he looked at her the same as the wounded who lay in the cells around him, waiting for it to end. But he was not waiting, she told him as she helped him into his shirt and bent low to kiss his brow. He had come back, and he would be well. He would have a life. A boy like him ought to be grateful. A boy like him ought to burn with new fire for the life he so nearly missed. She would sit on his bedside until he started to blush, and studiously tell him of all the good that was happening in the world, and studiously not tell him of all the darknesses that gathered in France and beyond. Once, his mother arrived just as the nurse was sitting beside him – and William's embarrassment was palpable. That was when they knew he would soon be good to go home.

But even as the trap came to take him away on that, the fifteenth night of his new life, William knew that he was not yet his old self. The nurses clucked around to make their farewells, but William barely heard a word. He was looking, instead, at the barnacles of ice that grew like frosted flowers on the windows, and imagining he could see his brother's clouded face standing beyond. There was something else burning in him now – and sleep and rest would never be enough to bring the old times back.

There was chicken that first night, a bird freshly killed and blooded only hours before. There was a party to greet him as well: his mother and his father and a motley collection of neighbours and schoolteachers that he had thought he might never have to see again. There had been a trap to take him home, and they had ridden down Woodhouse Lane from the infirmary with the Moor on their left and the endless terraces of Woodhouse and Meanwood on their right. It was a sprawling collection of towns that made up the city of Leeds, with streets and snickets that William had mapped and planned, but as he had come from the infirmary it seemed that the townships had shifted, that everything was vaguely askew, like a painting scoured from its canvas and a forgery daubed in its place. The spires of the city were behind him and the bulging slate towns reared from the hills in front, but all that he had seen as he rode the little trap back into the terraces was the heathen scrubland that looked down upon it all. Rags of snow had turned in the sky, and William had watched with squinted eyes as the scrub came into view. His mother had curled her arm around him, as if she might have been able to protect him from that stretch of frosted earth, and he had seen, walking there, one of the ragmen who trawled the streets of Hyde Park. He was looking for treasures up there, just as he would spend his days looking for treasures in the gutters and the gardens, and perhaps he craned his head at the trap as it passed. William fancied that their eyes might even have met then, the wounded soldier and the ragged veteran, and it was like he was staring into a looking glass.

There was wine. William could not remember another day

when the Redmonds had shared wine, but here it was, a gift from one of the wealthier families of Victoria Road. It was red and it was dark and William's father said it was the colour of the Lord's blood. William's father was the sort of man who slobbered every Sunday over the image of a God recording each man's sins in a vast, leatherbound ledger – and he beamed wickedly at William as he raised his glass for the first toast. William saw, then, that even the glasses were new, crystal goblets that he had never seen before, even when he and Samuel had rooted around their father's precious cabinet. He supposed that they were heirlooms from his mother's side of the family, for there had never been wealth in his father's line; his father still took his trap to trade up and down the tanneries of Kirkstall Road. All the faces at the table grinned and lifted their glasses, and they sang his name in chorus. It was hellish good to have William back.

There were clots of neighbours from Brudenell Mount and the streets that snaked thereabouts, and there was Mr Finlay – a weathered old face who had once been William's master at school – and family members from the furthest reaches of the city: Sheepscar and Allerton and darkest Otley beyond. Even Uncle Joshua was there. He had flashed William a look like benediction when he had first followed his mother into the room, but since that time he had been still. William wondered what had changed that Joshua was suddenly welcome in their home. He could not recall another day like it. He saw, across the table laden with silverware and ancient porcelain, the way the looks were cast between Joshua and his mother, and he was thankful for the wine that clouded everybody's thoughts. Tonight, his father would see nothing he did not want to see.

William did not think he would have an appetite, but he stomached his first helping of chicken and quickly his plate was refilled. It still felt strange to be turning real food in his gums, sometimes his throat still gagged as if in reflex, but he tried not to be conscious of what he was doing and somehow he managed to forget. He did not drink his wine – he had never liked that dark, oily taste – and listened intently to the conversations that rose and swelled about him. He was aware, for the first time that day, of the persistent ache at the back of his head.

They spoke of the streets and the snows – and they spoke of the darker clouds that gathered even now across the water. There was talk of forward offensives, of tactical retreats, of men honoured for their bravery and others sent, gibbering, to the great hospices at Craiglockhart, and the more ragged ones at Mirfield. Every day the newspapers hollered the news. People spoke of it in the snickets and the yards. Out there, monsters rose in the deeps and iron hulks roared through the skies, while boys crouched in the dirt and held to their guns and put their faith in a God that none of them could name. The men around the table remembered the wars of their own youths well, but none had dared imagine a campaign such as this. None had ever dreamt of this new world of howitzers and mud in which their sons now shed blood. On the fringes of the room, they shared stories of a cleaner, more honourable time, when men would look into the eyes of the soldiers that they killed, and feel the life trickle out of their foes. It could be a good thing to kill a man, somebody remarked. William looked at that man, a sallow creature who lived in one of the redbricks on the Otley Road and made sacks for a living. It could be an honourable thing, to take a man's life and lay him down and go back to your girl – but now the world was changed, and not a man among them knew what was right and what was wrong.

There were boys coming back to the streets tomorrow, soldiers from the Chapeltown Rifles sent back to see their families. It was the battalion William would have joined, and he listened more carefully now. It was Mr Finlay who had stood on the conscription board that sent them away, and it was Mr Finlay who was orchestrating their welcome at one of the local inns: the Royal Park, where William and Samuel had often taken furtive drinks. It was to be a grand affair. All the men agreed. They talked in lower voices now, and listened to Mr Finlay's words. There was to be drinking and there was to be feasting and there were to be glasses raised in celebration of the boys who had returned and in memory of those who had not. It would be a night not to be forgotten.

'You'll be there, of course?' smiled Mr Finlay.

It was a moment before William realised that it was he who was being addressed. He lifted his head from his plate to see the crowd gaping at him, waiting for his response. Slowly, he nodded. Yes, he began, of course he would be there. Of course he would go among them – those boys whose names he must once have known, but who had drifted beyond memory. He remembered those men lying in straps in the infirmary beds, and began to dread the coming night.

'The whole town will be there?' he asked. 'Everybody?'

If anybody knew what he meant, none of them showed it. William's eyes flitted instinctively at the rafters above. It had not escaped him, that though the room was crammed with people, still it seemed empty.

'The whole town,' said one of the neighbours. 'We'll all be there. We wouldn't miss it. We wouldn't do that to our boys.'

Not one man that night asked William about the wound that wept at the back of his head – and not one man that night could tear his eyes from it.

It was the thick of night when the party fragmented and the neighbours who had flocked to watch William return donned their greatcoats for the homeward trek. It was cold, the sky creaking with snow, and William wished each of them well as they lifted their collars to the frost and went out into the night. There were stragglers, men with the stains of dark-red wine about their lips, but William could hear his mother harrying them into the hallway. In turn, they lurched past him, bawling out their drunken best wishes. William had kept the company of drunkards before, but never had he seen them like this: spewing out laughter and joy instead of horror and bile. They cut comical figures as they pushed past him and staggered into the street.

Mr Finlay and Uncle Joshua were the last to go. Finlay paused briefly in the doorway, the cold wind gusting at the folds of his coat, and laid a hand silently on William's shoulder. It was a thin, papery hand, and its touch was cold. William understood what the old man meant. He said his goodbyes softly, and implored William to come to the inn on the morrow, when the whole town would turn out to see their sons return. William nodded, then, and said that he would try. It was all that he could say, and the old man nodded fairly. He whispered a final word, and then he disappeared.

There was only Joshua and his nephew in the hall, then. William could hear his parents shifting on the other side of the wall, their words muffled by the bricks and mortar. Joshua was silent, too. He shuffled oddly into his boots and laboured over every button on his coat. His lips turned.

'It's hellish good to have you back,' he whispered. He whispered it lowly, as if it was a dirty thing that he had said.

'What is it, Uncle Joshua?' William asked.

The old man paused, then. He was only slightly built, and his thin shoulders were hunched in the stoop that he had learned from years of working the mills. The hair on his head had been plastered back with grease, and though it was thinner than in years past, still it hung in lank strands around his shoulders.

'It's nothing,' the old man rasped. 'William, you've always been a good boy. Remember that. Promise it to me, William.'

That was all that he said before he drew his scarves around him and trudged into the yards. William watched him go until long after the old man had disappeared, his hunched frame sloping slowly into the gloom.

William closed the door to the wind, and turned back to the hallway. Beyond the brick, his parents still talked, their voices as low as ravens at roost. He took a step, but he could take no more. Suddenly, the staircase loomed above him. He turned towards it. It seemed to ripple and shift. He fancied he could hear the footsteps of boys as they clattered back and forth upon its ancient slats. He heard the tell-tale creaking of the third and fourth steps, as if somebody stealing out on a midnight mission was treading upon them. He saw one of the doors at the top of the stair flutter slightly, as if caught in a draught – and then he heard the cry of his own name.

It was only his father. That was all. His father, barking his name from the other side of the wall. William did not know if he was disappointed. He waited only to discern if footsteps truly fell on the floorboards above, and then he moved slowly back to the doorway, where the shadows of the fire still flickered on the wall.

William paused on the threshold. He tried to picture the scene again, how it had been while he was asleep, and this time he saw his mother and his father standing above his recumbent body – while, outside, his face pressed grotesque against the glass, there stood Samuel. He was not wearing a coat, just as he had not been wearing a coat on the day when they walked upon the Moor. Samuel's features craned to catch a sight of his brother lying in those sheets, but the snow whirled viciously about him and soon the window was caked in ice. Quickly, the veneer thickened, and as snow glanced upon it, it stuck there too, and in that way barnacles grew between William and his brother. There was a cry, and William's body tensed, and then the nurses clucked around him, checking his pulse, loosening his sheets, rolling his tongue back to save him from choking.

'Mother,' he ventured as he took a step into the room. 'Why wasn't Samuel here tonight?'

'He isn't here.'

William looked at his father. He was glowering at a point somewhere beyond William's head, gazing at him and yet not gazing at him, his eyes glassy and blue. William's father was older than his mother by twenty years or more; it had been said that he had taken a first wife when he was young, but it was a secret long buried and never to be unearthed. He was a stout man, neither as tall as William nor Samuel, and in spite of his years, the hair was thick and wild upon his head. His only signs of age were the crow's feet that gathered at the corners of his eyes, and the three deep lines carved into his brow.

'We haven't seen him, William,' he went on. His elbows were poised on the table now, and his thick fingers joined. 'Not since the day after it happened. He hasn't been here since.'

'How much do you remember, William?'

William looked back at his mother. She was wearing a smile, but the smile did not reach as far as her eyes. He could feel his parents watching him. He felt accused. It was a strange thing, the way he saw it: two boys heading, one after the other, heads bowed as if walking into a storm. He saw it from strange angles, as if he was a starling perched high in the trees, or a clod of earth lying in the ditch at the side of the trail. That was all it was now: a sequence of ancient engravings that

24

told a simple, stark story; a series of stoic captions printed underneath.

'I remember,' he replied. He went to sit down.

'We thought you were dead when we first saw you,' William's father began. He stood and moved to the window, where wet snow lanced upon the little stone yard. 'It was much like it was today. Grey, and wet and already growing dark. And there you were, lying in that space between the trees. Your body cried out to us from the ground. Cold to touch, William. I thought you were dead.'

'He came in that afternoon,' said William's mother, 'and told me there had been an accident.' Her voice, already trembling, trailed off then. William could imagine the rest: how Samuel had led them to that place upon the Moor, how his father had hammered at doors demanding help, how the three of them had first gathered at his bedside in the infirmary and dared not speak a word.

'He didn't cry,' William's father went on. 'Later that night, we were all together, and he just didn't cry. I remember you cried once when he sprained his knee and we wouldn't let him follow you into the streets. And you were crying for him, William, not for yourself. Crying because your brother was hurt. That's always been the difference. So I said to him, "Why weren't you with him? Why weren't you there?" I kept saying. And do you know what he said?' William's father paused, then. 'Nothing,' he went on. 'He sat and glowered, like he's been glowering since the day we first lay him in his crib. It was then that I knew.'

William wanted to remain silent. There was only one thing he wanted more than that – and now it seemed that neither thing could happen. He moved the big grey potato from one side of the plate to the next, marking wide trails in the congealing gravy. He was picturing, then, a time when he had been twelve and Samuel ten. It was a clear day and his father had taken the trap out into the streets, and perhaps their mother was there, too. The house had been empty, and he and Samuel had turned it into a battlefield. Fortresses of chairs had been erected. Trenches of cushions and poles. In that way, they spent the afternoon waging war against each other. Late on in the battle, having already relented in his quest to contain the scullery, William had fallen and shattered the looking glass that hung at the bottom of the stairs. That was the end of the war. They hurried to put the house in order, but they would never be able to disguise the looking glass. When their father returned, there were still shards of it embedded in the floor. He had flushed red with rage and looked at his sons. He had gone straight for Samuel with his belt in his hand.

'You didn't have to keep asking him that,' he said.

His father studied him oddly.

'How is your head?' asked his mother.

'You didn't have to keep saying it to him, like he didn't know already, like he didn't know the second he came through the door that you already knew, like you'd have known even if it wasn't him. If there's a reason for what happened, there it is.'

There was another silence. It gaped.

'Could I be excused?' asked William.

'Yes,' said his mother. Her eyes might have moved towards her husband, then. 'William, you need your rest.'

Upstairs, and the hallway was silent. On the ledge at the top of the rails a plant wilted in its pot, unnourished since the day William fell upon the Moor. He studied it before moving slowly through the doorway and breathing in the unfamiliar smells. Through the floorboards he could hear the murmur of his mother barracking his father.

It was not the room he had always known. The curtains had

been laundered and rehung, the rugs lain at different angles. On one side of the room there sat his bed, made up with clean sheets and turned back the way that his mother insisted; on the opposite, the other bed squatted sullenly beneath the windows, its blankets taken, its body flayed bare. William went to sit on his own bed – and saw, then, that the wardrobe was only half-full, that the boxes beneath the bookshelves had been opened and then resealed, that there was only one lead soldier sitting on the shelf. He fancied he could feel the sting of the air, the same as it had been that day when he and Samuel walked upon Woodhouse Moor. Bitter and flecked with rain, it was, a flurry of malicious gusts. For a moment he was back there, his brother crouched, the sky churning.

They had shared the room since a time when his memory was mist. Samuel had lain in the crib where his naked bed now sat, and each night William had watched him sleep, filled with awe at this squalling bundle that was his brother. It felt strange, now that his childhood was fragmented. He could remember it only in snatches, as if some mischievous spirit was sifting through his past and deciding which memories he should shred and which he should keep. William supposed that it must have been the same for Samuel, too. He supposed that Samuel must have had a malevolent spirit ghosting through him, cultivating every memory best forgotten, repainting and recasting and revising everything that had gone before.

And so, they flitted through him: the times they had spent in this room; the things they had done. The first night, when he was nine and Samuel seven, that they had dared venture out of the house after dark, and had seen for the first time the moonlight shining on the smokestacks and the illuminations along the viaduct on Kirkstall Road. His memories came in a thunderous deluge, now. Each time he remembered one fragment, it ran into another, until soon a river rampaged through his thoughts: the days after he had finished his schooling and he would wait every day for Samuel to come back through those doors; the day his father had taken him, for the first time, on one of his rounds up and down Otley Road. The night, only a month later, that Mr Finlay had come to the house and told his father that there was a place at a college for William, if that was what they wanted, a place where he might learn of things beyond tinkers and traders and horses and carts. He remembered how thrilled their mother had been. He remembered tramping back up the stairs, not knowing what to think of it himself, and telling Samuel it all after the lamps had been snuffed. It had been pitch black, then, and he had not seen the expression that formed on Samuel's face as he whispered his congratulations. It was taking shape in his mind, now, a grainy picture of his brother picked out in motes of dust. He saw Samuel's pained attempt at being pleased. He heard him shift in his bedclothes, so that he was facing away, head bowed to the fluttering curtains. He must have lain awake for a long time that night, alone beside William, unable to sleep for the thing that festered in his breast.

'William?'

William looked up. His parents stood in the doorway, but they did not cross the threshold.

'I'm fine,' he lied. 'I'm tired. I just need to rest.'

They smiled – as if they understood – and then they retired. William listened to their footsteps retreat and waited for their bedroom door to close. Countless were the times when he and Samuel had lain beneath their covers waiting to hear that sound. He heard the lilting whisper of their continuing row, and his head throbbed. He put a hand to the wound and thought how useless it would be to make a wish.

William crossed the room and curled to sleep on his brother's naked mattress.

II

He woke before dawn the next day and went out into the streets. The terraces were empty, but he could hear the sounds of a man and his trap shifting on the other side of the rooftops, some Romany on the look-out for whatever treasures the streets cared to give up. Snow iced the coal heaps in the snickets between the yards. On the crumbled wall of a garden across the street a family of starlings looked sullenly up and skittered after him as he started to walk.

He had decided, when he woke in the night, that this was the first place he would go. He had decided, then, that he would end this now. Alone now, he followed Brudenell Road deeper into the sprawl. Though it was early, the streets were already awake. In spite of the low wind that whipped across the terraces, whole families were turning out in preparation for their sons' return: grandparents and parents and children too young to know anything of the trade their brothers plied. William passed gardens where mothers had hung their streamers, brightly embroidered Union Jacks rippling in the gusts that tore at their gutters. The people were glad to see him, and they drifted to the end of their yards so that they might share a few words and ask how he was feeling and how his family had coped. He asked each of them what they knew of his brother and when was the last time they had seen him, but not one of them ventured a response. They told him the same things: that his brother was gone now, that they did not know where, that there were celebrations tonight and wasn't

29

that more important than where his brother was gone – that boys had been out there, across the water, and played their part and come back to tell the tale? William listened to it all, but absorbed not a word.

She was called Lucy, and she lived in the crook of a dead-end street named Beechfield Mount. William knew each crack in the stones of that street, but never had he walked them with such trepidation. He stopped at the bottom of the garden – a thin ribbon of land with low bushes and a flowerbed encrusted with deep snow – and looked at the window directly above. William could still recall the day that he had first spoken to Lucy, on the corner of this same street. Back then, hers had been a new family on the terrace, and new families always demanded attention. It had been scant weeks later that he had introduced her to his brother. In his most honest moments, William could vividly remember the look that Samuel had given when he walked with Lucy along their terrace; like something wounded, he had been, knifed in the back to think that his brother had been the one to have found this girl first. Even after she had been drawn towards Samuel, his brother had not lost that look, had spent his evenings jealously guarding the secrets of the times they spent together, disappearing on long walks with her and not breathing a word to William of where they had gone.

William was not so courageous to think of those moments today; he wanted nothing to blight the memory of his brother before he was found. It was an odd thing, standing at the bottom of that garden and not knowing if he should take that first step over the low wall. He recalled, now, that he had seen Lucy on the night before he had fallen on the Moor. They had drunk tea together and sat upon the steps of the Corn Exchange, and spoken of what it would be like when he was in France.

Curtains rustled in the bay window downstairs. William saw figures shift beyond. He braced himself. He thought about running, then, but his hand was upon the gate and his knuckles whitened against the rail. He waited until he heard the latch. The door swung slowly inwards, then, and he saw Lucy's mother standing in its frame.

'William,' she said, wringing her hands on a dishcloth as she came to the top of the steps. She waited there, high above William, and looked down upon him. 'I'd heard word you were being sent home in time for the celebrations, another boy back from the fight . . .'

She smiled the last words almost ruefully, pulling a shawl about her shoulders as she stepped into the wind. Lucy's parents were younger than his own, had borne Lucy when they were children themselves, and perhaps it was this that had made their daughter so wild and inscrutable. He could hardly believe that she had been birthed by the same woman who stood before him. He looked back at the window above. A thin sheet of ice stretched across it, so that even the curtains were obscured.

'I'm here to see Lucy,' he began.

She came a little further down the tall steps, but William shielded himself with the gate. He saw, now, that Lucy's father lurked in the doorway. He traded, often, with William's own father, and had the same guarded look of all the men who rode their traps up and down these hills. His head held high, he studied the figure in his yard.

'Could you tell her I'm here?' William ventured. 'Mrs Rose?'

'William, your mother and father won't have you upset.'

Lucy's father emerged from the scullery and they stood against him, twofold in the doorway, arms crossed before their chests.

'Lucy wouldn't upset me,' he retorted.

'I'm certain of it,' Mr Rose stated. 'But we aren't here to rail against your father's wishes.'

'I just want to see her,' he began.

'That's what your brother said,' Mrs Rose breathed, shuffling tighter to her husband.

William took the crumbled steps two at a time. He stopped when he was half-way there, steadying himself on the hawthorn that grew untamed in the garden.

'Is my brother here?' he demanded.

'There's nobody here.'

'Did my brother come?'

William's knuckles tightened around the rail. He turned, as if to go, but just as swiftly turned back to eye them one final time. As he did so, he shot a glance upstairs. He wondered if she was listening. He wondered if his father had cornered her, too.

'William,' Lucy's mother began. 'You're a good boy. You always were. We were broken, really, when it was Samuel she took up with. We always hoped she was burning a candle for you.' She stopped, then, and broke from her husband, coming down the cracked steps to meet William in the middle. 'But she's already gone. We don't keep her captive, up in that tower; she has a part to play tonight as well – we all do, we who were left behind.' She paused. 'We'll tell her you came.'

William turned, and descended the steps.

He did not want to go home. Back there, it was warm and it was dry and there would already be a pot hanging over the stove, but as he trudged to the end of the row he knew that he would rather be anywhere but there. Though it was not yet snowing, the sky above him creaked with the weight of all that it carried. There would be a blizzard tonight. The soldiers would tumble from their trains and see the city cloaked in white, would march in formation through the streets for all to see and all to adore. William would flit through the crowds and search each face in turn, but already he knew he would not find the one thing for which he searched.

Had William known it was coming? Had he known that Samuel was capable of taking a rock in his hand? The questions were like wolves baying at the moat of some prehistoric fortress. He trudged in circles through the unordered spiral of streets around Cardigan Road, and though he did not want to think upon it, the memories of the months before he woke were seared upon him. It had been two years or more since the proclamations, two years since people first clamoured to buy the newspapers and hear each sorry story that came up from the south. For a time, it had been as if the fighting was part of some other world to which the men of these streets were not in debt; it took weeks for news to find its way over the water, and longer still for it to leave London and those greater cities where lives were made and undone. By the time it reached these streets, it was already history. It had been a year or more before they started to marshal men from this part of the island. William remembered it vividly, for he and Samuel had been there to see the procession pass through. They had thought of it as some vile incursion from a barbarian land, a band of medieval slavers bearing down upon their streets to drag good men away.

They had been boys, back then. Strange to think that it had taken scant months for the world to shift on its axis and consider them men, as the first of Kitchener's New Army were summoned from their streets. It was happening the same in all the other little boroughs of Leeds; in Sheepscar avenues lay barren, and in Chapeltown men poured into the church house to scrawl their names upon the register. Samuel and William had traipsed from one end of the city to the next in those first days. They had never been boys for talking, but that week they had spoken freely of all that they thought. 'Will you go?' Samuel had asked. 'Of course I'll go,' William had answered. They were crouched together on a roadside, half-shrouded by an outgrowth of gorse, and together they watched the older men of their terrace flocking into the stations. 'And you want to go?' William was not as swift to answer that question, but at last he nodded. 'There's people dying,' he began. 'And more dying to come. Yes, I want to go. It's the only good thing to do.' He paused. 'And you, Samuel?'

William remembered it starkly, the look that Samuel had given him, his brother's face wrenched rigid. It was not that there were tears glistening in his eyes; only that his eyes were opened wide, as if in realisation.

'No,' he had said. 'They'll come for me, and they'll put my name on the roll, but I don't want a part in it, William. And look at them all,' he went on, gesturing wildly through the clawing gorse. 'The only good thing to do? Not for me, William. It isn't for me.'

William was replaying the memory as he came, alone, to the corner of Queens Road. It might have been midday, for the fires in the Royal Park Inn already burned. He paused for a moment on the edges of the yard. He and Samuel had been drinking there more than once, when their father allowed it. He thought he could see familiar faces through the frosted glass: groups of boys and old men, a huddle of them waiting nervously on the threshold as if uncertain whose sons would be coming home tonight.

He was walking away, the snow rising over the tops of his boots, when he heard his name. When he turned, he saw the glut of boys standing in the doorway of the inn. Orange light from within shone upon their backs. He moved towards

34

them, stumbling slightly on the ice, and then he recognised their faces: boys from his school, clamouring to come towards him. He reached them, and the first boy eagerly took his hand.

'William!' he exclaimed. 'You've got to come in. They bought us beer. I think it's a kind of parting gift. An up-and-at-them . . .'

His name was Matthias, and his huge hand closed over William's. William had once known him well, though since school had ended they had only rarely met. He had a mane of brown hair and was handsome in an ordinary way. His teeth were set straight and, though his nose had been broken in some childhood accident, somehow it gave him a noble bearing. William returned the greeting and found himself shaking each of the boys' hands. He did not remember all their names: there was Alexander and there was David and a host of others he could not recall. They grinned and patted him on the back and put arms around his shoulders – and then, he found, he was inside the inn. It was an old building, but great fires burned in its hearths and the air was dry and warm.

Smells hit him in waves: breads and cakes and meads and spiced ale, larders raided and cellars emptied so that the coming night might always be remembered. The room was bedecked in banners and streamers, tinsels not yet packed away from Christmas still twisted around the rafters and the pillars that held them in place. There were drinkers here already, interminable hours before the festivities were due to begin. An old man dressed in his finest clothes nursed a tankard of ale, idly rolling tobacco between thumb and forefinger and yet never completing the cigarette. He had been waiting for long months already, but it seemed that these last few hours stretched infinitely on.

William shook the snow from his overcoat and unwound

the scarf from his neck. In his boots, his feet were wet, but he stretched his toes and took a seat in front of one of the ranges. Soon, there was beer in front of him – and, soon, the conversation had started.

'It will be a grand night,' Matthias began. 'A return, but a send-off as well.' He drained the bottom of his glass and eagerly looked for another. 'We're to go to Catterick next Sunday,' he went on. 'All of us together. I'm sorry as hell you can't come.'

The other boys agreed. It would have been a grand thing, they all said, if the whole team could have been there. William recalled, then, the summers that he had spent playing cricket with these boys. They had waged a campaign against a gang from Armley: thick, cumbersome boys with arms like great apes but nothing in-between their ears. Samuel had kept wicket and William had bowled spin.

'I still remember your brother when he was a boy,' said Matthias. He lifted his eyes from his glass, and they fell upon William.

'There was something wrong about him, even then,' one of the other boys added.

William shifted.

'There wasn't anything wrong,' he said.

He remembered it, too, his brother as a toddler and, after that, a young boy. He played alone, but he never got bored. That was Samuel. And then, when he had been twelve or thirteen or maybe even older – William hated himself that he could not recall – he had appeared on the fringes of their gang. It had been a day at summer's end, when there was still sunlight long into the evening. He had followed them on forays over the Moor and into the city, loitered on the steps of the Corn Exchange as they drank Matthias' cider, started asking questions about horses and guns and girls.

'How long do you think it will be, William, before you can come out and find us?'

It took a moment before William could register the question. He had not thought upon it. He thought he saw one of the boys peering at the wound on the side of his head, but the boy quickly averted his eyes.

'Soon enough,' he said, and took his first taste of the beer.

They talked about the little things, then: the stories they had heard from their fathers of what it was like to be a soldier; the things they might miss about the terrace and the things they were longing to escape. Then they shared stories. It was a thing they had always done, because to share stories was to share a thing about yourself. Matthias had always been their teller of tales. His father was the local minister, and for years now he had taken pleasure in relating the bloodiest of the Bible's stories. This afternoon he lit upon the fable of Isaac. William had heard it told several times before, in varying degrees of blood lust. He had never liked the story. God summoned Abraham to slaughter his son on the mountainside, and only as his son was lying there on the altar did God let Abraham stay his hand. William had never believed in it as fervently as Matthias. He could not put any faith in a God who would put His subjects to such a test. He could not understand any father who put his faith in God above the love for his son. A man turns his back on his family, and he is one of the Devil's men. William had heard that said once, and it had lingered thereafter in his thoughts.

'No more Bible,' chipped in one of the boys. 'We'll see enough of God's work when we take to our guns.'

The others agreed. Matthias muttered some oath, insisted he had a wonderful story as yet untold – of Nineveh City and the ruin God wreaked upon its inhabitants – but nobody cared to hear it. There were others, he went on: men washed

37

up in the bellies of whales, or marked for their evil by God and damned to wander the earth for countless generations. But still nobody would listen. They jeered at him, and when Matthias opened his mouth to protest they only jeered louder. There was laughter at the table now, and William found that he was laughing, too.

After that, it seemed like they were back in school. They made the same dirty jokes; they told the same second-hand stories; they remembered that final speech that Mr Finlay had given, in which he told them of everything England expects. Somebody had with them a little hip flask of brandy, and when the barkeep was not watching they shuffled it round, under the table, taking furtive swigs or spicing up their beer as each saw fit. Soon, William felt light-headed. He drained his glass, and Matthias urged him to go and get another. It was the least the barkeep would do, Matthias insisted, after everything that had happened and all that was yet to come. At first, William was reticent – but he saw the faces of the boys who had once been his friends, and he stood to go to the counter.

She was standing at the door. As soon as he turned, he saw her. He looked back at the boys who gathered in front of the fire, and then turned to take in the rippling banners and streamers hung high. He weaved between the tables, and when he looked again she was gone.

The sky was bible black when he came out of the inn, and he could only dimly discern her silhouette as it climbed Royal Park Road. At the top of that rise, he saw the corner of the scrubland, and the Moor that glowered down upon it. He started to run, but the ground was hard-packed ice and he flailed to keep his balance. Further on, up the road, Lucy stopped and looked back. She was enticing him to follow.

He caught up with her, at last, at the top of the hill, where the edge of the scrub met the road. She was standing in the shelter of one of the great oaks, by the edge of a pond thick with ice. She stared as William approached.

'I'm not supposed to be out of the house,' she said.

She was just as William remembered. He did not know why, but it struck him as peculiar now, that she was exactly the same as before: the same curled hair, the same creases painted delicately about her eyes that made him think of a hieroglyph on a tomb. She was shorter than William, much shorter than Samuel, and though she still bore the plumpness of her youth, there had always been something pretty about Lucy Rose. Tonight her cheeks were rouged, lit lowly in the circles of gas lamps, and her blonde hair hung freely over her shoulders. Normally, it was bound back in curls – but, tonight, she had sloped into the streets without the time to lift her looking glass.

'Lucy,' he began. He saw that she was wearing no coat on top of her dress. Only a loose knitted scarf hung about her shoulders. 'You'll freeze.' He went to offer her his overcoat, but she lay a hand on his arm and held him back.

'You need it,' she said. She had a low, knowing voice that stirred a hailstorm of memories in William. Each time he heard her, he could not keep at bay the recollection of the first time he had kissed her, long months into their friendship and just as he was beginning to feel that such a thing could never happen. And each time he remembered that moment, he could not stop himself from thinking of the first time he had seen Samuel take her hand. He had never told Samuel about that kiss, though he was certain that he knew. William often told himself he had been a gracious loser. He took a certain pride in it.

'I haven't got pneumonia,' William said, squirming out of the greatcoat despite Lucy's protestations.

39

'You soon will have,' she grinned, donning the heavy coat.

They stood in silence for a little while. Through the trees, where the scrubland was lit in the halo of the gas lights, a street dog watched them with its head hung low. On the valleys that fell away from the Moor, they could see the gas lamps of each little borough starting to burn. Woodhouse was already lit up in orbs of fire, and beyond it Sheepscar and Little London were beginning to flare.

'Is it true?' William asked her. He paced a little, deliberately following the edge of the frozen pond. 'Was it my father came to your house?'

'I wasn't there,' Lucy answered. She nodded, then. 'But he came. I think he came for Samuel.'

'And?'

'Samuel wasn't there.'

'God damn it, Lucy.'

'I know.'

Lucy moved after William, further into the scrub. The grass was frosted beneath their feet, and it crunched with each step. Birds skittered in the trees, and the dog began to moan.

They walked, together, into the trees. Lucy had with her a little canteen – brandy siphoned from her father's cabinet – and they passed it between them as they trod the path into the scrub. It was for courage, and it was for warmth. Lucy took William's hand, and by the first fork in the path their arms were around each other. Snow, thick and wet, broke intermittently through the branches.

Hand in hand, they came to the edge of the clearing where it had happened. Where Samuel had taken the rock in his hand. Where William had fallen. William teased his fingers from Lucy's grasp, but quickly she took them back.

'Does it hurt?' asked Lucy. She was tentative, at first, and she tried to move nearer.

'Most of the time I can't feel it,' William replied. 'Most of the time,' he went on, 'it isn't even there.'

She stopped, and fixed her stare on the ground. She hesitated, then.

'Why did you do that to him?' she breathed.

William turned at her. Fleetingly, he caught his reflection in the tablets of ice beneath them. Wretched, he was, with that wound still weeping on the side of his head, and the hair growing back in ugly clumps around it, like weeds reclaiming a stretch of scorched land. She was staring at him now.

'He didn't mean it to be like that. That's not what he wanted. What was it you did? What was it you said to him, up here? Was it me? Did you tell him about me and you?'

'There's nothing to tell.'

'You know that's not true.'

'It's only not true because you say it's not true. It was nothing. It was before he'd even lain eyes on you.'

William wanted to say more, but he stopped. It was true that his lips had brushed hers that night, that it was at his side that she first came to their door – but there, for William, the story was finished. She was Samuel's now, and Samuel's she would remain. He knew how much it clawed at his brother, the thought that it was William who found her, but for long months he had not breathed a word of it. It was William's belief that disharmonies could disappear if they could only be forgotten.

'You have seen him, haven't you?'

She tried not to smile, then.

'I think my house was the first place he came.'

William pictured his brother going there, to her doorstep, and pitching stones at her bedroom window that she might let him within. In his head it was dark, and rags of snow turned across the terraces. He fancied Samuel had hidden throughout

41

the day, sloping from haunt to haunt, hurling sticks for the stray dogs that lived upon the Moor, wandering idly from one stretch of scrub to the other. Perhaps he had waited until dusk, when the bulging sky finally broke, and then – under the cover of that gloom – stolen back among the terraces. Perhaps Lucy had drawn back her curtains to see him standing, trembling, below – and perhaps, even then, she had smiled that it was her to whom he had come. She must have turned from the window, then, and made for the front door, straightening her bedclothes, checking her hair in the mirror as she came. It must have been a peculiar kind of warmth that she felt.

'Maybe he did it to protect you. Did you think about that, William? That he didn't want you to go and he took you up on the Moor and he laid you down so that you'd never have to leave?'

William might have smiled at that. Slowly, he shook his head. 'He didn't do it to protect me,' he said. 'He did it because he hates me.' He stopped, wary of the way Lucy looked upon him. 'But it's not his fault that he hates me.'

She turned from him, then, and wandered a little further into the scrub. For a moment William watched her go, wondering whether he ought to follow.

'Did you hide him?' he called.

'He wouldn't be hidden. I tried to make him stay. There's a cellar and an outhouse where he might have gone to earth . . . but it's Samuel, William. He just turned and went back into the terraces. I made him drink some soup, and then he was gone.'

'He can't just be gone,' William breathed. He had wanted to yell it: that men did not just disappear; that his brother could not just leave through an open door and walk into the ether. Such things did not happen outside of stories.

'There was others saw him, too,' said Lucy. 'Matthias and his

42

gang. Yes, they saw him. Cornered him in the streets the day after it happened. They went after him, William, Matthias with a stone. As if it was his right to cast the first one. The whole city knew by then. From Burley Park to Woodhouse Moor.'

William flushed hot. He had been there with them, and soaked up their sympathies and drunk their ales, and all the time they had had a story of their own. An eye for an eye and a tooth for a tooth and if your right hand offends thee then sever it with your left. Fuck Matthias and his teachings. Matthias did not have a brother. He walked a little along the crumbled trail, while the leafless branches surged overhead. Instinctively, he curled a hand around the bald sprawl on the side of his head.

'Are you always going to hate him?' Lucy trembled. 'Maybe if you didn't have to hate him, it doesn't have to have happened. Think about that, William.'

William waited. He did not know what she wanted him to say. He did not know if it mattered. 'It wasn't me who said hate. I didn't say I hate him. I hate the Moor,' he answered. He looked up and, through the darkness, he could see the tops of the trees that marked the path along which he had followed his brother. There were birds roosting up there: ravens and rooks and flocks of famished starlings. 'That's all.'

Lucy said that she understood, that truly she did, but still William cringed from her when she tried to put her arms around him. She stood at a distance from him while the wind gusted through her hair. The moon appeared from behind a low reef of cloud. It sat there now, like a ship beached upon some ragged shore.

'Do you know where he is?'

After he said it, he stared at her. He had meant to say it all along, but even as the words came from his tongue, he was uncertain what he meant. He thought, for a moment, that he did not want to know the answer. He imagined coming back to the Moor, to this place between the trees, and finding Samuel sitting there, waiting for him in the scrub. Their eyes would meet, and neither would say a word, and then they would part.

'I know he was at your uncle's.'

'Joshua's?' William swallowed. 'He's there now?' he asked.

'He tried to go home. He told me he just stood there under the windows and . . .'

Lucy's eyes caught the dull light oddly, and her face crumpled. William saw, then, that there was pity in her eyes for him as well. Vaguely, he remembered a summer when the three of them had walked the townships from end to end, following paths for no reason, tracking cats and watching strangers because they had nothing better to do. He looked at her again, and thought how wasted those days had been.

'William,' she said, the wind lashing fallen leaves at her legs, 'we have to go.' She tried to direct his gaze down through the trees, over the rooftops, along the glimmering gas lamps. There were hunched figures tramping to the revelry from all corners of the heath, proud parents blazing trails with their youngsters in tow – but William saw nothing of that. He peered, instead, into the darknesses of the Moor. Joshua's house was not so very far away; over the scrubland and through the ledges of Woodhouse he would go, deeper and deeper into the nightscape of chimneystacks and slates.

'Come with me,' he said, turning again to face Lucy. 'We'll bring my brother back – we'll walk into the tavern with him standing between us. We'll flank him and we won't let it mean a thing.'

William's eyes implored with her, but Lucy's own were downcast. They darted from side to side, refusing to be fixed as, slowly, she lifted the overcoat from her shoulders and pressed it back into William's hands.

'Your uncle will be at the inn tonight.' She said it so softly that the words were almost drowned by the chorus of wind in the branches above. 'Find him there, William. Talk to him before you go.' She stopped. 'It wasn't everything that changed in those three weeks you were asleep,' she breathed.

III

The Royal Park was already thronged when William descended upon the inn's great doors. As he and Lucy approached, they could see the shapes of soldiers cast upon the frosted glass, families huddled about them, gangs of young boys clamouring for the attention of their brothers. There was something in those pictures, framed there by the window slats, that made William uncertain he could bear the night among them. He stopped and looked back along the narrowing road. Up there, the Moor glowered over the rooftops. The boughs of the great trees, leafless now and still bearing the vestiges of December's snows, surged in the wind that wailed over the terraces, and ribbons of sleet turned in the air.

William did not know when the soldiers had arrived, but they swarmed the halls now, boys who had been raised on these same streets and snatched from them only a year before. If the families that had greeted them were reticent at first, afraid of what their loved ones might have become, their faces now were plastered in joy. The soldiers, too, could not contain their mirth at being back in these familiar halls. Conversations soared, jubilant, around him. He caught only snatches of words in the din: 'Edward, you young bastard!' an old man beamed, clasping the hand of his grandson and hauling him near. A huddle in greatcoats by the staircase were telling tales of the things they had seen at Mons, a fable Matthias would have killed to have claimed as his own, of unseen hands that groped from the ground and sculpted the low mist into an angelic host to lead them from the guns. Somewhere, another raconteur span the story of the Virgin at Albert, who still stood atop one of the cathedral spires, refusing to fall in the face of the shells. People sat rapt around them. The wine flowed.

As Lucy disappeared into the rapture, William became aware that his father was at his side. The crowd heaved against him as soldiers flocked through to the arms of their families and the calls of their sweethearts, and William struggled not to be swept away. There was a song erupting from one of the tables: 'Take Me Back to England', sung in an unordered but ardent round.

'Where did you go today, William?'

A passing drunk caught William's shoulder, and for a moment he thought he might lose his balance. When he looked back at his father, the old man's face was set in a scowl. He looked grey among the joyous faces around him.

'I wandered. I had to, Father. I couldn't just sit there.'

'You went looking for your brother.'

William would not deny it. There were too many things being denied in this town tonight, and he did not mean to be a party to it.

'I didn't find him, Father, if that's what's troubling you.'

A sudden cheer exploded in the corner of the room, and William turned to see one of the young soldiers rise, victorious, from an arm wrestle with his comrade. Beside them, a girl with auburn hair began an applause that spread around the room. The soldier was taking his bows now, grinning back at his groaning friends.

William's father turned upon him.

'You leave this thing now, William.' He paused. His face did not flinch. 'It was finished while you were sleeping; that's the way the story goes,' he breathed.

He joined his father at a table close to the stairs, where

47

already men were gathering for want of seats. In one of the back rooms, musicians blasted practice notes on their bugles, coming together intermittently for bursts of a song or a march. Some of the girls had started to dance; their fathers stood to rebuke them, while their mothers cried out that they should not listen, that they should dance and drink and sing while the wine still flowed, for nights like this did not happen often and ought always to be remembered. William's eyes flitted across the room. He saw that his uncle had taken up with a pair of other old men, with ragged hair and ragged clothes, trouser cuffs tucked into their boots, lengths of rope instead of belts. They stood at the back doors now, bent low in conversation like ravens at roost.

William moved as if to leave, to confront his uncle, but his father's gaze had him pinned in his seat. There was a dull silence at the table, and he turned to see a bank of faces staring at him. His father lifted a glass.

'To our boys?' jeered one of the men.

'To William,' his father announced. 'To my son.'

They drank a toast, and William found himself joining in. There was a glass pushed in front of him, and he lifted it to chime with the others.

'We're glad to have you with us, William,' said one.

'Never a finer word,' ventured another.

William looked from left to right, considering each of the faces in turn. He did not recognise them, and though he knew they were his father's friends, he also knew that they were the caste of friends who did not have wives and families of their own, who were not permitted to cross the threshold of his house when they came to call on his father. William knew that his father resented it, though the old man would never breathe a word of it to his wife; there were some things a man was bound to lose if he dared to marry out of his set.

48

William took a draught of his drink. One of the men was looking at him intently. He was a pallid creature, and there was no pretence in the way he craned his neck forward. William moved warily in his gaze.

'He got you good,' leered the apparition. 'Let me see?'

William shifted. He lifted his pint and drank a measure slowly, as if somehow that was his defence. He did not intend to let any man who asked see the ugly marks at the back of his head.

'Why won't you let me see?' the old creature crowed.

William placed his glass firmly on the wood.

'It just isn't any of your fucking business.'

For a moment the old man was cowed. He craned his head, in mock incredulity, at William's father.

'He got that tongue from your side of the family, I shouldn't wonder.'

'Just show him the stitches,' muttered William's father. He curled a hand around his pint, and steadied himself against the table. 'To keep the peace,' he uttered.

William did not reply; nor did he turn to look at the drunk. He looked, instead, from one end of the pub to the other and searched, in vain, for Samuel's face in the reeling throng. Out there, eyes were locked in looks of longing at last fulfilled; hands were clasped and voices joined in song. Alone among them, William could feel none of their joy. It was not his brother who had come home.

'I used to see you two up and down these streets!' the old man scoffed. 'Up and down and back and forth. Him always on your heels, if I remember. Yes, that was it – first came the knight, and then came his squire, always skulking on your trail, a spiteful little pageboy plotting on his master's life.' The face broke into a toothsome grin. 'What was it you did? The girl? Was it the girl?'

49

William saw, then, that Lucy was on the other side of the room. She was surrounded by boys: Matthias and Alexander and the rest who would soon be leaving. She was laughing, and she lifted her hand to rest it on Matthias' shoulder. William bristled. He thought of his brother, the times that he had seen him and Lucy with their fingers entwined, and he motioned to stand. He pictured Matthias, hunting his brother along thoroughfare and snicket with a stone in his hand.

The drunkard's hand was on his shoulder as he stood.

'Your brother,' the drunkard slurred, 'he was just a little boy when the Devil called his name. You could see it in him even when he was tiny. The sullen look. The silence. Ticking. Ticking. Ticking like some old grandfather clock, he was, the pendulum inside him slowly counting down. A quiet little thing, even then, just biding his time.'

'It wasn't like that.'

William pushed past the drunk, and tried to pick a way through the crowd to where Lucy stood with Matthias and the rest.

'William!' Matthias beamed, extending his hand in the way he always did. 'Did you get yourself a drink? Lucy was just wishing us well for what's to come. And do you really think they'll send you out to join us? Do you think it'll be you and me and the old boys rising out of the earth to drive them back?'

William's head rolled. He stared at Matthias with narrowed eyes.

'When was the last time you saw my brother, Matthias?'

Matthias looked at him, oddly. His head was cocked at an angle, in the same attitude that William often saw dogs looking at their masters. He decided that it was supposed to express some sort of concern.

'You know she's worried about you, don't you?' Matthias

50

said. 'She said you went walking together, up on the Moor. She says there's something different about you. Ever since they set you free from the infirmary, stalking from Burley Park to Woodhouse Moor like . . .' He paused. He did not have the right word. '. . . like a dethroned king,' he decided. 'What are you doing, William?'

'It's a hard thing to kick against the pricks,' William answered.

'Don't sneer at scripture like that. You sound like Samuel.'

'Why did you go after my brother with a stone?'

Matthias' hand was on William's shoulder now. They stood square against each other with the crowds heaving around them.

'Isn't it obvious?' Matthias pleaded.

Somewhere in the din: the shattering of glass. William peered around, and when he looked back, Matthias was gone, slunk back to his disciples in the crowd. A frenzy was rising in one of the corners. In its eye Mr Finlay stood alone, shadowed by one of the soldiers. William had seen him like this before, facing the boys in his schoolroom, when all there had been to worry about was numbers etched onto a board. But the boy who had once sat meekly before him was roaring now. The boy who had once called him Master would not cower.

'How old are you, Finlay?' spat the soldier. He was before the table, now, and William thought he had never seen a boy look so abominable. He remembered the face, from the days when there had been schools and schoolwork to think upon. His name was forgotten, but William could still see the face as it had once been. He pushed forward that he might see the man more clearly.

'Old enough to know better than this,' Mr Finlay began, his words spoken softly and not for the crowd.

'Over forty-one, I'll wager,' the soldier smirked.

The boy stalled for a second, and slowly his head curled around. It seemed, then, that he was suddenly aware of the crowd. He fumbled with a glass that still bore dregs of red wine, and brandished it aloft in a monstrous toast.

'You're proud of him, aren't you?' he grinned. 'Proud that he had the guts to send us out there. Proud that he could marshal us with his war cries and his choirs and his songs, and his words in our fathers' ears. But shall I tell you? Shall I tell you what the bravery of your sons really looks like?'

Not a man around them spoke – but Mr Finlay refused to look away.

'Three weeks ago we found an old Boche dugout. It was a still land through which we had marched: trees left without branches, railings crumbled and mired in the earth. I remember there were crows and there were rats – because some beasts will always find a way to flourish. We came down shelves of earth carved as steps into the trench, and there we found an oasis of calm, a stretch of the trench untouched by mortars and shells. We looked greedily at each other, then, as we thought of the treasures we might find in this abandoned trench. We imagined ammunition and rations left behind, canteens full of Bavarian whisky and bedrolls and meat. I suppose we fell like scavengers, then, tearing into each dugout in their warren, salvaging everything we could find.

'We were not alone. It was my misfortune to find him. My misfortune that I was the first one to go, unshielded, into that chamber. My misfortune that it should fall to me. He was cowering in the corner when I came in. There was a moment in which he might have surrendered. He was wearing only rags, and at first I thought he was left behind for dead. Then he bawled something in that guttural tongue and came for me.

'I jabbed and I parried and he was weak, he was starving and soiled and he was cold to the bone, and perhaps I thought

52

it would be easy, perhaps I thought that because I had eaten and slept in the warmth of our border fires for three nights on end, I might have the upper hand. But what strength can a dying man muster?' He stopped, and it seemed that he might even be laughing. 'What spirit rides upon a man when he is staring into the barrels of his own end? My bayonet broke in my hands, and it fell between us – and then, it seemed, there was only me and him in that channel. He was only a boy. I could not understand a word that he uttered, but that did not matter. There is a language in this world greater than words. He was crying out in it as I closed my hands around his throat. He was bawling out in it as we fell together into the mire, me on top of him, and I pressed his gaping mouth to the dirt.'

The onlookers shifted uneasily against each other. Those closest to the raging soldier had shuffled backwards, and now a moat of empty space lay between the speaker and his spectators. William was at the back of the room, pinned against the brick there by the clotted crowd. He strained to find some space, and saw his uncle motion to join him where the tavern opened into one of the back rooms. William was clawing through the drinkers when he heard the soldier continue. And if there was a message at all in what he was saying, it was that he knew that his end was coming, that there was only one place he was bound to go. 'When I reach those gates,' he was saying, 'I hope He turns me away. I hope He can see it written on me, that there's only one trade I know now. That there's only one trade a man like me can ply. And I hope He sends me down below, to serve in those volcanic halls with every other angel who fell. When men turn on men like we do out there, there's only one master they can serve.'

Joshua was at his shoulder. He trembled, oddly, as he pushed past. William followed him deeper into the alcoves at the back of the room as rags of men donned their greatcoats and, turning their backs on the soldier, went back into the night.

'Joshua,' he said. 'Is it true? Is Samuel hidden at your house?'

William looked at the old man. His eyes, too, were fixed on the soldier pressed back into his chair and flanked by his comrades.

'Not here,' said Joshua. 'Not in front of your father.'

A glut of men who worked on the Kirkstall Lane trooped past, reeling as they came, thrusting Joshua upon his nephew. William fell, then, against a pillar – and the wound in his head screamed out. He felt it lance upon him like the claw of some fell beast. For a second his eyes were filled with violent colour, and a sound like shrieking exploded in his ears – and he saw, there, in those bursts of black and vermilion, the stark silhouettes of the trees on the Moor and the chimneystacks and the redbricks that were his home. There were voices too – voices in the maelstrom. He strained to pick them out. He knew, then, that he was being watched.

'William? William, can you hear me?'

Joshua held him.

'Are you OK?' he said.

William gulped, a man drowning in dry gas, at the air.

'Where is he, Joshua?' he choked.

Joshua looked up. William followed his gaze to the soldier who had silenced them all. The wine glass was still in his hand, its red stains slashed down his front.

'Is he dead?' He could see the room clearly now, though his head still burned and he could not shake the dull droning, like that of flies, that still sang in his ears. 'Is that it?' he asked.

'Not yet, William. It isn't finished yet.'

There was another shattering of glass, and William turned to see that one of the soldiers had fallen, drunk, against the windows in the back of the room. A bitter wind, flecked with ice, whipped within now, and men rushed to pick up the mirthful drunk and shore up the broken frame. William winced when a gust of wind caught the wound at the back of his head. He turned back to his uncle, the thought of his brother's death still burning on his tongue – but, too late, he realised that he was alone.

Joshua was already lost in the crowd, drawing his collar high as he went into the night.

IV

He was in Woodhouse before the thickest of the snow started falling. He took to the paths that skirted the edge of the Moor instead of those that cut through the scrub. At the top of Rampart Road, he dared a glance back and saw the trees bowed under the wind. He felt that memory rampaging towards him, and quickly he turned away. Head held low, he started to run.

The ground beneath him was cased in black ice, but he kept his balance and he went deep into the sprawl. He did not know how late it was, but few people moved in the streets now, and fewer lights shone beyond the curtains and the drapes. The terraces here were uglier than the ones in which he and his family lived. Here the houses were like the trees of windfallen fruit that have been forced to claw at their brethren to reach the light. Down alleyways where cats were coupling he hurried, back and forth through deceiving snickets and streets.

The redbricks rose above him in ledges as he came, at last, to that meeting of roads where Woodhouse and Meanwood and Little London flowed together. The alleys were tangled here, a snarl of streets – and, at last, he emerged onto the green before his uncle's house, where trees laden with snow loomed starkly above. Under those trees he went, his legs pitching knee-deep into the snow. On the other side of the grass, he bowed his head low and crossed the crumbled street, fumbling awkwardly to lift the gate and go beyond. The house was above him now. There was only one light burned within, a rack of candles in one of the upstairs bedrooms throwing strange shapes on the window and its barnacles of ice. A thin trail of smoke still came from the chimneystack, but was quickly snatched into the gale.

William tried to remember the last time he had been there, but the memory evaded him. He could dimly recall a time when he and Samuel, barely old enough to be set free onto the streets, had set out for Joshua's house as if on some grand colonial errand. They had reached their destination, as well, which was more than could be said for many of the Empire's most celebrated adventurers. He could remember the surge of pride he had felt as he stood, side by side with his brother, and rapped on the old man's door. And was Samuel really there now? Had Samuel found sanctuary there, just as they had when they were boys? Was he sitting in that back room, wrapped in those bedcovers, petrified to step outside and face the town that was baying for his blood?

William tried the door, but it was bolted from within and would not give. He thought about the windows, bent low to search for a stone in the snow, but something stayed his hand.

He looked again at the candles that burned in the bedroom above and kept his head rigid as he took his shoulder to the wood.

Inside, the smell was strong. Somewhere, Joshua had been sick. William went quickly from room to room, crying out his uncle's name. He did not dare cry for Samuel; the idea of silence in return was more than he could stand. He took the stairs two at a time, striding over the landing to push open the doors of Joshua's room. Inside, the candles flickered in the window, but the man was nowhere to be seen. He retreated slowly, dared to venture into the room next door – and felt a fresh hailstorm of memories launch themselves upon him.

57

This had been the room to which he and Samuel had come every time they escaped from their own home. He remembered those days vividly: holed up here while their parents and their schoolmasters fretted over their disappearance, rolling dice across boards and fighting fiercely over which roll counted, the smell of their uncle's tobacco curling up through the floor. But again the room was empty: not a sign of his uncle, and not a trace of his brother.

It was the same in the living room below: books piled haphazardly upon each other and plants in terracotta pots growing, untamed, from their clods of soil. He checked quickly in the scullery, in case the man was lurking there in the dark, and stood for a long while at the foot of the stairs, where the carpet curled from the walls and the skirting boards were flaking and loose. Then he heard the murmuring. He was disorientated at first, thought perhaps that it was the stones of the building itself that whimpered. He trembled as he turned a tap in the scullery, pouring water into one of Joshua's cracked mugs, and brought it gingerly to his lips. His head was crying out.

Behind him, a cellar door fluttered in the winter's draught, drumming regimentally against the stone. His hand was not trembling now, but still the wound at the back of his head moaned. He tried to fix on the door. It seemed to swell towards him and then slink away, growing and then retreating like a taunt. He threw the mug back to the counter, where it shattered among the unwashed plates. Snow, thick and wet, plastered itself against the window, obscuring his view of the yards without.

William crouched at the door, listening to the voice beyond. He had thought, at first, that Joshua was not alone. He had allowed himself that flight of the imagination, and as he pressed his ear to the wood, he got to imagining that it was

Samuel who lay in the dungeon down there, that it was Samuel who shared that conversation with his uncle. His hand fell upon the handle, and slowly he descended into the ruin.

In the darkness, it seemed that the stones beneath his feet hissed at him wherever he trod. Were they singing out a warning? William advanced, ledge by ledge, and heard the sobbing rise in the cellar beneath him. Behind, the door snapped shut and a latch fell. He imagined that he was descending into some medieval dungeon. He wanted to see withered skeletons shackled to the walls – but, in truth, all that he saw were rolls of chicken wire and bicycle parts, a sideboard with two legs missing, an old iron range that somehow looked in better condition than the one burning logs in the scullery above. In the furthest reaches of the room, beyond the collected detritus of Joshua's life, stumps of candles cast their light upon bare stone walls.

He came between two banks of chicken wire, and there it lay: a stale mattress, a generation old, bulging and torn and stuffed with old newspapers where the feathers had spilled out. William saw, then, that the old man was sitting, slumped in the nest. He had drawn rags around him and sobbed into them, as if he could still smell his nephew on them, as if somehow Samuel still lingered. He looked old. William had never thought of his uncle as a man approaching death, but here he was, withered and withering further with each tearful breath. William cringed whenever the old man gagged, and though he wanted to put his arms around him, he was not here to comfort old men.

'Joshua . . .' William whispered, advancing with his body hunched beneath the empires of silk that clung to the beams above. 'You sat in my house, Uncle Joshua, and you didn't say a thing.'

'Your father told me not to say a word.'

'Since when did it matter to you what my father thinks?'

'It's always mattered,' the old man choked. 'I always cared. He thinks it doesn't mean a thing that he's the one with the wife and the children and the stories to tell. That it's his stories that will go on for ever. But it does. It did. It always mattered.'

William stepped forward, coming at last from the edge of Joshua's hoard. The stubs of candles still guttered against one of the walls, but the light that they cast was dim and did not reach far. He could not see into the recesses of the room. Did some vague part of him still dream that Samuel was here, hidden in one of those alcoves? He could not see how far the cellar stretched. Perhaps it went further, deep into the ground. Perhaps there were catacombs beneath this, and sewers far beneath that. Perhaps his brother did still lurk in Leeds.

Joshua shifted in the nest of blankets, dipping his head out of the candles' ailing light. When his face re-emerged from the darkness, it was a horrible smile that the old man wore. It was crooked and yet it was elated. He shifted forward a little, and William found himself instinctively retreating. His head caught the silk webs, and across the ceiling they rippled, shimmering in the candlelight as if enchanted.

'Where is he, Uncle Joshua?'

Joshua opened his arms, drawing himself from the blankets in which he was wrapped. 'It's where he slept,' he relented at last. 'He insisted on it. He saw nothing but these walls for three days and three nights. He just wouldn't come up for air.'

It was like he was an animal gone to ground, thought William as he kneeled at the nest. Like some wolf, its paw mangled in a trap, licking its wounds in its den and wondering if it might ever go back to its pack. He slowly traced the map of his brother's body in the creases in the sheets.

'If he was hiding here,' he said, imagining his brother alone here in the dark, 'you must know where he's hiding now.'

William looked up. The old man was shaking. He thinks I'm hunting him, thought William. He thinks I'm out for his blood. It was there on Joshua's face. But I'm not Samuel, he thought. I haven't got time for revenge.

Slowly, Joshua stood. He stooped low beneath the cellar roof, and when he moved he did so awkwardly, a man of long and brittle limbs.

'When I last saw him,' he breathed, 'he was with your father.' William turned. They looked at each other. They were still. 'Sitting in the back of your father's trap, wrapped up in blankets there, drinking tea from a canteen your mother had given him. Cowering there, looking back hopelessly at me, as they took him into the night.'

Joshua tried to tell him all, then, but his words fragmented each time he parted his lips. On the day after William went into his slumber, Samuel was there on the edge of the Moor. They both knew why he was standing there. They both knew what he was looking at. He had spent the night in a hedgeback, curled like a question up there on the scrub, and he was in shirtsleeves with no coat and no scarf. He looked a ghost, said Joshua. Some otherworld wight. Together, they had crossed the Moor and dropped through the redbricks into Woodhouse beyond. Men looked at them from their gardens. Women craned their heads from their scullery windows.

'It was already rampant, rumour spreading like typhoid through these terraces,' said Joshua. 'Mortar speaking to slate. Slate speaking to shingle. All those people, out there, leering over their fences to share the horrid news. Flocks of starlings shrieking it out as they moved from garden to garden. You'd think they wouldn't want to hear it any more. In times like these. Like the boy in the Royal Park tonight. You'd think the things we see and read every day might deaden the lust for that sort of news. But no. This was different. This wasn't England's brave sons crushed under the heels of their Prussian cousins. This wasn't three friends from Penrith buried together in the dirt to the sounds of their comrades singing some soldier's lament. This was two brothers. This was blood. And blood spilled on our own streets. And boys we had watched since before they could walk. Out there, families fought alongside each other – but here, they turned upon their own. People started telling the story, and it spread like plague.'

'So he sheltered here, and you shut him off from all that . . .'

'He didn't have to come hammering at my door, howling for sanctuary. There isn't a thing in the world I wouldn't do for that boy. I'm sorry, William, but it doesn't matter to me what he did.'

William wanted to smile. It doesn't matter to me either, he wanted to say.

'There are people out there,' he said, 'who think he must have had a reason. Lucy and Matthias and Alexander and the rest – all the old men gathering in the tavern tonight, leering to see this thing on the back of my head. The truth is, Uncle Joshua, they've been expecting it since the days when we were boys. And Samuel, spending all his life looking over the angels that looked over me. Well, it wasn't fair then, and it isn't fair now.'

The words seemed to stir Joshua, for when he next looked at William there was something different in his eyes.

'He'd have gone on just the same, if it hadn't happened,' he began. 'The shadow of your shadow. The boy next to the boy next door. William and Samuel, it would have been, for ever in that order – and the pause between you and him would have lengthened with each telling until he was nothing. Less than nothing. Forgotten. That's how it would have been,' said Joshua. William knew, then, that Joshua was thinking of his own brother. 'But still,' he sobbed, 'it wasn't meant to be like this.'

His hand trembled oddly as he reached into the folds of his greatcoat. For a moment he paused, as if his body was seizing, but then he saw the way William hunched forward, eager to know, and onward he went. When he produced the letter, he set it sadly on the stone. It was a stained and tattered little thing, and yet it lay guiltily between them. Neither one of them spoke. William turned the envelope over and saw that familiar hand: *Joshua Redmond*, it read, with an address scrawled below. At last, he took it in his hand and drew the creased page from it, like pus from a wound. He did not look at it at first, but stared at his uncle instead – as if, even now, he might be ordered to look the other way.

'Your father would hate me for letting you see this,' Joshua said.

'What difference should a little thing like that make?' asked William, and unfolded the letter.

Uncle Joshua

I am sorry about the way that I left, that I did not make my farewells, but I think that you will understand. I didn't want to say goodbye. It is such an odd word, isn't it? I had become strangely superstitious in the few days since William fell, and to have said goodbye might have meant something I did not want it to mean. I hope you do not think too ill of me because of it. There was so little time in the day before I left that I hardly said a single farewell.

By now you must know where it is I have gone. The wind is mournful over Flanders tonight. I am sitting in one of our support trenches, which only three days past I helped exca-vate myself. There are countless men here, the whole Empire living like rats in these holes in the dirt: there are Indians and there are Arabs and there are blacks, and they sit with us lads from Burnley and Leeds just as if we had been raised on the same grey streets. It is a strange thing indeed. At nights we can hear the shells, and always there is the distant rumble of men screaming as they come from their holes, but since I first came here I have been assigned supplies and maintenance duties, and I have not yet had the chance to show how well I can wield a bayonet. At training in Southampton it was said that I was naturally born to brandish such a weapon. It makes a man feel proud to think he has some natural skill in him.

Did William wake, Uncle Joshua?

I must go for now. Some of the lads – three friends from outside Oldham, come up together and straight out of school – have been given ration duties tonight, and since today the caravans came up the trench we may even have some meat – if, of course, we can keep the rats at bay.

Your loving nephew, Samuel Redmond.

The letter hung limply in William's hand. He resisted the urge to crumple it and cast it aside. He was remembering, now, a November's night when he had been eleven and Samuel nine. Snow had lain in drifts against the houses and the banks of Hyde Park, and across the terraces children had flocked out to build their fortresses and barricades. Fathers and grandfathers had hung from the windows high above Chestnut Avenue, nodding in mute encouragement as their children formed gangs and cornered their enemies along the snickets between the streets.

'The night you came out of the infirmary, your father tried to tell me this story was finished, that the world had to move on.' He paused. 'But it isn't done between you and Samuel. It might have finished, that day on the Moor, but there was something that stopped it. And I don't believe in that God they're shrieking about out on the terraces – but if He is there, William, if He is basking up there, looking down on us, He sent you back for a reason. There was a reason you didn't die up on the Moor. There was a reason that stone wasn't heavy enough, or wasn't true enough. There's a chance it could all be right. Isn't there, William? Isn't that so?'

It seemed, by the end, that he was pleading. William nodded dumbly. He looked back at the letter in his hands and saw, now, the way that the paper had strained and creased beneath his fingers. Some of the writing was smudged, but that did not matter. The words bled.

It was said that I was naturally born to brandish such a weapon. It makes a man proud to think he has some natural skill in him.

He traced the words with his hand over and again.

V

'He signed up, Lucy.'

She had been asleep when he arrived on the terrace, but a rock pitched against the window had woken her in the same way as it always did. They stood in the scullery now, Lucy still wrapped in her night shawl, the wind playing spiteful percussion upon the windows. William was not cold. They shifted against each other in the cramped darkness, their heads cowed, their voices hushed.

'God damn it, William. Who told you that?'

'There's a letter,' William said, brandishing the creased page as if it was a weapon. 'Do you want me to read?'

She curled her hand about his, and the letter remained sealed. Her fingers were cold where they touched William. She looked up, but she did not look at his eyes. Instead, she fixed her gaze upon that wound on the side of his head. He felt her gaze, and shifted awkwardly that she might not see. Drawing away, he brushed against one of the tabletops and set hanging pans to clatter.

'You'll wake them,' she said, shooting a look at the stairs that wound from the hallway.

He ignored her.

'Do you want me to read?' he demanded.

Uncle Joshua had said little after he gave up the letter. William had tried to tease it out of him, but he knew as he went back into the night that the old man had nothing more to say.

'I don't need you to read,' she whispered.

'Three fucking weeks I was gone, and everything went to Hell.'

'It's been going to Hell a lot longer than three weeks,' Lucy retorted. 'Or maybe you'd forgotten?'

She turned to close the scullery door, wary that they might be listening in the bedrooms above. When she turned back, William was bent over the sink, his hands trembling as he filled a mug with water.

'William?' she began.

'I'm fine,' he lied.

'You can't stay here,' she said.

'I didn't plan on it.'

'I won't be numbered with it. Your parents and my parents and everyone else in these streets. You know the way they look at me already, don't you? Because of you and your brother and I. You know the things they say.'

'But you did know, didn't you?'

William looked up from the sink, his head craned at a crooked angle.

'Of course I knew,' she said. She stood for a long time, her lips parting intermittently as if there was something she might say, the fingers of one hand teasing through the fingers of the other and then freeing themselves, over and again in a strange, anxious dance.

And then: 'That isn't the only letter he wrote,' she said.

She smuggled him upstairs. She made him swear that he would not say a word, and she showed him the stairs that he should tread on so that the floorboards would not betray he was there. Then she took him into her bedroom. He had been here only once before, that first time when his lips had touched hers, and he no longer recognised the place. It was only a small room, and the ceiling was low where it sloped to the roof, but Lucy kept it pristine. Beneath the window there sat a little dresser, on which she lit a small lantern. As the light of the candle refracted through the glass, William saw strange, spidery shadows cast against the wall. He saw himself as an eight-foot insect, bent low upon Lucy as she rifled within the dresser. In the air, there were the mingling smells of perfume and rising damp – and, to these, there now came the dry odour of smoke. He thought about sitting on the unmade bed, but though he was tired he remained on his feet. In the corner of the room, he saw Samuel's lute. Although it had been several years since he deigned to play it in William's presence, Samuel had once been a talented player.

Lucy reared up from the dresser with the letter in her hands. She turned at William.

'It was lying on the doorstep when I woke in the morning,' she said. 'I got to it before my mother and my father had stirred. They'd have shredded it if they got there first.'

William took hold of the envelope. It strained between their hands for a moment, before Lucy relented and William turned the thing in his fingers. There was no stamp on the envelope, no address scrawled upon the front. It had been delivered by his brother's hand.

He opened it and, in the glow of the lantern, he started to read. His eyes rode across the words, but his lips did not part.

Dear Lucy,
This letter must never leave your hands. Swear that to me,
Lucy. I think that you know why I'm writing. I think that
you know that you're the only person I can stand right now.
I thought about writing to Joshua. I thought about leaving
him a note. Over and again, I started, but I could never

finish. I still haven't ruled it out that it was Joshua sent me back to my parents last night. After everything that has flown between my father and him, I still cannot discount the idea that it was him sold them back to me to make his own reparations. They told us in church that there is a strange kind of honour in the groves of sinners, but it is not something that I am ready to believe.

It has been six days since William fell upon the Moor, and now I am back, here in the house from which I ran, here in the holds of the family from which I was cast. They came for me last night. It was late, and snow moved sluggishly across the terraces, and though I lay wrapped in the sheets of that cellar, I knew that I would not sleep. I suppose it was the wheels of the trap that first stirred me. I suppose that, before his fists rained at the door, I knew already who had come. There was nowhere for me to run, then. I suppose I would not have fled even if there was. Joshua's footsteps sounded on the rafters above, so that I might discern which way he was tramping through the house. He would not put up a fight. A door was opened and a door was closed, and then the voices, low as crooks, sounded in the hallways above.

I lurched into my trousers and went to the foot of the stairs that I might listen more closely to their conversation, but already I was too late: they were coming down the steps towards me, my father in front and my uncle behind him. I had never thought they looked alike before, but here they were, as if one was the other's twin, or some canker in the shape of a man sprouting from the other one's shoulder. My father met me beneath the low cellar's roof and, there, we looked at each other. 'Samuel,' he said. 'Something has to be done.'

And that was how it happened. That is why, in only a few

hours' time, I will be numbered with the Chapeltown Rifles. My father took me back home and he sat me at the kitchen table while my mother milled in the passageway outside, and he brought from his greatcoat a sheaf of papers. I opened them, though already something in me knew what they were. There was a place for me to sign, and there was a signature already in the next box – and then, hidden behind, there was a certificate of my birth. 1899, it read. March 1899. Two years before the day I came into this world. A lie. My father pushed the papers at me, and for a long time he did not speak. 'If he does wake,' he said at last, 'you can't be here.'

Three hours ago, I put my name to the page.

I know what it is I have done, Lucy. And I know what it is I must now do. This morning, before it was light, I walked back across the Moor and cut a path to the infirmary. These last days have been like a dream, and as I looked at the infirmary walls I started to think upon what dreams might be flitting through William's head, even now. And . . . were you and he together, Lucy? And if you were, would you dare say it to me? I know that you kissed. It's three years gone, I am certain it means nothing to you and that it only rarely crosses his mind – and, yet, still I think on it. When I am with you, it is always with the knowledge that it was he who found you first, that without my brother I might never have known you, that he directs me even in something as beautiful as this. What is it about him, Lucy? What is it that makes people smile at him in the streets? He might know the things to say and the way to say them, but is that all it takes? God damn it, Lucy. And God damn me, if He hasn't already. If I ever return, I'll be different. I swear it, Lucy. I'll be good and I'll be a man and I'll be everything William is when he isn't even thinking about it. I'll do it – but Lucy, I need you to be waiting. And still, I don't think that I can ask you to wait. I don't know why, but it just doesn't seem right and proper to ask such a thing. At least I can see that. There must be some shred of goodness left in me.

I think I love you. If I know what love is, I do. But it's like my mother said to me last night: there's just something in me that doesn't think right. She was crying as she said it, and it knifed at me that she was saying exactly what she believed. 'Even dogs know when they've sinned,' she said. She looked at me, then, and I could see that it was not only William I had struck down. 'Even a dog knows when it's done wrong. It drops its head and it slinks away and it looks at you with those big, shining eyes. And what do you do? Well, you just sit there.' She said nothing after that, and I said nothing, and my father said nothing. My bags were packed and I helped my father scour clean my bedroom. William's room, they called it now. I took my lead soldier from the shelf and I emptied my wardrobe and I flayed bare my bed. And now there is a trap ready and on its way, and tomorrow I might be in Catterick or I might be in Burnley, and after that I might be almost anywhere they send boys like me.

Lucy, I'll write. If I can, I'll send you letters. But never tell a soul. And never tell William. I'm not like him, but I do know him. I think I know him better than anybody else – and I know what he'll do if ever he knows where I am gone. Don't let him. Don't give him that chance. Don't give him the chance to be so fucking good. I need to do this myself.

My father is at the door. I can hear him shifting on the stairs. He must have delivered the papers already. They must be stamped and sealed.

I'm going to miss you,
Samuel

71

William folded the letter and looked at Lucy. Though he said not a word, he did not have to. Both knew what he was thinking. Both could hear the hum of his hatred as it swarmed in the air between them, like a cloud of flies cut free from the carcass in which they had been hatched. She had known from the first day he had awoken what he had wanted to know. She had known he would come looking, and still she had kept her secret. No doubt she would have been proud of that. No doubt she would have been thrilled at the strength of her loyalty to his brother.

'How can they hate him like that?'

'It's not about hate.'

'The hell it isn't.'

'They didn't think you'd ever wake.'

'I woke.'

Exasperated, at first Lucy did not reply. She groped out to take back the letter, but William retracted his hands and held it close to his chest. It did not belong to her. Not really. Samuel had addressed that letter to her, but surely it was meant for somebody else.

'It isn't about revenge,' she hissed at last.

'I never asked anybody to avenge me.'

'How much did you ever really know him, William?'

It was William's turn to be silent, then. He breathed, measured and deliberate.

'You barely knew a thing. To you, he was just your brother. To everyone, he was just your brother. If there has to be a reason he did what he did, there it is.'

'I didn't come here looking for reasons. I came looking for him.'

William ripped at the letter and pressed it back into her hands. She flinched only slightly, as if she had been steeling herself against it. Quietly, she turned and placed the ragged halves of the envelope back in her drawer. William stood for a long while, and fixed his eyes on the back of her head. She must have known how withering was his stare, for she did not turn to face him. Reasons? he wanted to say. What did a little thing like a reason matter? He was not concerned with what his brother had done. He was only concerned with what his brother was doing.

'You've got to leave it, William. It's what he wants. Didn't you read it in the letter? He knew what he was doing when he signed those papers.'

'You don't care what they did, do you?'

She turned to face him, then.

'You don't care that they sentenced him?'

'You're a sanctimonious bastard, William Redmond.' Although she hissed the words, William was certain that they echoed throughout the house, guttering along the terrace. 'Something had to be done. And you, you're intent on ruining it, aren't you? It wasn't malice that made your father go to him that day. It wasn't with malice that your mother brewed him tea and spread butter on his bread and cracked eggs on the side of a pan. There wasn't the sort of glee you're imagining on their faces when they sat together around that table, and your father brought out the papers and showed them to your brother and told him how it would happen. Oh, it wasn't forgiveness either. But it wasn't theirs to forgive, was it?'

'No,' William hissed. 'It's mine.'

'So if it wasn't forgiveness and it wasn't malice, do you know what it was, William? Did you think about that? Or can you even think any more, with that . . .' She fumbled for the word. '. . . that *thing* on the side of your head?' She stopped. 'It was love,' she went on. 'It wasn't easy love. And it wasn't only love for you. But it *was* love, William. They're not monsters, your parents. And they didn't breed a monster, just like in you they

73

didn't breed a saint. They know that, the same as you or I. So they went to him and they didn't forgive and they didn't forget – but they found a way through.'

There was an aching silence. It seemed to throb in the air between them.

'He might die out there,' said William, at last.

'You might have died up on the Moor,' Lucy retorted.

William looked at the window, where the net curtains rippled in what little wind could claw through the ancient frames. He could just see, through the fogged glass, the roads that wound to the top of the mount.

'If he does die,' he said, 'it's on you. If he does die, it's on you and it's on my mother and it's on my father.' He stopped, and the way he looked at her was withering. 'If he does die out there,' he said, 'I'm coming back for you all.'

He cut a quick path to the house on Brudenell Mount, his collar lifted high against the evening's chill. In the small yard in front of the house his bicycle still sat, alone where there had once been two. He bent low to check the tyres, and scrape the handlebars free from the thickest snow. He did not know how long it would be before he would need to take saddle and ride.

Inside, and the house lay empty. He moved silently from room to room. Like an intruder, he walked. Coals were still glowing in the grate, and on the range a teapot was still warm to the touch. He saw that his mother's overcoat was gone. Both his mother and his father, roaming those streets in the night, out on his trail. He slumped, for a moment, in the scullery, and tried desperately to think.

He saw the photographs on the mantel.

They had been taken each year, the whole family trotted out to a photographer in the city who would line them up and make them pose and adjust his lenses and demand that they smile. And that was what William saw now: four faces lined up and being coerced into smiling. That was what this family was. He picked up the first of the portraits, and slid it from the frame. His mother had once taken such pride in these pictures. He went along the mantel and gathered all of them together.

There was a tin pail in the cellar, and William took it to the yard at the back of the house. He was sheltered from the worst of the wind here, and the only snow that reached him curled from the guttering high above. He set the pail down and dropped the photographs inside: his mother and his brother and his father and himself. There were matches in the scullery, and he fumbled in the wind for one of them to light.

He dropped the match in the bucket and watched as the images started to wilt. There would be new photographs now. There would have to be. All that was finished. It could not be any other way. He knew that, now. Everything that he wanted was gone.

You've always been a good boy. Remember that. Promise it to me, William. Those were the words that his uncle had said, that first night out of the infirmary. You've always been good. William watched the flames lap at the sides of the bucket, heard each hiss where a stray snowflake settled on the rim of the tin. He had always tried to be good. He had held open doors and carried bags and lain down his coat. He would have gone from one end of the city to the other to gather the things that might have made his mother and his father and his brother happy. He would have gone further, if that was what was needed. But the world had changed, that day on the Moor. There was only one path to take from here on. He watched the last of the photographs disappear in the flames – first his father, then his mother, then his brother's face melting in the heat – and knew, at last, what he would do. I'll be low down, he thought. I'll lie and I'll cheat and I'll connive, if that's what it takes. I'll turn into everything that Samuel is, if that's what it will take to go out there and bring him back.

He did not move when he heard the latch fall. He was transfixed by the flickering pail as the footsteps came through the house, and the shadow fell upon the yard. He could smell the perfume already, and still he did not look up.

'William,' his mother breathed. 'William, what are you doing?'

She was aghast. She shook William by the shoulders, but he stepped away and withdrew the letter from his pocket. He moved as if he was unsheathing a sword.

'*The wind is mournful over Flanders tonight,*' he read.

She groped out for the letter.

'Did he write to you as well?' he demanded.

When she did not reply, he shouldered past her and back into the house. For a moment she remained without. In the mirror that hung over the hearth, William could see her reflection. The wind whipped at her skirts and made them billow. She was holding herself.

'Mother?' he said. 'Was it Father got the false papers and made it happen? Was it him did that to Samuel?'

She did not move. The wind tore at her. She was frozen.

'Mother,' he pleaded. 'He isn't dead yet.'

She looked up at him. She came, then, into the doorway and peered within.

'You let it happen,' William hissed. There was venom in that voice. 'You took him in and you showed him those papers, and you brewed him tea as he put his name to the page.' It was worse than what Samuel had done to him. They had calculated it. They had arranged for him to die out there for what he had done. 'Well, I don't intend for it to go that way,' he breathed as he backed out of the room. 'I don't mean for it to happen.'

* * *

76

He fell against the bedroom door. The room turned before him. He thought it was the way he had rushed upstairs, he thought it was the blood beating black in his veins – but that scar on the back of his head was throbbing again, and he felt as if he might fade away. He took measured breaths, braced himself against the floor, and waited for the feeling to pass.

She did not come to disturb him. Not at first. He had imagined she would thunder upstairs, he had imagined that she might rain her fists at the door and drag him from his den to face the damage he had done – but there were no footsteps in the hall, and there were no footsteps on the stairs. After a little while, when the heaving in his chest had settled, he stood and opened the window. Gusts of wind brought on them flecks of ice. He began to imagine what it was like for Samuel, sitting now in a hole in the ground with his comrades around him. He got to thinking, then, as the picture unfolded before him, of what it had been like in those days when he and Samuel shared a class at school. He remembered the times when the cricket was over for the evening, when they gathered on the grass to share drinks and talk of their victories and dismiss their defeats, and how Samuel had been, then – sitting among them, but never one of them, sharing their jokes but never quite believing in them. Was it like that now, on the other side of the water? As men broiled their stews for the night and stoked their border fires and checked the lines of barbed wire, was Samuel sitting silently among them, opening his mouth to share a story but never quite making it, offering each boy his help and recoiling each time it was dismissed? Or had his brother finally found out there what he had clawed at for so long here on the streets?

William studied silently the naked wardrobes, the empty shelves, the bed flayed bare. This was not his home. Scant weeks ago it might have been his home – when the wardrobes were full and the shelves overflowing and the bed fully made – but now it was only a shell.

He scrambled in the boxes beneath his bed and produced an old knapsack, a thing of flaking leather that had been passed on to him from his father, and his father before that. He started to pile some spare garments inside: a scarf and some gloves, a battered canteen, a roll of string he had kept and not used since he was a boy. He would not need much. Where he was going, he would be well provided for.

I won't leave him, he thought. They sent him to his slaughter on the mountainside, but I don't mean for it to happen. Loves come and loves go, but there's blood to think about; a man turns his back on his family and he is one of the Devil's men. He'll come back and he'll be with Lucy and maybe he'll marry her and maybe Joshua will be at the wedding. William would be best man. He would see to it. After all that had happened, it was the only thing he could do. He would need help if he were to do it properly, and though it seemed that these streets offered up few men who would stand up for a truly good cause, William knew at least one. He would need papers and he would need his medical forms doctored, but it would not be a problem. Of all men in the terrace, Mr Finlay would understand.

The door fell slowly open.

William turned to see his father standing there, his greatcoat drenched and spotted with snow.

'I went looking,' he said. 'When you didn't come back, I went out on your trail.'

William was slow to reply.

'It isn't a good night to follow somebody's footprints,' he stated, gesturing to the snow that plastered itself against the windows.

His mother appeared in the hallway beyond them. She looked cowed as she stepped into the doorframe. She tried to weave her arm into her husband's, but William's father did not respond.

'What's the matter with you?' snarled the old man. 'Don't you understand what we did for you? It's finished. You don't have to go. Your brother is gone, and you're set to stay.'

William fixed his father with a glare. He felt his brow tighten. His eyes shone.

'I heard you,' was all that he said.

'Don't you have something to say?'

William tried not to smile.

'Thank you,' he breathed.

A savage silence. William's father looked, incredulous, from his wife to his child.

'What kind of boy did I raise? Why don't you ever fight back? What Samuel did to you – don't you care? Don't you care that you would never have done that to him? You're a fucking man, William.'

'I haven't earned my spurs.'

His father advanced. William stood. They froze, then, only inches apart, his mother moving, like a hunted beast, in the corners of the room.

'I didn't raise you to be a coward.'

'It's you who won't have me at war.'

'I'm not talking about war.'

'I'm not the one being a coward here, Father.'

William's father looked suddenly huge. He strode forward. He was silent, and he looked down at William, his neck wrenched, every muscle up and down his body rigid. William felt the scar on the back of his head start to sing. He would have to cover it up, but that would not be a problem. The baldness on his head was disappearing already, and perhaps when the time came not a man who saw him would know how he was marked.

The old man breathed, laboured and dark. Perhaps he was going to say more, then – his lips curled in the beginnings of a snarl, and William knew at last that Samuel's blood was in them all – but William's mother came between them, her fingers teasing into her husband's hand. She spoke softly, then, and William's father hissed something in return. William studied the way that they stood.

'It's finished with,' she said – and, as they retreated from the room, William was not certain whether she had meant the words for him, or whether she had meant them for his father. He watched the shadows as they tussled in the hallway. A macabre kind of dance, it was, like marionettes in a summer show he had once seen, as one puppet beat the other into submission. He stared as they tumbled from the hallway and into their bedroom, and then he listened until the words were too dull to comprehend.

Alone now, he sat upon the naked mattress and brought the letter back from his pocket. The page was crumpled and some of the words were already gone, but that did not matter. It was scrawled all over him now. He waited a long while for the fighting to end that night – and as he lay there, as sleep refused to ride to his defence, as the lone lead soldier on the shelf peered down and the half-filled wardrobe gaped wide, he thought only of Samuel.

It was in the smallest hours of the night, when he was certain his parents slept, strangled in each other's arms, that he drifted back down the stairs and found his boots outside the larder. They were old boots, but they were strong, with hard heels and iron caps in the toes. Samuel had a pair just the same, though where they were now William dared not imagine. He spent a long time, sitting in front of the dead fire, tightening those laces, loosening them again, adjusting the tongue as it sat upon his foot. He went from the living room to the scullery, to the larder and the cellar beneath. In the room directly above, his parents slept. He did not know how much longer it would be like this. He did not know how much longer they would go on, not speaking his name. He knew only this: it could not go on for ever. People were not born to be forgotten.

William took up his satchel, and vanished.

Part Two

SAMUEL

I

The message came from the communications trench: they were safe for another night. Somewhere, orders had been rescinded or orders had been changed or orders had been forgotten. It did not matter which to Samuel. He propped his rifle against one of the support beams, and stooped back into the dugout. Three of his battalion lay slumped against each other, snoring greasily, their rations of rum wasted for another long month. He crept close to the makeshift table at which they sat – two splintered supply crates tacked haphazardly together – and lifted a crust of biscuit from one of their hands. Half of it was sodden, but half of it was still dry, and quickly he poked it into his gullet. Like always, it tasted of nothing. There was little more to eating than refuelling in these channels in the earth.

'Redmond?'

Samuel started. A rat skittered away from his feet as he turned, disappearing into one of the earthen walls. Once safely concealed, it turned its snout back at the dugout and emitted a squeak.

Captain Arnold's head craned into the quarters. He was a huge man, the sort Samuel had once considered an ogre, but his blue eyes always dispelled any fear he might have induced.

'Sir?' Samuel replied.

'What duty are you on?'

'Sleep, sir?'

It was a hopeful remark, and Samuel betrayed himself by a smile.

'What would you have me do?' he asked.

'I've a run for you. The rats are through our communications lines again. You up to it, boy?'

'I am,' Samuel replied.

He took the instruction – a roll of paper, sealed with dark wax – and stooped out of the dugout into the light. It was nearing dusk, and the sentries were changing on the parapets in the furthermost trenches, tramping back in for food and rest. Samuel watched them come, men who might have been standing knee deep in the dirt since before dawn. Two of them were helping each other over heaps of sandbags. They were caked in earth, and whether they were old or they were young it was impossible to say.

Samuel wondered what kind of message he was carrying. He turned it in his fingers, studying the crest in the wax. Then, quickly, he set out. He followed the support trench, cut like jagged teeth into the earth, and climbed from it into a little dell of reeds and windblown grass. The grasses grew in a depression in the land, and if he stood still he could almost imagine that there were no warrens carved here into the earth, and no parapets and no banks of snarled wire. He imagined, as he walked through the reeds, that he was standing on the moors at Ilkley, or on the ribbons of green that marked the Meanwood borders in Leeds. This was what he was thinking as he carved a path to the next line of holes in the ground: that everywhere was the same, when you stripped it down and flayed it bare.

He dropped again into the earth, and the smells rose around him: sweat and shit and piss and dirt. There were fires burning in the maws of dugouts along the body of the trench, like the night fires prehistoric men might have kept to ward off the savage creatures of their land. Three young soldiers stood hunched over their fire like crones in a coven, while a fourth circled their small camp fiercely, lunging with a barbed stick at each creature that peered out of the mud in want of their food. Samuel hurried past them, breathing deeply of the burnt onion smells that curled from their pot. Further along the channel – and two soldiers, stripped to the waist, took it in turns to pick the lice from each other's hair. Hunkered apes, they bent low upon each other, pawing at the pelts of each other's backs, crunching the parasites between thumb and forefinger. Samuel watched them as he walked past. One of them grunted and squirmed in delight, free at last of the vermin that had once feasted upon his skin. They clapped callused hands and drank greedily from their canteens.

He went on a little, following a thin trough into the furthest of the communication trenches. The walls were high here and the causeway narrow. As he went he imagined that he was walking the paths of some underworld abyss, as if he was the hero of one of the fables he had read when he was young. Those were stories his father had always forbidden, and all the greater for that: Greek and Roman odysseys of men and monsters and the wars they waged between them. He palmed the walls as he walked, and envisaged the dire wolves and hellhounds that might have come, roaring, out of that earth.

At the end of the furrow he emerged into a wide basin of boulders and sod. There was another battalion made their home here. Samuel saw them gathered around their fires. In one of the ditches two men were reading to one another from a book of French phrases, while in another, boys played at dice. Samuel listened to them singing. They were part of the Lancashire Fusiliers, a clot of Lancastrian grammar school boys who would have been devoured had they lived on the same streets as Samuel, and were cannon fodder in the trenches out here. Samuel had heard them crying at night, holding onto each other like girls. He had decided, days ago, that they would not be his friends. He was certain it did not aggrieve them wholly – they had read too many books to ever entertain the idea of befriending someone such as Samuel – but still he liked the idea that it was he who had scorned them, and not the other way around. There was more justice in it being this way.

He came over a shelf of upturned sod, and a huge basin carved by the shells of some past skirmish opened before him. The boys of the Chapeltown Rifles called it the Reservoir, a vast dome-shaped indentation in the earth that made Samuel think it could only have been fashioned by some comet falling from the stars. There were a hundred trenches that fed into the basin, channels for runners and traps and the ramshackle wagons that ferried cargoes to the boys closest to the wire. Even now, as dusk drew close, the place swarmed. Rags of boys were busy shovelling dirt into steep banks, while cauldrons billowed thick steam into the air. At the furthest reach of the basin, a parade of boys was forming. Half-naked and smeared with earth, they looked to Samuel as if they had crawled out of their dens in a frenzy. He watched the parade grow. Boys flocked from channels on all sides of the Reservoir. He heard a bugle sound, somewhere in the cacophony of voices: English and French, and a hundred other tongues that Samuel could not name. He held tight to the folded parchment and weaved through the herd.

They were leading a boy up the reserve trench, three men before him on horseback and two others bringing up the rear. Here they came, now, navigating the thin gauntlet between the two ribbons of boys. Between them the prisoner stood, head bowed low, walking with the odd attitude of the dancing bears Samuel had once seen at a fairground in Leeds. As they drifted slowly past, Samuel saw the way his face was smeared in dirt and blood, the chains that bound his ankles, the shackles that he wore around his neck and wrists. Often, the men on horse-back would lean low against their beasts so that their prisoner might hear their whispered words. Samuel watched their lips part to form their crude shapes and did not need to hear to know the kind of things that they said. The man in shackles shuffled pathetically on, while the horsemen sat proudly upon their steeds.

Somebody pitched a clod of dirt through the air and it arced over the captured man, exploding like a shell where it crashed against the rocks that sprouted from the earth. The man did not look up. Samuel saw, then, that he was wearing a muted smile. As he shuffled through the teeth of the trench, his head was bowed and that strange smile did not leave his lips. Samuel felt a small clot of men gather at his shoulder, staring at the spectacle as it came.

'Deserter,' whispered one of the soldiers. 'Poor sod.'

Samuel looked around. It was only Jacob, one of the other ragged souls of the Chapeltown Rifles. Samuel knew that he had been born and dragged up on the streets of Sheepscar, and that still he wore the proud marks of that childhood: a bulging shoulder where once he had been pushed from the arms of a tree; an ear that looked as if it might have been chewed by the dogs of the street.

'Who's the man with him?' he asked.

'That's Flynn,' Jacob replied. There was something in his voice that might have been awe or might have been disgust. Like a little boy, he slavered. 'Military Police. They send him out on the trails of men who run away. Now, some rangers, they'll get their man – but it always gnaws at them, the thing they got to do, that they got to bring their quarry back and watch them shot. But not Flynn. Flynn doesn't think the same as other men. Flynn doesn't have friends. He doesn't have guilt. He's just got a task. If we had a hundred men like him, we wouldn't be scrapping in any trenches. We'd already be overlords of this whole land.'

Samuel waited until the deserter was almost gone from sight before he pushed on along the channel. He turned when he reached the end of the Reservoir, and saw the men still gathered, peering after the ranger and his ward. He supposed it was a wretched thing, to be a coward. He supposed it was a dreadful thing that the man had done to his companions, that men might still have lived were it not for the night that he ran – but as Samuel watched the horsemen flanking him as he disappeared, he could not muster the same emotion. Surely there was some man among them who understood? Surely there was one boy there who felt the same thing as he: that there was fear in every one of them, that perhaps it burned more fiercely in some, that sometimes things just happened. The whole earth crawled with them: the spat upon and the shat upon. Why should one man turn upon another he was sworn to protect? It was a thought he had been trying to cling to since the day he first took up his gun.

He rose out of the earth, and into a glade where the grasses grew long. There were traps here, upturned and with their wheels removed, while horses stripped of their saddles stood tethered to the stumps of felled trees. Around a stone ruin, rebuilt with bricks and timbers, a shanty town of tents and lean-tos had arisen. It put him in mind of the plague towns he had been taught of at school that had once erupted across Yorkshire like the boils of the plague itself – and from which Leeds itself had been born. There were barrack buildings that had once been barns, banks of wagons propped high, wind-breaks built from branches and canvas. Men marched here, but they were not the same as those who crouched in the earth. Older and greyer, these were the weathered champions of wars that had raged in centuries past. Two of them stood proudly at the doors of the stone ruin. Already, they had spied Samuel. One of them lifted the rifle from his shoulder, like some medieval man-at-arms shouldering his sword. He met Samuel on the trail, where a low stone wall was crumbled and overgrown with weeds. The man lifted his hand in salute, and dumbly Samuel mirrored the motion.

'Chapeltown Rifles, sir,' he said. He lifted the roll of paper, and the soldier nodded. As he turned, Samuel followed him along the trail, under the charred oak arches and through the doors of the building. In here, fires burned behind the grates of a range, while men gathered about tables where charts were spread wide. Some of them wore uniforms – though they were unlike any uniforms Samuel had seen. They were stiff and they were starched, and they were emblazoned with emblems that Samuel could not read. When they addressed him, it was English that they spoke, but it was spoken in a way that Samuel had never heard in the streets – full and rounded, each word rolled proudly from somewhere at the back of the throat. At first, Samuel struggled to understand.

'I have a communication,' he began. 'From Captain Arnold.'

There was a low haze of smoke in the room, curling from the range. Where it mingled with the smoke of the pipes that the soldiers held, Samuel could see tendrils of grey. He stepped forward a little, holding out the parchment, and watched as the men shared a knowing look.

'Well?' one of the officers leered.

'Sir?'

'Well, what does it say?'

Samuel was still.

'Can you not read, Private?'

'I can read well enough.'

'They taught you that, did they, in whichever rotten little town it is they summoned you from?'

He pushed the paper into the officer's hand, and the officer turned it slowly before breaking the seal. His eyes glazed for a second, and then he looked back at the wretch who stood before him. There was something written there, on that face, but Samuel could not read it. Were there orders inscribed upon the page? Was there some news of when the next raiders might ride out, or some intimation of what the German boys were plotting on the other side of the wire? Was there some knowledge, concealed there, that might seal the fate of every boy who dwelt here in the dirt?

The officer's face crumpled as he refolded the paper. He looked to Samuel with an odd, mysterious smile.

II

In the days that followed, Samuel could not stop his thoughts from returning to the deserter who had shuffled so miserably into the Reservoir, his head bowed to the taunts and the stones hurled at him. For too long he stood and gazed at the mound that rose from the earth like one of the ancient tumuli that marked the dales back home, dwelling upon the man who lurked within. Samuel knew what happened to soldiers who ran. It was one of the first things the sergeants would drill into boys when the transports brought them to the line. You are here now, they said. You are counted as one of us. We live and die by one another – and, now, you will do the same. There were boys who had smirked at that, in the training at Southampton. They had been billeted in a carnival of places – a village hall, a seafront hotel, the cellars of an old seminary – and back then it must have seemed like a game to most. But it had never been a game to Samuel. He had known, when he put his name to that paper in the place that had once been his home, where he was going and what he was bound to do. He had known what he had done and what the world now asked. He had trained harder than the rest. He had not thought of sloping from the barracks at night to chase girls up and down the alleys of a new city. He had kept himself to himself and lain in bed at night, thinking of that day on the Moor and the harried days that followed – and, if the other boys had thought him sullen and strange, well, that was only to be expected. A boy like Samuel was not meant to care what other boys thought.

On the third night, he went to the captain. Samuel knew little of the man – it was said that he was once an officer of the law, roaming the streets at Kirkstall with an iron club at his side – but he had seen him walking through the channels, talking to his men, and he had heard the tales that were told. Somebody had claimed his Christian name was Martin, though using it was a liberty Samuel would never take. He was popular with the men of the Chapeltown Rifles. They did not pour scorn on him as Samuel had heard some men pour scorn on their leaders. He had faith in his boys, and his boys had faith in him. This, Samuel knew as fact. Samuel had often heard the men of the Lancashire Fusiliers bitching about their own fey leader, and he allowed himself some small pride in the fact that he served in the battalion of a good man.

The captain was in one of the oldest excavations when Samuel turned the tooth in the trench. The boys here called it the Mortician's Walk. It was a silly superstition, but this was a land that paid heed to superstitions, and even Samuel felt the chill as he walked that stretch of land. Perhaps it was just that the channel faced south, a trick of the ridges that funnelled wind along the ditch – or perhaps it was that these fields had seen battle a dozen times or more, had been conquered and reclaimed by boys from every corner of the continent. Perhaps it was the bones buried underneath the duckboards, the tombs on which he trampled that bore no inscriptions and no names. Samuel trod lightly as he went.

Captain Arnold was waiting there, by the opening of a thin dugout. Two of the older men were tramping away from him, heads bowed and arms swinging low. The captain's face was set. There were thorn bushes here, sprouting from the parapets and veiling the caverns that lined the trench. It put Samuel in mind of the older houses he had known on Victoria Road and the avenues that grew towards Headingley. He had

94

seen pictures once, of an excavation along the Pennine trails, where the ruins of a prehistoric fort had been uncovered. It was the sort of thing that had lit up his boyhood: men at arms defending their wilderness outpost. He imagined himself, now, stalking those ancient battlements.

'Sir,' said Samuel.

'Redmond,' said the captain.

A silence. It was as awkward as if Samuel had been talking to some girl he admired. It was not a small thing that the captain had remembered his name. It was more than the teachers and shopkeepers of Leeds had ever deigned to do.

The captain reached forth with his pouch of tobacco.

'No thank you, sir,' said Samuel. 'I don't have the habit.'

'You'd be wise to take it up,' the old man grinned. There was a low whistling, somewhere over the wire. 'Many a night, it's saved me, a lungful of the good smoke to remind me of the yards back home.'

'I heard it's got lads killed,' Samuel started. 'Some Goth out there seeing the light of his cigarillo flare – and all it takes is one bullet.'

The captain gave him a lopsided grin. 'You listen to too many stories,' he said.

They stood together, in silence, listening to the sounds of that part of the earth: the low grumble of men at rest, the creaking of a wagon on the other side of the channel. A lean, black bird lit upon one of the beams at the opening of the dugout, and stood there haughtily for a moment before disappearing back into the murk. No doubt it was carrying their secrets to the ravens and crows that skittered up and down the enemy lines.

'What is it, Redmond?'

'It's the man they brought in,' Samuel ventured. He wavered a little, then. There were spectacles perched on the end of

95

Captain Arnold's nose, and he looked over them like an old master at his school. Samuel knew better than to question the deserter's fate. He knew that there were Laws, and that Laws had to be obeyed. He knew that there were things against which no man ought to rail. 'I wanted to know when it might be done,' he said.

'A friend of yours?' the captain asked. His voice was warm, and he tramped a little in the trench. In a dugout along the channel, two boys were practising at parries with their bayonets.

'No,' said Samuel. 'Not a friend.'

'Then why?'

Samuel stifled a shrug. He did not mean to seem weak in front of the captain. He did not mean to seem a little boy. It was one of the things he had sworn to himself, as he scrawled his name on the forged paper at home: that he would not be a boy any longer, that he would leave all those spites and petty jealousies behind. That he would be a man.

'I saw him when they brought him in. There were boys lined up, like they were at the fair – and some of them had rocks in their hands.'

The captain's eyes widened, but it was not in surprise. It's little wonder, he seemed to be saying – little wonder that his fellows should feel so betrayed after the thing that he did. That was what Samuel read on the lines of the captain's face. And if the captain meant it to be harsh, he meant it to be humble, too. There was a horrible regret there that the old man dared not voice.

'Did you know him, Captain?'

'He's one of the old boys. He was in the Rifles when we fought at Aisne.'

'Before the excavations?'

Captain Arnold pitched the stub of his cigarette into one of the latrines.

'He was a horseman. That was what he signed up for.'

'Not this,' Samuel added.

'I was sorry when he fled.'

Samuel wanted to ask about him – who he was, from which town he had come, what he had been like before he ran – but he stayed his tongue. It did not seem a good thing to ask. It seemed a thing over which other boys might have gloated.

'I wanted to go and see him. It must be a frightful thing, Captain. To be sitting there, in a hole in the ground, waiting for a bullet. It must be a god-awful lonesome thing.'

Captain Arnold looked about him, at the caves cut into the ground, at the boys that laboured within, at the walls of earth that looked, in the shadows, to have the visages of men. 'A god-awful thing,' he breathed. He laid a hand on Samuel's shoulder. 'Tell him I won't be there, will you?' he said. 'Tell him I couldn't stand to see it done. Tell him that, Samuel.'

It was late when Samuel set out: the first watch of the night, when boys ran raids, and forays were launched, and the listening posts were manned. He knew that some of their own boys had already been felled, for he saw the stretcher bearers scurrying along the Dead Channels, those ditches carved especially for the ferrying of the fallen. He crouched at one of the ridges that overlooked the Channel and, though he dreaded what he might see, somehow still he looked. The stretcher bearers were the most courageous men in the battalion – men who dared brave the bullets without a gun at their side, who moved awkwardly and sluggishly and open to attack just so that their brothers might be rescued – and a huddle of them rushed, now, along the trench below. They were carrying, between them, a boy whose head was swaddled in dark cloth. He had been shot. It had once seemed to Samuel that if a boy was shot in the head, his life was extinguished in a whisper. He had since learnt that it was a lie.

He reached the mound, and though he explained himself, though he invoked Captain Arnold's name, still the guards there studied him with narrowed eyes. Finally, they deigned to let him pass. There was a small grille in the side of the mound, and as Samuel wrenched it open he heard the squawking of birds in the lone tree that stood, a skeleton, in the crater of earth. It held him for a moment, but then he pushed on, into the jaws of the passage. He did not look back. Even as the grille groaned shut behind him, he refused to turn.

The darkness was absolute. Samuel palmed at the walls and groped his way along the ledges that had been carved into the clay. There was scree scattered here. He could feel it grind beneath the heels of his boots. He staggered a little where the stairs came to an end, and took a moment to right himself. He did not look around. He thought that, if he looked around, he would not know from which direction he had come – and then it would just be him, alone in the dark. Slowly, he started to walk. The air was thick. He might have been walking in mist. He found that he was walking hunched, like a beggar or a cripple, his body coiled and cowering from the tunnel walls.

The passageway must have turned, for now Samuel saw light. At last, he stole a glance back at the channel from which he had come, and saw the way it sloped upwards to the grille and the gateway above. He squinted. He wished he was bearing a torch, or a brand – anything that he might be the one to control the darkness. He edged on, and there the narrow tunnel opened into a small chamber. There was a lantern here, flickering in one of the corners. He could see the walls and the roof of the cavern, the way the earth was marbled and textured with the roots of trees that had once covered the pastures above. The whole land was riddled with

98

the scars of what it had once been. Samuel was stricken with the sudden fear that he would not leave this den alive.

His eyes lit upon the figure propped against the furthest wall. He was slumped on one of the packing crates that furnished the cell. His face was banked in shadow, his hair long and matted with dirt and crushed leaves. There was a mess tin at his feet, but he had not deigned to touch the gruel of meat and potatoes that had been slopped within. Samuel supposed that a man such as he would have no appetite.

It was Samuel who spoke first.

'It's a real dungeon in here, isn't it?' he said. 'A real oubliette.'

The man in the shadows smiled.

'They used to lash the likes of me to a tree,' he breathed. 'I suppose you could say: thank the Heavens for small mercies.'

Samuel had heard of it. In the early days, after the first excavations of 1914, those deserters who were reeled back in would be bound to trees or posts, shackled there like yard dogs or circus bears. The other soldiers would come and look at them, and as the days and the nights flew they would watch the prisoner degenerate, each hour robbing him of a little more of his manhood until he crouched there, shivering and wild. Then he would be led out, still with the rope around his neck, and propped against a wall as the guns blazed.

'Who are you?' the prisoner asked.

'My name is Samuel.'

'A gloater?'

'Not a gloater.'

'Sometimes they send gloaters down to see me. I've had my fill of men who gloat.'

The boy said that his name was Jacques. It was a foreign name, he knew, but that did not mean a thing. He had a mother who was fanciful, and a father who was weak. That was all. Jacques was like Samuel. Jacques was an English boy, born in Mirfield and raised on a farm in that border country. He spoke with a lightness in his voice that did not befit a boy at war. He was tall and he was lean, and even in the gloom the blueness of his eyes was vivid.

Samuel moved a little further around the walls of the oubliette. It was not cold in here, though the clay walls shone with moisture. Perhaps some warmth was rising up beneath them, creeping slowly from the caverns at the centre of the earth. It would not be long before both of them were sent down there – Samuel was certain of that. He contemplated sitting on one of the crude ledges carved into the walls, but something made him remain on his feet.

'I saw you in the channels,' Samuel began. 'The day they brought you in. You were shackled and roped and some of the other boys were pitching dirt at you.' He stopped. 'I didn't pitch a thing,' he said. He remembered, starkly, then, that day on the Moor, when he and William had come between the trees and he had lifted the rock to hurl it far along the trail. He fought hard to stop the memory before it rolled onwards, before it reached the part of the second stone in his hand, and the way he had brought it down upon his brother's skull.

'The man who brought me in. Have you seen him since?'

'No,' Samuel admitted.

'He rode out?'

'I haven't seen him.'

Samuel did not know whether it was true or whether it was false. All faces looked the same, smeared in the dirt of these lands. More than once he had peered into a shard of glass and not recognised his own reflection peering back.

'He'll be on the trail of another now. Some other poor lad who was hungry or lonesome enough to do it.' Jacques paused. 'Why don't you sit?' he said, gesturing to the earth.

Jacques told Samuel of the days before he ran, and Samuel

sat, rapt, upon the earth as the fable was told. He had been in flight for twelve weeks. Perhaps it was slightly less, or perhaps it was slightly more. Jacques said that little things like time no longer mattered. It had been the day after a raid that he ran. He had not planned it. It was not something he had plotted and contrived. It was just something that he did, and something that he had lived and would now die by. There was no trace of anger as he spoke of his end. Samuel supposed it a grim sort of acceptance.

'It was the most horrific raid I served in,' Jacques began. 'There was a flight of gas, and there were mortars, and then it was the other boys pouring into our trenches with cudgels and daggers and entrenching tools. There hardly seemed a gun between them. They had come for our rations. Our boys had shelled their supply lines for four days and four nights and they were starving. There's nothing puts rage in a man's heart like an empty stomach. Six of my friends felled for want of corned beef.'

His lips curled as he trailed off, and it might have been that he was smiling at the nonsense of it all.

'You could repent? You could come back and serve?'

'Repentance isn't enough. There'd be no deterrent if a man could simply repent. Every one of us would run and we'd run and, if they caught us, we'd just look down the barrels of those rifles and hold up our hands and tell them how sorry we were.'

Samuel wanted to go on, but instead he braced himself against the clay and said nothing. He looked at Jacques, and Jacques looked at him, and then each tore their gaze from the other. In the corner, the little lantern flared. The flames in the glass hissed as they swelled. Shadows rippled on the walls.

'It will be OK, after it's done,' said Jacques. 'There's a transport that will take me up there. I believe it, even if the priests they send to forgive me do not. I've seen it. I've seen Marcus

Brutus and Guy Fawkes and Oliver Cromwell sitting with Saint George, singing dirty songs together as the wheels start to grind and the wagons start to roll. Mordred and Arthur, both of them clambering into the back of that wagon and drinking out of the same canteen like nothing ever happened between them. And there he is, the soldier who struck Christ with his spear. He did it just because he wanted to, just because he could, and still he's sitting there with every man who laid down his life so that another might live, or dedicated himself to his wife and his children, or stopped to help a ragman in the streets. There won't be any vengeance where we're all going. Just because I'm going there sooner, it doesn't make a difference.'

Samuel stirred at the words. His eyes narrowed. He was looking at Jacques, and though he could not bear the idea of him standing before the battalion's guns, he found that his throat was tight and his stomach clenched in rage. The walls seemed closer now. He thought that he saw roots twitching in the clay, like grass snakes drowning in dirt. For a moment, the lantern roared and the shadows loomed dark against the clay. And still Jacques just sat there, that same vague smile on his face, too drawn to stand, too calm to kick back or flail out or throw a single punch. He was not even crying. Perhaps that was what chilled Samuel; the boy was already entombed, and he did not betray a whisper. Surely he had a mother and a father who would wait on his news. Surely there were people back home who mattered. The lantern dimmed again, and Samuel saw that his own head had been bowed.

'Do you know what the Harrowing is?' asked Jacques.

Samuel looked up at him. He had heard the word before. Jacques was smiling now, for he thought he could see something written on Samuel. Here there was a story waiting to be told. He might never know how it went, but perhaps he could guess.

'Did you ever study Scripture?'

Reluctantly, Samuel shook his head. He remembered only the passages that he had heard in church week after week, those simple stories that had been drummed into him just as fiercely as the language he was trained to talk. A garden where all was ignorance and peace. A flood summoned to condemn all unrighteous men to a watery end. An ancient king bent on blooding every new-born child.

'You've heard, of course, of the Ascension?'

Samuel conceded that he had. This much, at least, was within his knowledge. He could vividly remember an old leatherbound tome that his father had once unearthed, and the paintings depicted within. On the yellowing pages, there Christ was, his hands and ankles still bloody from the Cross as the light lifted him from the earth and bore him aloft.

'What of it?' he ventured.

'He might have died on that Cross so that all living men might be forgiven,' Jacques said, 'but there was more. They won't tell it in Sunday School, they won't preach it in church – but there's something Christ did before he ascended. Some place else he had to be. Because even then the world was old, and even then generations of men had lived and fought and killed and died and been damned for just daring to be born. So before Christ rose, Christ descended. Went into those caverns below and smote down daemons and drove back devils, so that even men long dead might be forgiven. He scoured those volcanic halls and drew men out, and promised them their ordeals were done with, that there was a place for them now, up there where it is light.' Jacques paused. Samuel was studying him in that pallid light, and there was a look that sparkled like triumph in his eyes. Footsteps sounded heavily on the earth above. 'He went deeper and he went deeper into those caverns, and even when it seemed that every devil was vanquished and every trapped soul freed, still he plunged on.

He found what he was looking for in one of the deepest ravines, a nook where the man was cowering and had been cowering for days and would have been cowering for an eternity if nobody had come. He peered into the abyss and he held out his hand – and he drew Judas Iscariot back to his side.' He stopped, and he smiled. 'And together they were in the back of that transport, as it wound its trail to the Kingdom above.'

Still, Samuel did not understand.

'Don't you see?' Jacques said. He was content, and the simple contentment smothered Samuel. 'It won't matter soon. My friends were cut down on the parapets, but it won't matter that I ran from them and left them to the guns.' He paused. His body was slumped against the wall, but his eyes were wide. There was still life in those eyes, bright and unyielding. 'There are bigger laws than the laws of men. It's something my grandfather used to believe. He'd tell me it when I was only a boy. He'd make me repeat it, like it was an old monk's prayer: "There is a crooked shard in every good man's heart."' Jacques stopped, slumped against the earthen wall. He lifted the canteen to his lips. 'It doesn't matter what I've done out here. When I'm gone, it won't matter at all.'

He was smiling as Samuel left.

They shot him the next day. Samuel was there to see it happen. There were men gathered in one of the hollows in the deep, a big depression in the earth where none within could see the fields of green grass and wildflowers that flourished on the banks above. They led him, blindfolded, into that grim arena and there he stood, arms and legs bound in loose ropes. He did not need to prop himself against the stone wall that ran the breadth of the depression. He was standing as the shots rang out. Samuel imagined that he might even have been smiling behind that dark cowl.

III

Jacob was in the dugout when Samuel returned. He had been sleeping, but he had stirred and he was standing, guardedly pacing the ground. Perhaps it was the six gunshots that rang out which had stirred him. Samuel supposed that those kinds of gunshot would cut through even the roaring of the shells. He stooped under the earthen eaves and slumped against the wall, where the moisture ran cold against his back. There was a mess tin filled with the remnants of the day's meal, but Samuel kicked it aside.

'Is it done?' asked Jacob. Wearily, he kneaded his eyes.

'It's done,' said Samuel.

'I'm sorry.'

'You're always saying sorry.'

Jacob was one of the first boys who had taken Samuel's hand on the day he walked into the trench. It had seemed to Samuel, in those first days, that there was a mark on him – some scar or welt on his skin – that sang out to the soldiers of what he had done that day on the Moor. He had walked guardedly, his shoulders hunched – and perhaps it was only that that made the other boys eye him with suspicion. It was Jacob's eagerness to stand at his side that had made Samuel think he was wrong, that he might not be marked as a monster for all his days. He and Jacob – they had gravitated to one another like boys in a playground. Jacob had not been there to witness the execution, for he had seen such things a dozen times before and had no desire to relive the spectacle. He was older than Samuel, though he had the countenance of a spat-upon infant, and he had walked the line from the very first days of the war. He still recalled, with glee, being part of the teams who had launched themselves into the very first excavations after Aisne in 1914. Those had been glorious days, he said, when war was still good and right and men would flock into France just for the few shillings the King would send their family in Leeds or Wakefield or Poole, or whichever other little fiefdom it was from which they hailed.

'They were fine days, before the excavations,' sighed Jacob, with a kind of grim nostalgia. 'A man might even have enjoyed war at the beginning.'

He was saying anything now, just so that Samuel might not keep on seeing the spasms that had taken the boy when they shot him down. Samuel knew what he was doing, and he was glad for it. He had delved into his packs and drawn from it the little lead soldier that once sat proudly on the shelf at home. Nervously, he turned it in his hand, measuring its weight, tossing it from one palm to the other. It cut the same arc between his hands with each gesture he made. He was concentrating so hard on maintaining the pattern that he caught only snatches of what Jacob was saying, but he heard now that he was telling the story of his first Christmas on the line. It was a story Samuel had heard rumour of many times before. It seemed such a fanciful thing, that there might have been a truce.

'We could hear them on the other side of the wire. Singing carols, they were, except with different words. German words. 'Silent Night', except it sounded like it was being sung by rats. Terrible strange thing, it was. Then somebody had a ball, and suddenly there was people out in the middle, out in the dirt, kicking the damn thing backward and forward as if this was the green outside somebody's old house. Damn strange night.'

Samuel squinted at him. 'You played football?' he said.

'Oh no,' sighed Jacob. 'Not me. I didn't get picked. I never did get picked at school neither. You'd have thought they'd have given me a kick, wouldn't you? But I just never got a game.'

Samuel wondered what school Jacob had been condemned to. He had heard of them – the Woodhouse Halls, the Chapeltown Mill – but to him they had seemed distant places, as far away as the lands in which he now walked. It might have been that they would have been friends, if they had been born on the same street. Samuel found himself warming to the thought. It might have been that he would never have had to follow on the heels of William with Matthias and Alexander and David and Jonah.

'They used to set on me at school, sometimes, so it isn't too bad out here. At least here there's the Bavarians to worry about. I'd rather they were bayoneting the Boche than throwing my shoes in a tree.'

They were talking like that in the dugout when the cries went up. At first, it was just a lone holler, one of the battalion crying out in the deeps. Samuel and Jacob stirred, and turned together to the maw of the cavern – but that was all. They did not go out. They went on, as they had done before, flicking stones from palm to palm, gouging pieces of clay from the ground – anything that would stave off the boredom of those interminable hours. Then, the cry came again: louder and more shrill, closer this time, filled with fire. There were other boys bellowing as well, a chorus of them bawling as they stampeded over the land above. Samuel sensed the support beams starting to shudder. Jacob was already standing, snouting forth from the opening of the dugout, and Samuel went to join him in the trench. A ribbon of boys cascaded over the ridge.

'Is it a raid?' Jacob breathed.

Samuel took hold of his shoulder and heaved him back into the den.

'No,' he said. 'It isn't a raid.'

Samuel had seen it already. Men were fumbling with straps and buckles. Faces were wrenched in private agonies. In some parts of the channel, they scrambled over one another in their haste to retreat. Samuel and Jacob hung there, in the opening of the cavern, and waited for the first rags of the stampede to pass. Then, tentatively, they emerged. Was there something different about the air in which they walked? There were some stragglers in the trench, urgently pawing their way along the walls. Two of them were holding each other, as if they had been shot, or knifed, or worse. Jacob set off as if to run, but Samuel's hand on his shoulder held him underneath the eaves.

Footsteps thundered on the boards above. Samuel looked up, and saw Captain Arnold's face appear over the ledge. His jaw was set tight, his cheeks bunched and red.

'Gas!' the captain yelled, tumbling wildly into the trench. He caught sight of Samuel and Jacob, loitering there in the dugout, and bawled at them. 'Gas! Quick, boys!'

Samuel emerged. Clawing wildly at the ledges, he hauled himself to the duckboards above. Alone there, he turned his gaze to the advancing reefs. To his ears, the world had fallen silent. The sky was torn, and from it the gases poured. It was a magical sight, really. It turned and it shifted and it churned. It looked, to him, like a thousand yellow spirits had risen from the deeps, and now mingled up there, swirling around each other as they advanced. He started to see shapes in the colour. He thought he saw hands groping and faces form. He thought that the gas formed a phalanx of spectres, leering as they charged, each one of them some tortured soul who had lost his life in the dirt.

'Samuel!'

It was Jacob. Jacob tore at Samuel's sleeve, as below them men thundered past.

'What?'

'Samuel, your mask . . .'

Samuel looked around. The shadow was almost upon them. It was thin, like the shadow of tinted glass, and all about him boys fumbled with their masks. Otherworld creatures, they scrambled like rats in a flaming nest. Jacob pressed the ugly contraption into Samuel's hands and implored him to press it to his face.

He did so. The world changed.

Even the land seemed distant. He pulled, fiercely, at the straps that bound the mask to his head and forced himself to breathe. The air was warm and tasted stale. It had not been like this in drills. He had not known that the sound of his own breathing would be so loud, a roaring torrent in his ears.

He watched as the world withered. Grass perished under the tendrils of the gas. He saw it come like a flight of ghosts whose fingers drew the life out of everything they touched. Some boys were still streaming out of the trenches closest to the wire, but others were trapped out there, huddled down in the earth together as the first bullets tore through the cloud. Most of the boys were wearing their masks, but for some the horns had sounded too late. They were thrashing now, flung upon the earth like fish snatched from water. Drowning. Samuel saw it. He reeled a little forward. The yellow mist was thickening about the fallen boys, but there was one he still saw, lying low there in a depression in the ground, a pocket of clean air that the sepia did not touch. There was a mask on his face, but the buckles were loose, knotted and tangled, and in his panic the boy writhed. Groping hands of gas curled about him. The phalanx of spectres howled.

Samuel strode forth.

'Redmond, back into the earth!'

The words were muffled. Perhaps that made them easier to ignore. The boy was sinking out there, scrabbling like a rat. Samuel had watched rats die before. He remembered it vividly. He had been five, or perhaps he had been six. It was his father who had lain the poison, but it had been Samuel who had crouched there, in the shadows of the cellar, watching the rats lurch in their strange little circles; watching them turn, at last, upon themselves; watching the way the feet kicked and the nose twitched as death finally came. William had found him down there, watching the rats. William had cried to see what his brother was doing. William had sobbed for the rodents.

Samuel vaulted the sandbags. He heard the thunderous yell that summoned him back to the trench, but it was only a distant thing, the voice of some anxious mother snarling at her son to come out of sleep. He ran. He saw the world warping in the fog, tinted yellow and dark. He could hear his breathing, heavy and all about him, could feel the moisture that grew on the inside of the mask.

He reached the boy. He saw who it was. His name was Peter. He was thin and he was slight, and he was sprawled there with the mask hanging half off his face. Although the bullet had only found his shoulder, still he did not move. He was rigid with fear. Samuel looked up, and saw the gas curling towards them with outstretched arms.

He drew the buckles hard around Peter's face and hauled him aloft. He was not heavy. Boys rarely were, out here where there was nothing to eat. Samuel shouldered him and stood. When he turned he could see the banks of boys staring at him through the sandbags, each masked man identical to the last. Even through those masks, Samuel knew that they had fixed their eyes upon him. He heard his own breathing pounding as he took his first step.

Gunfire. There was gunfire around him. He heard it only distantly, like stones pitching into sludge, but he knew without turning that it was upon him: boys gathered on the other side of the gas, loosing their rifles at whatever dim shapes moved out there in the murk. He sank for a second, his shoulders hunched over the boy that he bore, but quickly he found that he could not move, and quickly he righted himself again. He lurched on. Through his mask he saw, in the peripheries of his vision, one of the bullets find one of the boys who peered over the sandbags. The boy was standing, and then he was flying, and then he was still, a dark fountain pumping from his breast.

Another bullet. Samuel heard its hiss as it rent the air at the side of his mask. Startled, he reeled around to see the dim outlines of boys on the other side of the gas. He knew that they had seen him. One of them shifted, his silhouette rippling in the haze, and then another bullet ripped the air above Samuel's head. He turned, and staggered forth.

'Samuel!'

There was a boy rising from his own ranks now. Samuel saw hands grappling to draw him back, but somehow the boy summoned strength beyond his size, and scrambled over the sandbags to meet Samuel on the ridge. It was Jacob. Samuel could not see through the mask that clung to his face, but still he knew that it was Jacob. The boy had produced his pistol now, and he lifted it to loose bullets into the veil. There must have been shadow men advancing from all directions, for Samuel saw him whirl wildly with the barrel, driving them back from all corners of the earth. There was a muffled roar, and Samuel pushed on.

Bearing Peter aloft, he descended the ledges alone. The gas was thick above them now, and he kept low as he charged along the channel to where the air was yet clear. There were other boys here. Most of them had fled, but the stragglers still remained. Samuel picked out Captain Arnold among them. The old man was unflinching, the mask strapped tight about his grizzled face. There were tubes and visors between them, but Samuel could envisage the expression that clouded the mask. He felt the gaze bore into him – but he did not care. He turned back only to see Jacob throw himself into the trench and then, gently, he stooped low to the ground.

Samuel lay Peter on the duckboards, and looked up to see the gas ghosting over. The other boys were gathered about him, each one of them masked and unknowable. Some of them saw the yellow vapour creep over, and retreated into the dugouts, as if that might save them from the mustard shroud. One by one, they left. One by one, they fled – until, at the end, only Samuel was there, crouched over the boy he had saved, wrapping a length of his own shirt around the arm to stem the blood that still spilled. And it seemed to Samuel, then, that he was back on the headlands of Woodhouse Moor, stooped over another body, tending to another fallen boy. In his mind, he walked again the journey from the heights of the scrub through the ledges of his streets, heard again his echoed words as he came through the scullery doors: 'Mother, there has been an accident!' Tears did not well in his eyes, then, for there was something older, more mysterious in the way that he felt, something that mere tears could not answer for. He looked at his hands; they were red and they were sticky – and, in that moment, he believed that he at last understood the crime for which he had to atone; in that moment, he believed that William was already dead.

It was said that Peter would be well, that perhaps he might even rejoin them in the earth in a scant number of weeks. Some of the men said that it was a terrible thing, that perhaps he ought to have been left to suffer just a little longer, that then he might have been sent back home. Though they said it with a grin, Samuel would not suffer it. He left them to their stories and he paced the reserve trenches alone, kicking idly at the clumps of grass, now crumbled and brown, that grew between the boards.

There were boys there who saw what he had done, and brought him cigarettes and brought him whisky, like men making up their offerings at church. There were others who looked at him with suspicion. Samuel had not expected it, but he was not surprised. They kept a distance from him in the channels. They bowed their heads as they passed, so that he might not catch their eyes and engage them in conversation. They need not have worried; Samuel was not a boy for idle chatter. He did not mean to speak about what had happened on the day of the gas.

He was alone in the dugout, flicking shards of stone from the soles of his boot with the end of a dagger, when the summons came. It was only a few words, spewed from the lips of some rat-faced runner, but even as he heard them for the first time, Samuel knew that something was amiss. 'The captain wants to see you,' were the words that the boy declared – and, softly, Samuel set down his knife.

Slowly, Samuel came along the ditches in which the captain was stationed. They were a mile or more from the wire here, though still the shells could be heard whining as they rocketed overhead. The trenches here were higher than at the front, and in places wildflowers flourished in the cracks between the duckboards. Tethered outside the mouth of the dugout, a lean donkey scuffled with the rope that bound its neck. Samuel lay a hand on its snout as he pushed inside, and the beast opened its eyes to him as if in communion. Bending low, Samuel palmed some of the grasses it could not reach into its lips. It turned them gratefully and brayed out its thanks.

Samuel stood there, in the shadows at the entrance to the dugout, for a little while. Inside, the captain was shuffling papers. There was a pencil in his hand, gnawed to a stub. He might have been forty years old, or it might have been that he was younger, weathered by the years he had spent with a rifle in his hand. Samuel wondered that a man like that could ever have lived on the terraces of England.

'Samuel,' Captain Arnold began, stirring at last. 'I've been wanting to see you.'

Samuel moved a little further into the cavern, entering the halo of a lantern that hung from the beams. It was bigger than the holes in which the rest of the boys dwelt, but not by far. There was a rifle propped against the wall, just like in every other den; a rack of stones on which to sit; a trough against the furthest wall that would act as a latrine.

He knew already, by the way the captain looked at him, what it was that was wrong. He hoped it might have been spared him – but, really, it was a futile hope. He heard, again, the donkey braying in the channel outside – and wished that he were as dumb and set for death as that brute.

'What is it, Captain?' he asked.

'I've been asking questions,' said Captain Arnold. 'After what happened on the barricades, after what I saw, I knew there was something amiss. I could see it in you as you thundered out there. Wild and unstoppable, as if a hail of bullets wouldn't cut you down like it would the other boys out here . . .'

Samuel did not know if there was anything he could say. He looked at Captain Arnold, and it was as if he was daring him to say more.

'I heard about what happened to your brother.'

114

Samuel wrenched.

'What in God's name do you mean by that?' he spat.

'Secrets leak in a place like this,' said the captain. 'Maybe there was a lad from your streets, down in one of the other trenches. Maybe he was a runner. Men can't live like this without talking. Men can't live like rats without telling their tales.'

'It wasn't their tale to tell.'

Samuel wavered. He stared at the captain, and the captain stared back – and nothing more was said. Outside, a trail of men tramped past, propped awkwardly against each other with their canteens in their paws.

'How old are you, son?'

Samuel did not reply.

'I could have you discharged. Back to your streets. It could be over for you, and if things go right this year they need never call on you again.'

'What makes you think I oughtn't to be called on?'

It was a challenge. Samuel started forward and peered down with venom, while Captain Arnold lay back in his chair and considered his charge. For a moment, Samuel did not know in which direction to look. His eyes flitted nervously from one corner of the dugout to the other.

'You could go home.'

'Sir, I want to fight,' Samuel began. He fixed his eyes on his captain, now, and the captain did not flinch. 'I want to be up there, on the barricades, with the others. I want to be standing with them when the gas comes tumbling over. I want to look around and see someone fumbling with his mask, and I want to run out and steady his thrashing and fasten it good so that the gas doesn't get in. I want a rifle in my hands when we rush out to build back the sandbags. I want to go over the top.'

Captain Arnold stood. He was taller than Samuel, and his face was set.

'You want a bullet in your side,' he growled.

'I didn't say that.'

He sat back down, then, and there was a look on his face that Samuel could not read. He thought for a second that this was what pride might have looked like, but he quickly cast the thought from his mind; he had seen pride before, and this was not it. For a long while they looked at each other – until, at last, the captain tore his eyes away and began to wring his hands.

'The orders I had you carry. You remember? Did you stop to think on what I had written? Do you know what's bound to come?'

Samuel had turned away already. He supposed it was insubordination of a sort, but a little thing like that did not matter now. He was already in the ditch outside the dugout when he whispered his reply. The donkey tethered there was studying him with hooded eyes. It might have been that even a stupid beast like that could see straight through him. 'I know,' he breathed.

'Then you're a god-damn fool,' the captain said, repeating it over and again, a petition and a prayer: 'You're a fucking fool. A god-damn fool.'

Samuel strayed a little way along the trench. He had reached a parting of the ways when he heard the donkey braying out, and turned to see that the captain was following him. 'Please, sir,' said Samuel, imploring him with a look to leave, but the captain solemnly shook his head.

'Why did you come?' asked Captain Arnold, softly.

'I don't know, sir,' Samuel shrugged. 'I suppose there's some things a boy has to do.'

'Killing other boys isn't one of them.'

Samuel wavered. 'I didn't kill him,' he uttered.

'I didn't mean your brother.'

If it was meant to injure Samuel, the captain had succeeded. Samuel writhed a little, and pushed further into the dirt, before the captain's muted growl stopped him in his tracks.

'It was my parents.' Did Samuel's voice break, then? He had to stop talking. He had to wrest himself back. He felt coiled, like a spring. It was the way he had felt his entire life: ticking, ticking, counting down the hours until his own trap was sprung. 'After what I did, after what happened to my brother, they searched me out. I tried to run, like that boy tried to run – and they came for me, just like the ranger came for Jacques, and they sold me out.' Again, he stopped. He knew he had signed that paper willingly, but also he knew that there was no other choice. It seemed an odd conundrum, but that was the truth. He could not have stayed, he had wanted to flee – and yet, there was something in him that still wished it could have been his decision. 'It was supposed to be my brother in the Chapeltown Rifles.' He gave a sigh that might also have been a smirk. 'Well,' he said. 'At least this time I came first.'

'Does he live?'

Samuel pictured the infirmary. He was looking up at it, and it was dark, daubed like a child's painting in black silhouette against the sky.

'I don't know if he lives,' he admitted.

'Samuel,' the captain said. 'It isn't a sin to be alive. There's all men equal out here in the dirt. Don't forget it.'

'I won't.'

'You won't listen though, will you?'

'I said I would.'

'Don't forget it and you'll be OK.'

Samuel stopped. There was a whistling, and somewhere further up the line the ground started to quake.

'When it comes,' Captain Arnold went on, 'I need to know you're with me. Not lost in your own head, thinking about streets and red pillar boxes and suet pudding. When it comes, I need you here. And it will come, Samuel. It's been three months now. You get to know the feeling. You can sense things shifting on your shoulder. Runners going back and forth and back again; men summoned and battalions split apart without any pattern, like some demigod up there is playing with dice.'

Samuel understood. He had seen it, too. Men were being marshalled and men were being moved. In the last days there had been more movement in this part of the line than in all the long weeks he had been stationed here. The guns had been blazing further along the front, and it was said that the French boys at Verdun were, even now, tramping in trenches of their own blood. Sometimes Samuel thought about it, late at night, what it would be like, up on the barricades, if battle came to this part of the line.

'I'll be there, Captain,' he said. 'There isn't any doubt.' He stopped. 'That's why I came.'

'I'm glad of it,' said Captain Arnold. There was a wailing in the deep, as somewhere over the wire a cry went up. 'We'll be together when it comes, Samuel. We all will. I'm not like the other captains. I won't send you out there without me riding alongside. I've seen captains like that. I've served under them. But it won't happen under me. I still remember a unit of men scattered by shells, and their captain scared shitless, just saying to them, 'Boys, you'll have to make your own way back', before sloping off into the dirt. I wouldn't do that to my boys, Samuel. They mean more to me than that. You all do.'

He said the last words pointedly, and they lifted Samuel's eyes. He allowed himself to smile.

'Thank you, Captain,' he said, and felt strange warmth creep upon him.

IV

Though it was said, in the barracks back home, that a man might only be called upon once or twice in a long year of war, on the line the story was different. On the line, it was said that each new day visited fresh horrors upon any man unfortunate enough to survive. On the line, every soldier had a story of the things he had seen, or the depths to which he had sunk out there in the dirt. Sometimes, in the nights, Samuel would venture into the circles of soldiers as they shared those dark tales: men turned to fountains by strafing guns; a French girl found alone in a ditch with no tongue left with which to cry out. He heard of men thought lost, who erupted gasping for air from the corpses piled in the dead carts; of others stricken with a strange kind of awe as the yellow gases curled over their heads to claim them. He began to think that there must have been something magical in war, to make grown men talk like that. He wondered what it would do to him, when the time came and he tumbled over the tops.

On the fifth day after the gas, the men of the Chapeltown Rifles were billeted in the trenches furthest from the wire, and the old farm buildings that doubled as bunkhouses thereabouts. Captain Arnold went among them, then, delivering their instructions: for a day and a night, they were to be free. Some of the boys did not understand, so used were they to bedding down in the earth at night, but quickly they learned. For a day and a night, they were not to be soldiers. For a day and a night, they might wander and roam as they wished.

Some of the older men were suspicious, as if perhaps this presaged their final charge over the wire, but Captain Arnold allayed their fears. This was a kindness. That was all. And didn't men who found themselves in such lands deserve a simple kindness from time to time?

It was midday by the time Jacob and Samuel had grown used to the freedom, and the sun had already reached its peak and begun again to sink when they hit upon an idea. Jacob had often been told the merits of seizing the day, but until now he had never cared for it. For Jacob, days were dull things to be squandered in idling from one end of the town to the other – and so far he and Samuel had successfully squandered long hours, lounging there in the grasses that grew against the farmhouse walls. They had been watching the clouds shifting and parting over the glade, and for a while that had been amusement enough. It was a glorious day, with warm air and little wind – but there had to be something more.

They had seen the other boys, of course, piling upon the railcarts and tramping over the fields, but until now they had not thought that such things were for them. Samuel had not deigned to imagine where the other boys might be going, and though he had heard of the little township of Le Bizet, he had not spent his time picturing it as had some of the boys in the trench. Jacob was standing now, drawn proudly to his full height at the top of the hill, and he was staring at the little rail-cart that ground slowly along the tracks, on its way back from the village. 'It would be a damn fine thing,' he was saying, 'if we were to go out there. It would be a damn fine thing if you and me were to be like the other boys for once.'

And that was all it was. Just an idea. But soon it had claimed Samuel as well, and together the two boys were scrambling aboard the little cargo train, trying not to catch the signalman's attention as they grinned like girls and wondered what they might find in that foreign land.

The township of Le Bizet lay only a short ride along the rails, through fields where farmers still tended to their land, and along trails marked in wildflowers already bursting into colour. It sat on the edge of a glade, and as they approached it was easy to imagine that the land thereabouts was not ploughed by shells, and there were not men summoned from all corners of the world battling here in caverns carved into the fields. Indeed, as they came from the carts, Samuel and Jacob were both acutely aware of the dirt that caked their skins. It was the first time that they had felt it, and it stabbed at them – that here there were normal, loving people, getting on with the business of being alive.

They called the glade Cockerel Valley. It was what the English boys called it – another nonsensical, child's name, as if to suggest that what they did out there was nothing but japes – and even here Samuel could see the observation balloons floating above. Samuel and Jacob came through the grasslands now, towards the first of the buildings. There were low town walls, but no guardsmen to patrol them, not since the ages when these lands had last been conquered. There were people milling in the streets, and somewhere the sounds of music.

It was a pretty place. Samuel could think of no other word for it. It was not beautiful and it was not majestic, it was not grand and it was not striking – but it was pretty, and for two boys dredged from the dirt, that was enough. They followed the sounds of music along a wide thoroughfare of cobbles, and for a little while it was as if they were not soldiers at all. Donkeys were tethered along the edge of the road, and three pigs snouted in one of the yards – and the only sign that this was still the world from which they had walked was the wagon parked in a lane between two houses, and the soldier who stood alongside it, accepting gifts of flour and eggs.

Le Bizet was alive. If there was one thing that struck Samuel as they probed deeper into its pathways, it was that Le Bizet still lived. It was bordered by grey and it was banked by graves waiting to be filled, and yet somehow it throbbed. There were gardens full of flowers. Banners strewn across streets. Washing pegged to lines and drying in the breeze. The little things of life. It still went on. Samuel smiled to think that, only an hour from a land riddled with tunnels and mines, an old maid threw up her hands in disgust that the birds had made a mess of her washing. It was a strange country that could let such things happen.

They came from the spider's web of streets and into a broad square, bordered on all sides by stalls where tradesmen hawked their wares. The sun dappled the cobbles here, and in the middle of the stones a trio of fountains erupted from a dark, ornate design. This, then, was where the town gathered each day. They ventured on, peering dazedly at the milling people of the town: the women, and the girls. Samuel saw, then, that there were few men among them, and he remembered suddenly how it had been in Leeds, the streets dredged of young men to go out and grapple in the Flanders mud. He looked back, absently, through the stone abodes, at the fields through which they had come.

There was a building across the square. Boys were sprawled on the boardwalks there, clustered around little tables under the overhanging eaves, while girls brought them drinks and whispered to them their secret words. Jacob wrenched at Samuel's sleeve – and, without turning round, Samuel knew what his friend had asked.

The dance hall was already crowded when Samuel and Jacob

pushed through the doors. Though Jacob was the most eager, it was Samuel who went first. On the threshold, the boy was beset by nerves. He looked at Samuel and perhaps he was thinking about giving up the endeavour – and, in the end, it was Samuel who had to coerce his friend through the doors.

Half of the battalion was here. It was a dark room, its rafters low and its floor uneven, and girls were weaving through huddles of men, bearing drinks and trays and bowls of food so bounteous that Samuel was not certain they were real. He surveyed the room quickly, lest he be mistaking it for a mirage. There were men from all the battalions here, and not just the Chapeltown Rifles, men who had poured in from all points along the line: Englishmen and Irishmen and Canadians and, by the furthest shutters, dark-skinned men who must have been marshalled from one of those distant lands to which England had laid claim. They went a little further, and the crowd closed around them.

Across the hall, Samuel saw some of the other boys from their battalion, gathering around a group of girls. He and Jacob watched them for a long time. Samuel had once befriended an old accomplice of Joshua's from the lanes of Meanwood, who kept hives of bees on a stretch of land beyond the city walls. The summer before the old man had been taken to the infirmary, he had spent long hours at his side, learning of the ways the bees danced, how they sang out to their sisters of where the sweetest nectars could be found. Watching these boys and these girls was much the same. He felt as if he was studying them – how one of the boys would lean forth across a table and spread his body wide, how the girls would recoil in mock horror while secretly mirroring the actions of the boys. On the edges of the room, he and Jacob clasped their drinks.

'You ever kissed a girl?'

'Shut up, Jacob.'

123

'You've never even kissed a girl?'

'Have you kissed a girl?'

'Shut up, Samuel.'

An hour passed. Perhaps it was more. The warmth of drunkenness was upon Samuel and Jacob, but still neither of them made forays into the crowds that clogged the hall. It did not seem a thing that either of them could do. Conversation had died between them now, and even when one or the other tried to rekindle it, quickly it petered away. They were content to be together and watch. Samuel supposed it was a good way to be. He supposed that was friendship.

The day must have been dwindling – though the shutters had long been closed, and the air inside had long been a pall of dark smoke – when Jacob broke Samuel from his reverie to see the two girls perched on the neighbouring table. Jacob's words were garbled, then, but Samuel understood this much: that somehow Jacob had attracted their attention, that for the last five minutes they had been casting glances in his direction, before retreating behind cupped hands for a private deliberation. Somehow, Jacob had succeeded. He was proud of this fact. He called it 'making eyes'. This, he understood, was what boys did when they wanted to summon a girl. Was it really so simple? Was the incantation really so easy to master?

The girls lifted their glasses to Jacob, and Jacob saw, then, that the glasses were empty. Samuel was studying his friend's face when the idea flashed across it. Jacob would get them drinks. It came to him like the face of God. It was an epiphany like shepherds and wise men had once had. He would get them drinks and they would come and share those drinks, and in that way something wonderful would be born. It was just another part of the magic. Jacob understood that, now. He scuttled off into the crowd, Samuel looking hopelessly after.

The music picked up. Samuel had not noticed when it

began, but there were musicians here now, weaving through the crowds of young lovers, bearing roses and ribbons and an assortment of other trinkets the soldiers might have wanted to buy to woo their new-found sweethearts. It was the music of accordions, and little wooden pipes. Samuel had not heard music for a long time. He thought, suddenly, of a day on Burley Park, when buglers had played.

The table shifted, and the girls sat down.

Samuel was torn from his daydream to see them sitting there. Jacob had only just appeared, over their shoulder, and the most peculiar expressions were flitting across his face. The girls were pretty in a way that English girls were not. There was something different about them that Samuel could not name. They had drawn their stools close to the table, and the smaller one – the one with red hair, with green eyes – was leaning forward, long fingers arched against each other to form a kind of temple. Samuel straightened on his stool, and found that his throat was dry.

If Samuel found it difficult to believe that these girls had chosen to approach them, Jacob must have thought he was in a waking dream. He bustled forward with the drinks and groped clumsily for his own seat. He was looking from one of them to the other, and then to Samuel, and they were not words that came from his lips, but a sort of frothing joy instead. After a little while, the girls began to look confused. Perhaps it was the silence that confused them. Girls and boys were supposed to talk. This even Jacob knew. Samuel decided that he would break the deadlock.

'Samuel,' he said, indicating himself. 'Samuel,' he repeated, placing his hand on his breast.

'Samuel,' Jacob intoned.

The girls looked at him, puzzled.

'Samuel?' the second, black-haired girl questioned.

'Not me!' grinned Jacob. 'Samuel . . .'

'Samuel?'

'Samuel.'

The girls looked at each other. There might have been something knowing in that look. They began to say the word over and again, as if in the repetition they might discern its meaning. Soon, it seemed to Samuel that they were chanting the word. Did they understand it was his name? Might it have been that they were mocking him? He went to the bar, and when there was nobody watching he ferreted around for a scrap of paper and a pencil with which he might write a message. He might only have been away three minutes, but when he returned Jacob was proudly holding court with both of the girls – and it was a look of horror that came upon him when Samuel returned and the black-haired girl went to his side.

Samuel gifted her the piece of paper. He was trying desperately to remember the few phrases the boys had bandied about in the trench, but even English words were failing him now. He had scrawled his own name on the page, as if in some way that might help. 'Samuel,' the girl said, enunciating each syllable slowly and awkwardly. 'Samuel,' she nodded, and folded the paper to hide it in her blouse.

And that was how it started. That was how there were drinks, and how there were wild attempts at being understood – and how there might even have been fumbling underneath the table. Was it a thing these girls had done before? Surely Samuel and Jacob were not the only lonely soldiers to have wandered into their path? Samuel did not care, and it did not cross Jacob's mind. Together, they drank – and it seemed that their glasses were never empty.

The black-haired girl was the prettier. Samuel and Jacob

126

had both remarked upon it, though as Jacob was swept aside by the other girl, Samuel did not hear a yelp of complaint. The hair was short but thick, and she wore a dress that might have seen any of the girls from Burley and Sheepscar sent screaming to the stocks. On her shoulder there was a strange mark, a butterfly made of ragged lines scored into her skin several years before. Samuel wondered if they were the mark of some lover the girl had once known. He found the story was formed already in his head: the stolen nights in the long grasses outside the town, the father who had found them and dragged them back to the farm, the decree that they might never see each other again. He reached out to trace the line of the crude tattoo, and found that she laughed in strange excitement when his fingers lit upon it. She was smiling, and the expression was infectious. Samuel began to speak, tried to mouth the few phrases in French that he had learnt from the boys in the basin – but she pressed a finger to his lips, and he was quelled. There was no need to speak, she seemed to be saying. There was nothing he could say.

The girls led them outside. It was the end of the day and, though it was still light, the sun was low, turning the rooftops and the chimneystacks to copper. They followed a street of cobbles that narrowed as it ran, and at the bottom they turned into one of the houses there. It occurred to Samuel, then, that the girls were probably sisters. Together they harried and clucked behind him, and soon Samuel and Jacob had been shepherded inside. Like lost lambs, they were, their eyes wide and confused. Jacob looked at Samuel. He was struggling to suppress his grin.

It was a plain little abode, with curtains hanging in the windows and only a few chairs littered about the wooden boards. There was a hearth, but there was not a fire burning in it and there had not been one for many months. They went a little further, through an arch at the end of the room and into a little hallway. A bare set of stairs led into the chambers above. Jacob could no longer hold it at bay, and the smile erupted on his face. It frothed there and would not be dispelled.

At the bottom of the stairs the girls conversed in that same rush of unintelligible sounds that they had first heard only an hour before, and then the smaller one clasped Jacob's hand. Jacob jerked a little – but already he was following her up the stairs. Now the black-haired girl and Samuel were alone. Samuel watched Jacob disappear beyond the rail of banisters, and he felt for a moment as if he was being left alone on that stretch of land between the trenches. The girl said something that might have been intelligible if only Samuel was listening, and then she reached out to take his hand. Rigid at first, his fingers quickly slipped into hers and, together, they took the first step.

The room upstairs was small, with only a single feather mattress and burgundy curtains draped against the glass. She closed the door and bowed her head at him as she went to draw them closed. Already Samuel could hear Jacob and the other girl in one of the neighbouring rooms. It was Jacob that he heard, and only little of the girl. There was fumbling and there was chatter in English and chatter in something that might have been French – and then there was that awkward grunt of unity and all that followed. The girl looked coyly at Samuel. He thought she might have been apologising for her sister, but quickly he realised it was not that at all. She lit a candle stub in the corner of the chamber.

She was beautiful. There was little doubt of that. She had black hair and she had blue eyes. Samuel had not known many girls in his short life, but he had known a few – and this girl whose name he did not know was one of the finest he had seen. She was prettier than Lucy. Samuel had to concede it, though it tore at him to do so. Her head was slightly bowed, and she was tracing strange sigils with her finger upon his knee. Slowly, she moved from his knee to the inside of his thigh. The runes of Love, no doubt; Samuel knew what these foreigners were like. She must have had spells, for already he could feel them taking effect.

She said something in that strange tongue of hers, and he could not translate. A moment later, and she had planted her first kiss upon his cheek. She caught the corner of his lips as she drew away, and instinctively they followed hers. His eyes were closed and when he heard her whisper his name, he opened them, and she was close and he could feel the fog of her breath and it was sweet. She shuffled closer to him – and it was then that he ran.

He tumbled out of the building and he hurtled up the street. He imagined that she was hanging from one of the windows behind him, bawling for him to return – but he heard nothing, and he did not look back. It was difficult to run, but the further he flew from her the easier it became. He turned onto the wider thoroughfare, and there he slowed. His feet clattered on the cobbles. If any of the passers-by had noticed him, they did not let it show. He disappeared into a narrow lane between two of the streets and slumped alone there, thinking of what he might have done.

The stone was cold against his back. He braced himself there. He looked down. Saw the rock. Imagined it was in his hand as he brought his fist back and cut the arc into his brother's head.

He wondered what Lucy was doing now. He wondered what she had made of the letter he had left. He pictured her as she lifted it from the mat where it had fallen, spiriting it away to the bedroom where she could read it, safe from the prying eyes of her parents. No, they would never understand. Samuel had long known the way that they thought about him. Some things did not have to be said. He had seen the way they looked at William and he had seen the way they looked at him – and for many years he had known, without ever having heard, the things that they whispered behind closed doors.

He wanted to see her. It was the first time the thought had occurred to him so clearly – and now he wanted to see her as he wanted only one other thing. He was thinking, then, of that perfect day when he had first kissed her and told her the things that he thought he would never dare voice: that he dreamt about her at night, that he wanted to look after her, that he wanted to hold her hand. They had strayed onto the Moor, that day. It was spring, when the scrubland was not so forbidding. She had looked at him – puzzled, at first – and then she had taken his hand. They had lain together in the grass and he had dared to stroke her thick, curled hair. He didn't think he would ever want to stroke another girl's hair again. He had been dazed for days.

He was there for what might have been an hour, and when Jacob emerged it was with a triumphant grin that the boy approached his friend. He was holding himself tall and his shoulders were pushed back, and he clapped a hand on Samuel's shoulder as they met. Samuel tried not to think about that hand, and together they pushed back into the streets.

'What was she like, that girl?' Jacob beamed.

'She was nice,' said Samuel.

'Real nice?'

'She was good.'

Jacob's laugh was sticky with phlegm.

'Yeah,' he grinned. 'What was she called?'

Samuel admitted that he had never found out.

'You're an old wolf, aren't you, Samuel Redmond?' Jacob snorted as they disappeared into the streets.

They took the railway back to the end of the line, and from there they walked down through the dells to where the first of the shacks were erected. The evening was still, and though the sun was almost down, there was still light in the fields. There were few clouds left. In the grasses the first flowers of spring were coming into blossom, small blue and yellow buds that grew like weeds but were among the prettiest weeds Samuel had ever seen. 'It's a strange thing,' grinned Jacob as he stooped to pluck a cluster of the flowers and pin them to his lapel, 'but even a thing like a weed can be beautiful. Even something as ugly and useless as a weed.'

It took only a few steps for the grass to disappear and the ditches to open below them. They could smell the familiar stench of the reserve trenches now. There were fires burning on the ridges above, and in the dugouts men were eating. They dropped further down the earthen steps and followed the jagged teeth of the trench. Some of the men here were familiar. One of them clapped Samuel on the back as he went, as if the two of them had been friends since a time neither could remember. Samuel hesitated at first, but then he smiled back. He placed a hand on that man's hand, and then they passed on. Jacob was still chattering about the girls in Le Bizet, but Samuel did not hear every word. He did not have to. Sometimes you could understand the meaning of a man just by the rhythm of the noises he made. There were things, he knew, that you could recognise in a boy no matter what language it was he was speaking, or whether he was speaking any language at all. There was fear, of course, and there was anger and there was hate – but there was laughter, too, and excitement, and joy. Jacob leered back at Samuel as they turned into the next tooth of the trench. He was saying he would dream of that girl tonight, and the night after, and the night after that. He was saying that the next time they were billeted beyond the trenches he would disappear for nights on end, just to be with that girl.

They came, at last, to the channels in which they were stationed. There were new men up and down the line, shifting cargoes and crates, pouring out of the communications trench that ran all the way to the front. A unit of men had been laying new duckboards in the basin of the ditch, and as Samuel walked he pressed them to the earth, so that thick mud oozed in-between the slats. They stopped momentarily at the inter-section of the trench and watched a group of the newest boys tramp by. They were brothers – three of them, with the same eyes like pigs and the same jagged fringes where their mother had taken the kitchen shears to their heads – and they were sharing ominous looks as a sergeant led them about the warren. Samuel's heart went out to them. It had been different for him, when he first tumbled from the transports, but still he knew the fear that was worming its way through them now. He and Jacob stopped to watch them disappear along a tributary in the trench.

At the end of the tributary, they parted ways. Jacob was still squawking about the girl he had conquered as he disappeared, but Samuel did not hear the words. If Jacob was proud of what he had done that day, it dawned on Samuel that he too was proud. It was a strange feeling, and it took time before he could warm to it. It was an honourable thing that he had done, and more honourable for the fact that Lucy would never know. He saw Peter in one of the caverns he passed, and the boy nodded to him reverently, as always he did. He went on a little, towards his own post, and he saw there that a dozen other boys were gathered. More men brought in from the streets back home. More men who could hardly wield a rifle or a dagger. He stopped and studied them from a distance, and he started to think what a crying shame it was that boys ever had to leave the terraces in which they were raised. He moved a little closer, and saw then that there was another huddle of boys within the wider ring. He stopped, and then he took another step. He breathed. One of the boys started to turn.

Samuel recognised them at once. He did not need to linger on the thought to remember the last time he had seen them. It was with him in an instant: the wind that blasted his hair as he ran, the clattering of his boots as he careened along the edge of the Moor. He could still hear the way they had cried for him, that chorus of murderous voices whirling high on the wind.

'Hello, Matthias,' said Samuel.

'Hello, Samuel,' said Matthias.

V

Samuel did not know he was a monster on the day that he was born. He supposed the knowledge had visited itself upon him at the same time as he started to see hair sprouting on his body, and his shoulders had started to bulge, and his voice had started to harden. It was a slow process, or so he had come to believe. It happened in stages. He hoped, even after everything he had done, that the transformation was not complete. He hoped that it might one day be undone, and he might one day walk the streets of Leeds and not feel eyes boring into him and not hear stones arcing overhead.

It was different in those first days with Matthias and Alexander in the trench. Samuel remembered them both. He remembered the others as well – the boy called David, the other called Jonah – but it was Matthias who was driven, like a thorn, into his memory. He remembered the way that boy had wielded a cricket bat as they carved their way up and down the streets of Burley Park. He remembered how Matthias' grandfather brewed his own ciders in old tin tubs, and how Matthias once brought a stone flask of the brew to the Moor to share with his friends. He recalled how the bottle had been passed from boy to boy, and how even William had not noticed as the chain missed Samuel.

He found himself crossing Matthias' path, drifting through the channels to which he knew he and Alexander had been posted. More than once, he had to question himself: Was he going to them deliberately? Did he want them to see? He loathed himself for it. There had been good months before they arrived. Even in the hail, it had been good. Even with everything that had gone before. They had not been months filled with thinking and talking. For a while there, he had lost himself. It had been a glorious thing, to not have to think, to start and forget. But now he was found, and it was a dreadful thing to look in the mirror and see himself staring back.

He was drifting through those channels at the dying end of a day, groping along a narrow crevasse where the walls were bound by entangled roots, when he heard a voice he had not thought to hear. He pushed a little further along the ravine, over duckboards that had long ago been buried in the mud. There was a channel here, bordered by dugouts. Outside each of them, a little fire was burning. Somebody was roasting a rat. Some of the boys peered at Samuel as he stole past. One of them muttered a hello, and offered up a spear of meat from his spit. Samuel did not reply. He ghosted along the channel, and at the end he stopped. The boys were gathered in the maw of one of the caverns there. They had eaten together, and now they were drinking. Was that how they had lured him? Was that the way they meant to buy his friend?

Jacob was among them, sitting rapt in the circle. At his sides: Matthias and Alexander. The rest were gathered around. How had he come to be there? Samuel's chest tightened. He saw that one of Matthias' special canteens was pressed into Jacob's hand. They were all a little merry – it was written on their faces, in their eyes and in the redness of their cheeks – and there was laughter, and stories being told. Samuel writhed that it should be this way. He moved back a little, into the trench, and from there he watched the gathering unfold, framed by the cavern's beams.

At last there came a voice.

'What do you want, Redmond?'

It was Matthias. Samuel paused. He did not advance. He did not have words for the occasion. He looked at them, and felt as if it was he who had been stabbed in the back.

'It's OK, boys,' said Jacob, looking carefully around. 'Samuel's one of us. Samuel's my friend.'

Matthias' hand was on Jacob's shoulder. It was a protective gesture – or so it seemed to the little boy who sat among them. Hovering on the edge of the circle, Samuel saw it for what it truly was. 'Jacob,' he began – but before another word escaped his lips, he was cut short.

'We were just telling Jacob about the streets we come from,' Matthias intervened. His eyes were fixed on Samuel. They were knowing, cynical orbs. 'Sheepscar isn't so very far from us, is it, Samuel? We were just telling him about the terraces and the parks and the Moor. We were just telling him what kind of a land it is. The kind of things boys do back there.'

Samuel stalled. Jacob was looking from one to the other, and if he had seen that something was amiss, he was a master at keeping it concealed.

'He'd know it well enough,' countered Samuel. 'One street is the same as the next.'

'We were telling him we'd stay together, after it ends,' Matthias went on. He allowed a smile to curl upon his lips, but just as quickly he disguised the expression. 'That after it was done, we could go back and we'd know boys from all over the city – boys from Otley and Poole, and Mirfield and Batley as well. And, every year, the signal could go up and we'd gather there, up on the Moor, and we'd drink up there and eat and have fires and cook on spits and tell stories of everything we'd done.' Matthias paused. 'What do you say, Samuel? Wouldn't it be a grand thing, to have a gang like that?'

Jacob stood. He pushed between two of the boys – David

and Alexander, who raised their eyebrows as if to hurry him back – and he went to Samuel's side.

'I was telling them about the gas,' he began. 'I was telling them how it went on the day it came over.'

'Jacob, you shouldn't . . .' Samuel did not know how he was going to finish that sentence. Shouldn't tell them such things? Shouldn't be here? Samuel believed both of those things.

'You shouldn't be ashamed,' Jacob whispered. He was speaking in a low tone, and Samuel understood, then, that the boy truly was his friend. 'It was a good thing you did. A stupid thing, but a good thing, and that's what matters. You should tell the story.'

'I couldn't tell the story.'

'Samuel!'

'Not here, Jacob.'

Jacob turned, grinning in pride, at the boys who were gathered. He flung his arms wide. Rum sloshed from his canteen. 'You should have seen Samuel, that day of the gas!' he grinned, slobbering now over a fresh canteen pressed into his paws. Was it that he was drunk, or was it the memory that enlivened him? Samuel willed him to be still. 'Rushing out there like some knight of old. That's what it was like. Wasn't it, Samuel? Goths and Visigoths on our every side, and us in the middle, outnumbered and outflanked, two lost Legionnaires . . . "For Death and Glory!" we might have yelled.' He paused. He looked sheepishly about. 'We didn't,' he admitted. 'We didn't yell it.'

Matthias looked up. He was wearing his most contemptuous smile.

'Redmond, even when you do do something good, you do it to prove that you can, not for the goodness of the act itself. Men like you, they'll never get it right.'

'I'm not alone. I thought men like you did good things to

buy a ticket into Heaven?' Samuel retorted. 'Not because there's warmth and love in your heart for all mankind,' he smirked. 'Just to get your name on some celestial fucking register.'

'You wouldn't know a thing about it,' Matthias returned. 'When did you last say a prayer?'

'I've done my share of praying.'

'He isn't listening to you, Samuel.'

'No?'

'You'd better direct your prayers to those caverns below.' Matthias looked around at the other men. Some of them, they were laughing. 'That way, Samuel, you might get an audience.'

Samuel dreamt.

It had been a long time since he was plagued by dreams. He remembered thinking it a silver lining, when he was first asked to sleep in the earth, that he was too exhausted to dream. But now, here they were, back to assail him, a hag straddling his breast as he slept. He was on the streets of Leeds, and all was not well.

It was a stretch of the terrace unknown and yet horribly familiar. The redbricks leered at him. He was following the line of a road where the houses had long been abandoned, where boards had been raised in the place of shattered glass, and the yards grew wild with grasses and weeds. He was running. In the dream, Samuel did not know why he was running – and yet, it was with a fevered pace that he ran. He came along a snicket between tall walls of stone, and from there onto a thoroughfare that had not been walked in many long years. He saw, then, the faces of his attackers. They were gathered at the head of the street, where the houses had grown together like the trees of an entangled woodland: a pack of street dogs, birthed and raised here in the dens of abandoned homes. They saw him and he saw them, and for a second the world was still. There was no wind. There was no sound. Not a leaf moved in the gutters, or a bird wheeled in the clouds.

He ran.

They were on his heels. He took flight from terrace to crescent, but he knew he could not outpace them. He heard them baying. He had often imagined the baying of hounds. He had read of it in stories, of criminals broken free of their shackles and hunted on blasted heaths, of wild dogs that set upon them and – worse, still – of dogs trained by men to bring fugitives back in. He tore from a narrow lane and saw, then, that the road sloped before him, banked in tumbledown houses, climbing to a stretch of scrubland far above.

He stopped. He heard the dogs – black and brown and fierce and proud – screaming as they poured from the snicket. He felt them already on his shoulder, a horde of malevolent spirits whispering into his ear, and again he ran. The road was steep, and the scornful houses stared, but he felt certain, now, that if only he made the edge of the scrubland, he would be safe. If only he reached the edge of the Moor there would be sanctuary.

The Moor. It was the Moor that he looked at. The Moor that bore down upon him. And yet, he could not stop running. The wolves were almost upon him. They were howling and they were snarling – and now there were stones pitched through the sky, shattering like grenades where they landed, and now they were not wolves, but boys, who chased him – and now he was there, at the edge of that blasted heath, and the trees were roaring in a frenzy, and the hail was starting to fall, and every brick and slate and slab of mortar was crowing out in an insidious chorus: his name, hissed and spat and rasped and wheezed. 'Samuel!' the city called. 'Samuel!'

'Samuel?'

139

Samuel opened his eyes. He found that he was frozen, held there by some malicious terror of the night. There was a face peering into his – a face mapped by shadows and dark depressions of skin, gaunt and wild and with its eyes opened wide. Samuel wanted to flail out, to drive the daemon back, but his arms were held fast. He gagged. The creature stank of stale sweat. Again, he tried to move – and this time it was as if he was kicking free of his shackles. This time, his legs obeyed, and he struggled to sit.

'Samuel?' breathed the apparition.

'Jacob?'

The daemon was only Jacob. At last, Samuel straightened himself. His face was glistening with sweat. Outside, the trench was bathed in a silvery light. He shivered as he stood, and struggled into his greatcoat. Up there, the moon, a fang, hung in the sky, between two reefs of low cloud. He trudged up and down to ward off the cold, but it was no use; the dream was still rampant in his head. It played over and again.

That night was the last he saw of Matthias for several days. Perhaps it was coincidence, but Samuel felt it was something more. He thought that the captain might have known what it was, for more than once he caught his eye and the captain gave an almost imperceptible nod. It was making him feel dirty, now – that the captain knew what kind of a man he was, and still did nothing; that the captain could know about such a monstrous thing and still have told him that it did not matter, that he trusted him above all else. What kind of a man did that make the captain? What kind of a leader would lead a boy like Samuel out to war? Samuel did not pretend to understand.

Matthias had noticed the way the captain treated Samuel. The whispered words. The secret looks. Samuel knew that Matthias had noticed because he felt a new kind of guilt each time the captain walked among them. He tried to shirk the captain's hand on his shoulder, to avert his eyes whenever their gazes might have met – but it was to no avail. Everywhere he turned, he saw Matthias' face banked in shadows; Matthias' face emerging from the gloom of the dugout; Matthias' face emblazoned on each earthen wall. He thought he saw it in the clouds. He thought he saw it in the gas. Matthias and his followers hunting him through the terrace.

Jacob, too, knew that something was amiss. Though he dared not ask Samuel – and though he was uncertain if this secret was something he could bear to know – he too saw Matthias on every ridge and every tooth in the trench. He knew, though he did not know why, that he was numbered with Samuel now. He had thought that they were all numbered together, the English boys of Leeds, but the trench was different now that the others had come. Jacob might almost have forgotten about the foreign boys on the other side of the wire if it had not been for the shells that arced overhead each night, and the men he saw ferried back and forth between the dirt and the field tents. It was the English boys he was looking out for now. He had long heard it said that there was no worse devil than the devil that called you his friend and lay himself in your hearth. He only wished there was some way he could change things. More than once, he tried to talk to Samuel about it – but each time Samuel glowered at him, and each time Jacob slunk away, like a dog that knows it has done wrong.

At the dying end of the day, when boys were readying themselves to raid the channels over the wire, Samuel was sent back into the reserve trenches to ferry sandbags further up the line. There were boys already stooped about their cauldrons in the channels. Samuel had not eaten since the horns sounded that

141

dawn, and even the bland smell of those soups stirred something in his gut. He passed Jacob in one of the ditches, and the little boy threw him a wearied grin. It would be over before long: another day, the same as the last. The sun's light was already dipping behind the hills, and fingers of red cast long shadows where he trod.

He was in the dugout, stooping to shift sandbags, when he felt one of those shadows on his shoulder. It was long and it was dark, and he knew before turning whose shadow it was. He groaned inwardly. The muscles tensed up and down his legs.

He turned. They looked at each other, Samuel and Matthias, and for a moment it might have been that neither would say a word.

'Samuel,' Matthias started. 'I just want to talk.'

But already Samuel could see the shadows of Matthias' kin at the jaws of the dugout, and already he knew that it was a lie.

'We can talk in the trench,' said Samuel.

Matthias stepped forward. 'There's rain,' he said.

'A little rain won't hurt.'

The other boys came into the dugout, then, drawing near to Matthias like disciples crowding their king. Samuel did not consider them. His eyes were still fixed upon Matthias. He could see nothing of the trench beyond them, now. The only light there was filtered through the thin gaps between their heads and their shoulders. It was dark, and he felt for the first time that they were trapped in some collapsed mine far beneath the sod. The roof and the walls bore down upon him.

He breathed slowly. The boys were staring at him, but not one of them spoke. He decided that they were like every gang he had ever known. He turned his shoulder on them, and he bent low to heave another sandbag onto his back. It felt good to be doing something, but here was that wild feeling, swelling again at the back of his throat. He saw a stone on the ground beside him, and thought that he would take it in his fist. Then he stopped.

The shadows gathered. The last of the light disappeared. Samuel turned, and the boys had closed around him.

'Matthias?' he began, rising now. He saw one of the rifles propped against the wall on the other side of the den. Its barrels were broken back, but there was a bullet inside. He would not be able to reach it. He shifted a little, so that he might see the faces of each of the boys: Matthias and Alexander at the forefront, David and Jonah on their flanks. There was another boy lurking by the opening of the dugout, some neanderthal that Samuel recognised from the darker terraces on the other side of Kirkstall Lane. He was their look-out, then. Samuel risked a wry smile.

'Matthias,' he repeated. 'You're really going to do this, aren't you?'

Matthias breathed.

'You fucking coward,' Samuel spat.

Samuel could not move further away. One of the support beams had reared at his back, and the circle of boys was fast around him. He might have been in a backyard then, or some secluded stretch of scrub on the Moor. His eyes flared, and he caught the look on David's face. It was a strange, hollow kind of look. Samuel had seen it before. He had seen it when he peered into the looking glass. He managed a smirk.

'William woke,' said Matthias. 'Even after what you did, still he woke.'

It silenced Samuel. For an age, he did not speak.

'He lives?' he finally wrenched.

'He lives,' answered Matthias.

It started. The first blow caught the side of his head. He weaved a little, and the second glanced from his shoulder.

They were pathetic little boys, really. They did not know how to throw a punch. Samuel caught Alexander's first attempt, and wrenched his arms back so that his enemy reeled. If there was one thing that he had learned up and down the terraces of Leeds, it was this. He could take a hiding as well as any boy he had ever known, and if things were fair he would even have turned it on them. These boys knew nothing. He was not fast enough to meet Matthias' next blow, but he turned his shoulder to it and absorbed the shock. He was a little winded, but nothing else. He would not fall.

'You're not even sorry, are you?' Matthias scoffed.

'I didn't say I wasn't sorry.'

'If you were sorry you wouldn't have run.'

'Who teaches you this stuff, Matthias?'

'There's some things you don't need to be taught. Things like goodness, Samuel. Things like how to be a man and how to do good.'

Matthias jabbed him, then, so that he toppled into the beams of wood. He tried to throw his weight forward, tried to force himself back at the boys – but there was mud at his feet, thick and wet, and he found scant purchase on the earth. He crashed against the beam, and heard it splinter. He was showered in dirt, but the wall held firm.

He did not have time to dodge the next blow. They caught him as he reeled: first one thrust, then another, then a third, none of them blocked, none of them parried. He tried to roll with the punches, but the walls bore down upon him. His lip tore. He crumpled for the first time, then, and his vision blurred. It seemed to streak, as if he was peering through a window streaming with rain. There was a lull as no fists flew – these boys were not manly enough to finish it properly – and then, at last, he drew himself back.

First one fist, then another. He found Matthias' temple, and while the bastard cringed at the blow, Samuel brought his left fist around to drive him further back. He allowed himself to grin, then. He saw the way Matthias hung his head and he smiled. He took a step forward, pushed himself from the support beam, and launched himself at the next boy in line: the boy named David. David was slighter than Matthias. He stood there on the left flank of their little battalion and he trembled. Samuel had seen the fear flicker on his face already, and he did not mean to let it go unpunished. How dare he be frightened? Wasn't there a God on his side? Samuel fancied he could remember David from his time on the streets. He fancied he had seen him leer at Lucy. He grappled for the boy's throat.

Samuel felt a boot in his side, and though he tried to roar out, all the wind was gone from his lungs. Too late, he buckled and could not straighten himself. Through watery eyes he looked up and saw, hanging above him, David's face, banked in that wild black hair that was his mark. Shimmering it was, and like an angel's as it sparked into life, buoyed by the knowledge that he had been spared and that he might now do his duty. Quickly, Samuel's face turned to survey his attackers. They bore down upon him, like crumbling buildings. He saw David and he saw Alexander and he saw Jonah – and there, between them, he saw Matthias returning to the fray. There was a darkness on the side of his face where Samuel had dealt that vicious blow. It was little recompense as the boys piled onto him.

The boots and fists upon him, Samuel sank. He braced himself and swore to himself that he would not fall – but already he was limp, pressed against the earthen wall, hardly even registering each new blow. His whole body was consumed by it. After a few blows he thought it might end, that these cowards might see him bleed and lose their courage,

145

but still it went on. He began to feel numb. His ears were heavy with blood. They pounded as if he was swimming deep in a lake. And that was what it felt like, as he hung there and he did not fight back – as if he was drowning, flailing at first to get to the surface, and then just giving himself up to the churning waters. It was cold, and he was alone, and he could see, in that inky brine, the faces of everyone he had encountered in his short life: his mother and his father and his schoolmasters and the men who paraded up and down the streets where he lived. He was thinking of William as the last of the blows were dealt. He was thinking that William was alive and that that was all that mattered. Even if he never made it back to those streets where he had been raised and all their secret haunts, William was there now. William had not fallen for ever up on the Moor.

Samuel waited until the sound of their boots in the dirt was gone, and then he slumped against the clay. One of the rats had appeared from a hole in the wall, ferreting forth between two platforms of shale, and its eyes bulged horribly as its body contorted through the crack. Samuel watched it with shining eyes. Each considered the other: the boy and the beast. It pushed forth a little, and Samuel held out his hand. He gently kneaded his fingers and the rat, timid at first, grew bolder in its advance. It had a streak of white fur stretching from the nape of its neck to the highest point of its snout and, marked like that, it was unlike any rat that Samuel had ever seen. They were only inches apart now, and Samuel thought he could almost feel the way that the whiskers flexed. His face throbbed and he felt a trickle of blood cut a gully down his brow.

There was tramping outside. The rat tensed. Its eyes flickered from Samuel to the jaws of the dugout. It withdrew onto its haunches, nose furrowed at whatever new stench drifted in on the wind. Samuel had seen such things before. Even rats could tell when there was something dreadful afoot. Even rats could tell when they kept the company of stoats.

Matthias reappeared in the portal of light. The sinking sun had broken from reefs of thin cloud and it shone now upon his back. He had a canteen of water in his hand and a clean rag in the other. He had a little hip-flask pinned to his belt.

'Samuel,' he said, coming into the dugout. 'Let me tend to it.'

He knelt at Samuel's side. Already, the rat was gone, disappeared back into the earth.

'What?'

'Let me clean it up. Please?'

Samuel understood this. He had served his sentence well. He had been placed in the stocks and felt the lashes on his back and the stones in his face – and now he was free, and he was clean, and his torturers would stoop to pick him up and wrap their arms around him and welcome him back to the fold. It was common Christian forgiveness.

'I don't want you to touch me, Matthias.'

Matthias sighed. It put Samuel in mind of the times his mother had knelt to rub the dirt from his cheeks or knead the stones from cuts on his knee.

'Samuel,' Matthias began, uncorking the canteen.

Samuel's head snapped back. He stared Matthias squarely in the face. His swollen, bloodshot eyes met Matthias' clean white orbs. He choked a little as he spoke, but he did not flinch. His body was wrenched rigid against the earth.

'I mean it, Matthias,' he growled. 'Touch me,' he hissed. 'I dare you. Touch me, Matthias. Matthias, touch me. Matthias?'

It was Jacob who found Samuel. He was alone in the dugout where he had fallen, and he had crawled under blankets and rags so that he looked to Jacob more like a ragman from the streets than a soldier serving the king. It was dusk, and there was shelling only a mile down the line. The screaming rose from the trenches like the morning's mist, a ghostly vapour rising into the thickening night.

'Oh Samuel,' he whispered, stirring his friend from his nest. 'What did they do to you?'

Jacob teased back the blankets and, like a little girl rescuing her mangy kitten, he opened his arms to receive his friend. Samuel was limp and he was light. Even though Jacob was much the smaller man, still he could lift Samuel. He arranged him like a boy might arrange his wooden soldiers, shifting arms and legs into place, buttressing him on each side with the bedrolls and blankets. They sat together in silence for a little while, and Jacob scavenged for water and bread.

'It was Matthias, wasn't it? Matthias and Alexander and the rest.'

'They're boys from my streets.'

'They're English boys.'

'Good old English boys,' smirked Samuel.

'I'd rather face the Bavarians,' breathed Jacob.

Jacob busied himself about the dugout. The sole wooden cot was splintered now, crushed in the melee that had seized the chamber, but he bound its cracked legs with twine and, in that way, the rickety thing assumed its old shape. In a wooden tea chest he found blankets not caked in earth and, at the bottom, a small canteen. He unscrewed the lid and, like a rat, sniffed tentatively at its contents. It was whisky, and he tossed it to Samuel's side. There was a little leatherbound bible lying there as well, and he lifted it to gesture at Samuel. 'Yours?' he asked.

'Hardly,' Samuel replied.

Jacob hurled it out into the mud.

'Why are they out for you, Samuel?'

The two friends sat together, each cowled in the coarse blankets that Jacob had drawn from the chest. As they passed the canteen from one to the other, the white-streaked rat reappeared from its hole in the wall. It snouted forwards a little, and for a moment it might even have joined them: two ragged soldiers and a rat, communing like criminals in that wretched little oubliette.

The shelling was stronger tonight, and outside it was growing in fervour: stretches of land somewhere down the line targeted and relentlessly bombarded in preparation of what was to come. Samuel could picture it now, the way they would pour from these holes in the ground like rats erupting from a torched nest. Like those poor rats, half of them would be felled. He looked at the creature with the white streak and wished he could tell it to run.

'If you could,' said Samuel, 'which way would you flee?'

'You mean desert?' asked Jacob. 'Like Jacques?'

'Like Jacques.'

Jacob squirmed. Samuel could tell he did not like the question.

'I'd go to Le Bizet. That was a good day.' Even Samuel had to concede that it had been a good day, thought Jacob. There had been sunlight and there had been flowers in the vale, and there had been beautiful French girls whose words he did not understand, but who had spoken to him in a language that was nothing to do with tenses and verbs. 'You couldn't hide out there for long,' he said, 'but, gosh, I'd risk it for a night . . .' He smirked.

Though it was a lie and he had once sworn to renounce all lies, Samuel tried to return the knowing smile. It would hurt Jacob to know that Samuel had deceived him, that Samuel had fled from his girl and stayed true to the girl from Leeds, and he did not mean for the boy to be hurt.

'Yeah,' said Samuel, 'I'd go that way, too.'

'You can tell me, you know,' said Jacob as the canteen changed hands. 'Whatever it is you did that was so wrong, it won't mean a thing to me. Whatever it was, it can't be worse than what we'll do come the push. I haven't killed a man yet. It must really be something, to have to kill a man. Some man who's probably the same as you or me.'

'No one's the same as you,' winced Samuel, taking a draught of the whisky.

'You know what I mean, Redmond. Some boy from some terraces like ours, only terraces in Berlin or Munich or Hamburg or one of those little shacks in Bavaria. And he'll come at us and we'll go at him and then we'll cut each other down. It must be a fucking strange thing, to watch him fall and then just walk away.' Jacob stopped. He could see, now, that Samuel was shivering. There was a thin film of sweat on his face and his brow, and it was freezing there with the night's chill. He tossed him another blanket. 'Samuel? Will they come again?'

At first, Samuel did not reply. He strained to stand and he shuffled to the maw of the dugout. He could see, in the vaults above, the malign constellation that looked over him. Yes, he thought. They'll come again. Matthias and Alexander and David and Jonah and countless others like them. How could they not? How could a man hear a story such as his and not set out with a stone in his hand? He knew, now, that there would be no escape from it. It was on him, that birthmark, that welt on his skin.

'Jacob,' he said. 'I wish I'd never come.' He turned back, and looked at his friend with a torn, bloody grin. 'I wish to hell I wasn't here.'

He raised the canteen, and he drank.

VI

If anybody noticed the torn lips and bulging eyes in those few
days that followed, nobody breathed a word of it when Samuel
could hear. He imagined, as he went about his duties up and
down the line, that all men now knew what it was he had done,
and what justice had been meted out to him for his sins. He
thought he could see it, daubed onto each man's face, their
disgust at what he was and their righteousness in how he had
been set straight. He would not let himself believe that
Matthias and his followers had kept this thing between them.
He knew people better than that. It was a rare man who kept
secrets. Secrets festered in a place such as this. They bred and
spread like the rats to which Samuel now tended. He wondered
how long it would be before another gang set upon him.

On the third day after he was lain low, there came a letter.

It was Jacob that brought it to the den in which he lay. It had
been on one of the caravans that lumbered through, hidden in
a collection of other cards and newspapers and scraps, and
might even have gone astray if Jacob had not been there to
spirit it away. Samuel received it gently and thanked his friend.
Jacob did not blush, then, though he did pretend to be
affected. It was an affectation he had been rehearsing, a look
he had observed when studying the faces of the Lancashire
Fusiliers. It brought a smile to Samuel's face, and that was
enough.

'Imagine if one of those lads from your streets had got to it,'
Jacob grinned as he handed it over.

Samuel held the letter oddly as Jacob pressed it into his hands. He looked at the curled, precise script on the front of the envelope and a smile betrayed the fact that already he knew whose letter it was. Jacob was asking him questions about it before he had even broken the seal, but Samuel was practised at keeping secrets. He did not breathe a word. With Jacob's help, he took to the shadows of one of the hazel trees and opened it carefully so that the paper did not tear.

Dearest Samuel,
I have tried to write. Truly, I have. I have lost count of the number of times that I have locked myself in this room and pressed my pencil to the page, and then found that the words would not come. I have such a little thing to tell you, Samuel, and yet it feels vast. I miss you. That is all. I was not surprised when I rose that morning and found your letter sitting there, alone on the step. But, Samuel, I was hurt. I have thought, of course, on everything that has happened this winter, but still it pained me, that you would leave me and go out there when it was not yet asked of you, to ride out and be a hero and leave me here in a town that will never understand. It didn't matter to me what you did. I would have braved every scornful look for you. I'd have been the shadow of your shadow, if only you would have stayed.

But Samuel, my love, there is something else . . .
Samuel, he is coming to find you. He is seeking you. His whole heart is bent on it. Something was changed in William when he woke. There was something new. Some different beast in him. He would not let it go, and he forced his way upon your uncle's house and he drew the truth from him, Samuel. I am ashamed to say that he did the same to me. Do not think too badly of me, Samuel. I kept your secret

for as long as it was in me to do. But the way your brother looked at me last night, it made me afraid. I have known him a long time, and never have I thought that he had that in him. Because William is good and kind and has honour. Last night, Samuel, I was afraid. And tonight he is gone. I do not know where he is, but I know where he is going. If I am right, he will have gone to Finlay for the papers. You are brothers, after all.

Samuel, if he finds you, remember that. He is still your brother.

I love you,
Lucy.

Samuel folded the letter and slipped it within his greatcoat. Already, Jacob was at his side, peering over his shoulder as if he might still be able to read what she had written. Samuel looked up and caught his eye. He saw, then, that Jacob was grinning.

'You've got yourself a girl, haven't you?' he beamed.

'Shut up, Jacob.'

'You always did! You old dog. You never said. What about the girl in Le Bizet?'

Samuel shrugged. He was looking over the fields, and it might have been that he was following the line of the rails that led to the village.

'You old hound.'

At dusk, hunkered down in a hole in the earth, Samuel read the letter over and again. '*He is seeking you. His whole heart is bent on it. Something was changed in William when he woke. Some different beast in him.*' William was awake, and William was well. That was what it meant. He had known, of course, that William had risen from his slumber – how could he not have known, when Matthias and Alexander had so fiercely forced it upon him? – but to hear it from Lucy was a good thing. It made him feel warm. It made him feel that he might almost want to see his brother, if only somehow that could be.

What was the meaning of those few words? '*His whole heart is bent on it.*' It was not Lucy's declaration of love, but that simple sentence, that would not leave him as, long past the midnight curfew, he tried to snatch some sleep. His brother, alive and well, was stalking the streets of Leeds. Hunting him down. He pictured how it had been at Joshua's house, how William must have thrown his shoulder to the wood, how the two of them would have faced each other across the cluttered room. He saw William, head bowed low, descending the steps into the cellar just as Samuel had descended the steps into Jacques' oubliette, seeing the nest he had crafted there, trailing his fingers across each surface of dust in the hope that he might find some sign of his brother.

He wanted to write. He wanted to send a letter back to England. Something – anything – that might reach the people he had known. He wanted to understand. How was it that his brother was different? Did his brother hate him now? What was the beast that reared within him? Samuel tried to picture the way his brother looked now – head shaven bare, the skin dark and thick where the stone had found its mark. For a long time that night, he could not bear to close his eyes – for, each time that he did, he saw he and William together again, walking the streets together, from Burley Park to Woodhouse Moor. The silence was horrible. It wrenched and forced them apart.

He was holding the letter as he fell to sleep that night, and he was holding it still when he woke in the morning.

That was the final day.

There were bugles sounding in the trench before dawn, and rags of men not of their battalions descending into the dirt. When Samuel stooped from his dugout and into the light, he saw that the depressions already swarmed with the incoming men. Some of the new units were scarcely a dozen men or more, but each of them stood here, alongside their captain. Many of their leaders must have been felled, for Samuel saw men who could have been only months older than himself marshalling their men. And here there were men dredged from every corner of the island: farmers and lawyers and bankers and tramps; all men equal out here in the dirt. Samuel weaved among them, studying the faces, the blank expressions, the faces set and unflinching as if too scared to betray any feeling at all. That was what these men were now – simple, unfeeling folk, ready for the guns. Samuel spied Jacob along a wretched parade, and moved to join him through the murk. The rest of the Chapeltown Rifles were huddled by the mound in which Jacques had once been imprisoned. They were yet to form ranks, and through the unsettling murmur of men Captain Arnold barked at them to fall in line. Miserably, they shuffled together. Samuel was only a furlong away from them, Jacob gestured that he should turn and leave – but Samuel would not listen. He saw Matthias and Alexander in the file beyond Jacob, and pushed through a glut of Fen Country men to find his place in the order.

'You could get out,' Jacob hissed. 'After what they did to you, you shouldn't have to fight. Look at you, Samuel! Your face, it's still black. Your ribs, still cracked. They wouldn't send a crippled man to the guns. You should talk to them, Samuel!' he pleaded. 'You should find a way.'

Samuel shook his head softly, and Jacob's face wrenched. He bleated a little, aggrieved, as if somehow the whole thing was a personal slight.

'If your life was forfeit as mine is forfeit, why would some little thing like that stop you?' he breathed.

'Your life isn't forfeit,' Jacob hissed. 'Not yet.'

Samuel did not turn around. If he turned around, he knew he would sneer, and he did not mean to let the boy see that. That would not have been right. He knew that Jacob meant well, but even that little thing irked him now. Samuel's life had been forfeit since the day he smote his brother down. He supposed that he had known it all along. It did not matter that he had left Leeds. It did not matter that he had rampaged in the gas to save lives, that he had stayed true to Lucy, that he would lift his gun to defend any starving wretch. Whether you stayed or you strayed, it was bound to catch up with you. That was what had happened when Matthias and Alexander appeared in the trench. That was what had happened when he received Lucy's letter. He felt for it, now, in the folds of his greatcoat – and knew that it was safe there, kept against his breast. He felt a little further, and there – coiled in the ragged lining of the coat – lay the little lead soldier that he had lifted from its shelf on the day he left Leeds. He teased it out of the pocket and turned it to what little light remained. It was a sorry little trinket, a lone gunman cast from black metal and with its paint peeling away. William had had one, too. He studied it for a second, and then slipped it back into the folds of his greatcoat, there to lie with the letter Lucy had sent. He would carry them from here until the end of all things. He would carry them with him when they ran out in the morning.

When, at last, he turned, Jacob was still standing there. Throughout, he had not said a word, patiently crouching in Samuel's shadow while the guns rained above. Jacob was a good soul. Samuel knew he would not leave.

'Are you scared?' the little boy asked.

'I'm scared as hell,' answered Samuel.

'Me too,' said Jacob. 'I'm scared, Samuel. I'm scared to shit.'

It rained.

It started at dusk, a steady drizzle, but in the vaults above the badlands the clouds thickened and the downpour grew. As the gloom deepened, few words were exchanged. Out there, the rain was an assault on the land. Slowly, under that relentless barrage, the mounds and ridges changed shape. It was imperceptible at first: clumps of reeds crumpled and then flattened, roots exposed and driven from the earth. Then, through the veil of rain, the world was suddenly different. Mounds sank. Ridges shifted. Ditches turned into torrents of sludge. And everything that lay hidden beneath started to rise.

In the shelter of an ill-hewn lean-to, Samuel saw banks of wire that had long been trampled into the earth re-emerge, victorious, from the land in which they had been entombed. A tree, long dead but still standing, slipped at last in the torrent and had crumbled before it hit the ground. In pieces, it was torn away, moving sluggishly at first, but with increasing vigour as about it the mud deepened. What rose, then, seemed like the fragments of a different time, as if the rain was beginning the work now that the archaeologists of the future might finish. Whole huddles of men smothered by the dirt. The skeleton of a horse still standing when the earth dragged it under. Trailing flesh and mane caked in grime. There were guns out there, too, guns that had fallen with their men. They poked, now, out of the crust, like the saplings of iron trees. Against one of the furthest mounds, Samuel saw the gut of an ancient howitzer as the rain drew it from its grave. At first it was only an ugly brown protrusion, but slowly the rain washed it clean – and there it stood, the great steel behemoth, half-mired now in the earth, a useless thing from a battle neither won nor lost.

Not a man on the line said it, but all were thinking the same thing: that tomorrow, they too would be taken below as were the men out there. Through the lancing rain, they watched the remains of what had once been a man as he was washed clean of mud – and then, the mud the only thing to hold him together, as he came apart bone by bone. There were men like this all over now – soldiers caught in the waltz of battle, preserved there with howls of agony upon their faces, mouths open wide to breathe in the suffocating earth. If only there was some man here trained in the dark magics that Samuel once loved to read of in fables and books – then, perhaps, these men might rise again and swell their ranks a thousandfold. Then, perhaps, there could be a real war – and not just this dying in the dirt.

If any of the soldiers spoke at all, it was only in whispered fits and starts. Somewhere, somebody was praying. Men rushed past, carrying rolls of wire salvaged from the deeps. There would be a clean path when the bugles sounded. There were orders being sent now, runners scurrying back and forth with the words of their masters – and all around, boys were sinking back into the holes, gathering there for when the whistles blew. A rag of boys broke away on the right of Samuel, and he turned to watch them go.

Where the boy next to him had once stood, Samuel spied a single flower, seemingly hunched against the onslaught of the rain. When he shifted, and looked closer, he saw that there were others, a cluster of green shoots with blue and white buds, like the speedwell he had often seen in the summers at home. Some of them had been trampled by the boys around, but a clump still remained, beaten by the wind and the rain, but full of colour and full of life. It seemed a dreadful thing that, out here in the arse of the world, something so frail and beautiful could survive. The rain was like pearls on the leaves of those flowers.

'You ever done anything bad?' breathed Samuel.

Jacob squinted at his side. 'You mean like we'll do come the sun-up?'

'No,' Samuel replied.

'In life, then?'

'In life.'

'No, I haven't been that bad,' said Jacob. 'But, you know, I haven't been that good. What do you think's waiting, up there, for people like that?'

Samuel shifted, uneasily, against the sandbags.

'I haven't thought of it,' he said. 'It's none of my concern.'

'You think this is it, don't you?' Jacob smirked. 'You think we already died and went below. That's what you think this is. Hell.'

'I didn't say that.'

'No, you didn't have to.' Wind buffeted the sides of the lean-to. It clawed at the huddled soldiers through cracks in the wood. 'Samuel,' he said, 'you ought to have been a poet.'

Before dawn, the guns were still. They knew it, then, up and down the barricades, that their time had come. Perhaps Matthias and his followers had imagined they might see the clouds come apart and watch spectral horsemen ride out to lead the charge. Perhaps – but it was not so. There was only a cold wind, and somewhere a bugler blowing, to herald their approach.

Captain Arnold moved up and down the line one final time. He paused at each of his boys, and though he did not say a word, he rested his hand on each of their shoulders, and in that he said more than words ever could. When he reached

159

Samuel, perhaps he lingered longer. Perhaps – but Samuel could not tell. They stole a look, and Samuel felt the old man's hand knead at his shoulder. There's all men equal out here in the dirt, thought Samuel. Captain Arnold passed on, and then he was alone.

Along the line, the sergeants motioned, and each boy drew his bayonet. They checked their bindings, they checked their boots, they fastened the buckles of their coats. Some of the boys were thumbing through little books of verse, or bibles with lettering too tiny to read. Samuel did nothing but look down at Jacob, and help him to loop the final brass button on his breast.

'For death and glory?' grinned Jacob. It was a twisted kind of grin, and he was trembling as his hand curled around the rung of the ladder.

'For something else,' said Samuel.

'Yes?'

'Yes,' breathed Samuel. He took Jacob's hand and he squeezed it tight.

The bugles sounded for the final time.

What a life it must have been, to have been born a bugler. That was what Samuel was thinking as he heaved himself up. That was the nonsense that Samuel could not shake as he reared, for the first time, to the top of the scaling ladder, and hurled himself forth. What a life it must have been to sing out death.

The world opened before him.

The other boys must have known the time had come as well, for already they were streaming over the parapets on the other side of the dirt. They were only indeterminate shapes now, a rippling grey line that advanced from the horizon, but rapidly they were getting nearer. Samuel could see the shapes of arms and heads appear from the amorphous mass. He put his rifle to his shoulder. Some of the company were already loosing volleys into the mist. They did it in a frenzy, and without direction.

Around Samuel, his brethren started to fall.

It was just one boy at first. He was running, and then he was fallen – and that was all that Samuel knew. There was no howling. There was no screaming for a saviour. He was gone from the line, and the line ploughed on without him. They moved in formation, a phalanx as they had been taught in drills, and at the head of the charge Captain Arnold bawled out his commands. To Samuel, it was nothing but a mouth gaping and eyes flared wide. There were guns blazing now, artillery raised on the other side of the dirt, and all that he heard was the pounding of those shells. All else was lost in that sound. It was thick and deep and all around him, like the sound he imagined babies heard still curled in the womb, the sort of sound to which men fell to their knees and threw open their arms and offered themselves up.

They splintered before they reached the first ridge: rags of boys tumbling into craters carved by shells; others throwing themselves down behind a line of fence posts that still poked from the crust like bones from an ogre's grave. Samuel and Jacob and a gang of other boys found themselves sheltering, now, behind the hulk of a howitzer, long since abandoned to the dirt. The comet trails of shells lanced overhead, pounding into the trenches from which they had run. The earth erupted in waves around them. It quaked and it rolled. It undulated like the sea. Samuel could feel it pounding where he trod, as if some beasts in the caverns below were roaring out their fury at what went on above. Where the rain had formed its marshes, the water sprayed thick and dark.

'We can't stay here,' said Jacob.

'I know we can't stay here.'

'They'll kill us if we stay here.'

'I know.'

More than once, they tried to set out. More than once, the shells rained down and sent them darting back for a sanctuary that was not there. Then, in a second: silence. Samuel and Jacob exchanged a look. Some of the boys sheltering with them started to shift, as if rising from a trance. Two of them, neighbours and friends since they were babes, held to each other as they emerged from the shelter of the hulk. Where they trod, the earth oozed.

Two shots rang out, and they were dead.

That was it. It was not a lull. Samuel raged, his face wrenched rigid. If the shelling was finished, it was only so that they did not fell their own kind. This was not the end. Samuel put a hand on Jacob's shoulder, that he might at last be still. He stood up to peer through the gaps in their miserable fortress, and saw the German boys advancing over the ridge. Some of them barely looked like boys any longer. They were coated in the earth, like monsters dredged from the mire. The land that had once been so still was now a sea of fallen boys, groping out with bloodied arms, heaped there and crying out and never to be rescued. Across the wastes, Samuel spied another clot of the Chapeltown Rifles, fending off a brigade around an outcrop of rock. They were not to last long. Already, Samuel could see a huddle of Bavarians advancing, wielding a gargantuan black barrel that spewed flame like the jaws of some vengeful serpent. On the furthest flank, an iron hulk was surrounded by cavaliers on their wretched steeds. It was an absurd sight, to see them jousting with the barrels of the tank. There were more riders moving now. They seemed to emerge from a mist of dark brown spray: German boys on German horses, rifles tucked into their shoulders and sabres in their hands, a raiding party streaming down from the steppes. Samuel watched them come. He watched them tear into the English horsemen, while beyond that the spouting flames set boys engulfed in flames to flight. And there, with the mud whirling around him, came their leader: the rider upon his white horse, rampaging through the ranks – with all Hell following after.

The other boys hurtled past. Samuel threw Jacob against the hulk and, there, together, they lay in the earth, eyes screwed tight and breathing stilled in an imitation of death. Was this cowardice? Was this what it meant to have no courage? Samuel did not have time to consider it. It was a trifling thing, and in this hail it did not matter. Samuel had heard stories from the older men of the Rifles, those who had already seen battle, of the hours they had spent basking in the dirt, praying for a victory, praying that the stretcher bearers would get to them before their deception was unveiled. They were not the first, and they would not be the last. Samuel waited until the mud was choking him, touching his lips and his tongue, before he reared from that pose.

Jacob was gone. While Samuel had been sinking slowly into the sludge, Jacob had bolted. Samuel did not blame him. He looked for him fervently in the seething mass of men, but he saw neither his friend, nor his friend's fallen corpse. There was nothing more Samuel could do.

He tried to set out. The guns drove him back. He wrenched to get back his breath, and threw his rifle to his shoulder. Wildly, aiming at nothing, he emptied it into the squall. If any of his bullets were true, he did not see and he would never know. He turned again, tried to set out – but again the guns were blazing, and again the air was rent full of holes. High on one of the enemy ridges, a gang of English boys had fallen upon one of the mounted weapons. For a while it turned, uncontrolled, raining shells into the swarm. Then, at last, it was silent, just another corpse of metal to sink into the dirt. On top of that wretched knoll, the English boys cast down the giant barrel and streamed back into the frenzy.

Samuel kept his head down and ran.

He bolted, first, for the cover of a mound. There were boys there, and he hurled himself to join their pack. For a moment he lay, gasping, among them. Then he looked around. He choked. The boys – they were already dead. They were mangled and crooked, eyes wide and white, breasts soaked in scarlet. Against the knoll, they were holding each other, as if that was the way they had fallen. Only a yard away, a small German boy was sprawled alone. The bayonet at his side was dark with English blood, the back of his head destroyed by some bullet from afar.

'Samuel?'

Samuel heard the word. His head whipped back and forth, searching for whichever bastard had dared call his name, daring them with the knife in his hands to call it again. But there was nobody there. He tried to stand, and a flurry of gunfire forced him back. Why could he not move? Was he really such a coward? He stood again, and saw a horse roaring towards him out of the mist. Everywhere he looked, now, there was that mist: the earth and the rain forced up into clouds around him. The horse thundered towards him like some charger of old. Without a rider, it snarled. It had seen him already. Samuel could see it in the eyes. He stood there, frozen in its path, knowing he could not move, the knoll at his back and the cadavers groping at his feet. Was it an English horse that loomed, or did it belong to the others? It was a nonsensical thing that came into Samuel's mind. He saw, through the dark spray, that the beast's flank was soaked in scarlet – but whether this was the brute's blood or the blood of its vanquished rider, he could not say. It was bigger now, almost upon him, its teeth bared wide, its body thrusting, front legs reared with every lunge the monster made. Samuel steadied himself, and drew his gun.

A tremor. The land rose. He stumbled back, staggered through the limbs of his fallen kin, saw the ball of blackness as it hurtled into the horse's flank. The beast did not roar. Instead, it flew. It was ripped from the earth, and it whirled, and then it landed – and Samuel was coated in the foam that erupted where it crashed. He looked around, saw another black orb skittle men as they poured over the enemy wire. The beast started to snarl, and Samuel's eyes lit upon the cannon-ball that had cut it down.

A cannon? Surely in these times men did not still use cannons? Samuel staggered forward. The horse, bloody and braying, was already half-taken by the earth. Its head flung wildly from side to side, its eyes yellow and large. It kicked its legs, but quickly its legs were caked in dirt, and quickly they were too heavy for the dumb brute to lift. The screaming was more than anything Samuel had heard come from the lips of a man: demonic and anguished and unreal. He reeled around and saw, for the first time, the gaping wound in its side. Dark and red and wet, its insides squirmed.

He lifted his gun and he shot.

The Rifles who still stood were already streaming over the final ridge. Samuel was alone. He clawed on, and saw his brethren fallen around him: boys he had seen on the streets, boys he had seen gathered in the tributaries of trenches, boys with whom he had sat about fires and eaten and got drunk. He saw Peter sprawled there with only half a body, shoulder ripped and shredded, mouth agape to the horror above. Perhaps it would have been a better death to drown in the gas. He looked desperately to catch sight of Jacob, thought he saw the small figure disappearing into the enemy trench, and bent low to carry on. The rain forced the dirt into fountains around him. He heard the bullets shrieking and sobbing as they hurtled past.

Somehow, he reached the wire. A boy he had thought dead reared up at him from the dirt. He was startled, but Samuel held his ground. He kicked out, and the boy sprawled back into the earth. He did not move. He was not dead, and yet still he lay there, curled and unmoving. Samuel surveyed the land around the wire. There were others here, hidden among the fallen. He could tell by the way their hands were held, the way their knuckles whitened as they held to their guns. These boys were stricken with something, but they were not yet finished.

The wire had been obliterated by the guns, trampled then by the English boys who poured into the trench. Samuel found a gap where the barbs were low, and he kicked his way through. The mud was thickening at his feet, and his boots found scant purchase, but he staggered forward and he came, at last, to the sandbags that had been spilled and torn apart. He looked down, into the melee, and for a moment it might have been that he wanted to flee. He saw Matthias grappling at a German boy. He saw an old Bavarian with eyes black and wide tearing down one of the English old-timers. Captain Arnold was nowhere to be seen – but perhaps even that would not have helped. Perhaps even he would not have been able to salvage any order from this chaos. A gun exploded, and it seemed for a second that silence seized every boy among them. Then, as before, the killing went on. Samuel looked down, caught sight of Jacob as he turned his shoulder against one of the foreign boys – and he launched himself into the horde.

A punch to the left. An elbow to the right. Samuel had thought it would be different, a game of guns, but already in the dugout daggers had been drawn. Men leapt at each other like the savages of ancient times. He fumbled to draw his own blade. Jacob was crying out for him, one of the ragged Bavarians clawing at his throat, and Samuel strained to reach him. As he came under the earthen eaves, he was hit by the horrific stench of the chamber. His feet sank into a sludge of blood and shit.

It was dark. A boy reared below him, his face already torn and streaming black blood. His eyes were big and white. Samuel's dagger was in him before he had time to think. He felt the terrible grating as he drove it between the ribs, saw the boy's body suddenly twitch, the hands scrabbling to grapple something that just wasn't there. Then the boy fell forward, still now, his entire body and everything he had ever been suspended there on the blade. It was over in a second. That was it. It was a simple thing, really. It did not take any thought. Samuel struggled to draw back the blade, and the boy's head lolled back. Scarlet foamed on his lips. His eyes rolled back. It was done.

It was harder to draw the blade back out than it had been to drive it in. Samuel flung him aside, the dagger still buried in the breast, and clawed out to reach Jacob. They stood there, backs against the corner of the dugout, and saw now that the chamber was still. Heavy rain lanced down outside, a rippling curtain against the maw of the cave. The earth was heaped with those who had fallen in that skirmish: English boys and Bavarian boys both. In one corner, somebody still laboured to breathe.

'Is it done?' gasped Jacob.

'No,' said Samuel. 'It's not done.'

They held each other and they staggered to the trench. Thunderclouds stampeded above them. The rain was a torrent. In the shifting gloom, they saw that the battle still went on: a dirty, interminable thing of unending grappling and crying. One of the German boys rushed upon them, and Jacob instinctively turned his shoulder to the assault. Samuel reached out, and the other boy fell. He was struggling to regain his footing when Jacob fell upon him, panicked and wild as a beaten dog. Samuel stood and surveyed the narrow causeway. Along the line, in the savage confusion, he could see Matthias, his hands around one of the German boys pressed against the wall. There were neither knives nor guns between them. It was only fingers and fists and thumbs. It was almost over, and the foreign boy was gone long before Matthias released his grasp. Their eyes met across the melee, and for a moment each boy held the gaze. Was there some understanding between them, then? Did Matthias finally understand? Did Samuel?

There was an odd kind of stillness came upon the channel. Matthias and Samuel drifted to one another's side, trampling on the boys who had fallen. Jacob stood there, in Samuel's shadow, his eyes darting back and forth like a cornered rat. He was still shaking. The rain streamed unchecked down his face.

'Where's the rest?' gasped Matthias. 'Is this it?'

David lurched around a tooth of the trench, Alexander draped across his shoulder. Alexander was hurt. He cradled his arm, and there was blood there, running in the rain.

'I can't find Jonah. I don't know where he is.'

'Did he come into the trench?'

'He was behind me when we tore through the wire.'

'There has to be more.'

Samuel picked Jacob up. The little boy was shivering. He was chattering, too, words streaming from his lips too quickly and too quietly for Samuel to pick out a single one. Samuel hustled him into the dugout, and forced him onto one of the crates piled therein. They sat together for a little while, but they did not speak. It was a mausoleum in which they had sheltered, a tomb for the freshly fallen and the yet to decay.

The earth was a carpet of limbs and faces frozen at the moment of death. Eyes, open but lifeless, peered up at them from the grime. The air was cold and shimmered with rising ghosts.

Samuel left Jacob there with the dead and went back into the trench. But for the rain, the world was still. He stalked up and down each tributary, and he did not feel the rain that lashed him. He began to think, then, that he was some hero of ancient times, navigating the Labyrinth and seeing every man who had gone before him to face the monsters that dwelt within, the Minotaurs and chimeras and beastmen that could never be conquered. He saw English lads and foreign lads sprawled upon each other – all of them alive only minutes ago, all of them dead now and never to return – and he got to thinking that this was some nightscape of his own imagining, crafted from every sin he had ever committed, fevered and without sense.

He looked back at Matthias and David and the huddle of boys still standing. He stumbled through the outstretched arms of a fallen boy, his body half-sunken in the earth. How was it that they had come through? Again, he locked eyes with Matthias. Whose God was it that had decided which ones were killed and which ones did the killing?

That was when he heard the shouting.

It was not words. It was not English and it was not German and it was not any of the other languages that boys spoke out here, and yet still Samuel understood. He pushed through the survivors, and hauled himself over the sandbags. The ladders were crumbled here, but still he fought his way to the parapet. The rain sliced into him. A low wind was howling now, tearing across the dirt with all the ferocity of the bullets that still flew. The clouds were low. They shrouded the land. All around, the hail made fountains out of the earth. The land erupted in thousands of tiny explosions. He screwed his eyes to the onslaught – and saw, out there, the man grappling in the dirt.

It was Captain Arnold. Samuel saw that, now. He was on the other side of the wire, trapped out there by the battle, and around him the cascading rain was a distorting veil. It made him look ethereal, like some ghost risen from one of the fallen boys. Samuel did not know if he was hit, but he was wailing out. He pushed forward, hunched low so as not to be seen, and felt his feet plunge suddenly into the quagmire. He stumbled back, and drew his boots out. The mud had reached his shins. So that was it. That was why the captain cried. Samuel put his hands to his eyes that he might see more clearly, and saw, then, that the earth had already risen to his knees. He was reaching out, arms flailing wildly, but there was nothing to grasp but the wire. It was cutting and tearing his hands, and yet still he held to it. His howling rose. Somehow it was louder than the rain.

Samuel turned. The other boys were still huddled in the trench below him. He could hardly pick them out from the dead in which they were mired. If they had heard the scream- ing at all, they were deaf to it now. Samuel did not blame them for it. He saw, through the thundering rain, the earth erupt on the farthest side of the wire. It was a spectral image, cast in strange strafing shapes by the deluge, and for a moment it stayed him. But Captain Arnold was still out there, and if his screams were slighter now, that did not mean they were any less desperate. Samuel heaved some of the sandbags into the dirt. They lay there like stones across a river, slowly sinking into the sludge. He took one step, balanced himself, and then another. On the other side of the crumpled lines of wire Captain Arnold's eyes locked with his. It was a wraith's face that Samuel saw. Samuel ached. He fancied he could still hear the scuffling of Matthias and Alexander and Jacob and the rest – but they were too far away to be of any use. Samuel steadied himself. He would not let the old man die. There's all men equal out here in the dirt. That was what the captain had said. Those were the words that sang, now, in Samuel's head.

'Captain!' Samuel cried. 'Captain, give me your hand!'

Samuel leapt from his makeshift bridge and hurled himself forward. He grappled at the barbed wire. His boot, entangled in the spikes, tore as he wrenched his foot free. He thrust out his arm, tried to reach the flailing arm, heard the final strangled cry as their fingertips brushed together – and then Captain Arnold was gone, entombed even before he was dead, given at last to the ground.

VII

They had won the land. Later, that was what the people would say. Later, when new border fires were burning and men were tending to their wounds and burying their dead, that was all they could say: the land is ours; the land is won. It was left to the writers to fill in the detail: the heroes and the villains and the courageous and the cowards. It was always that way, said Jacob to Samuel as, together, they joined a detail of men sent back into the dirt to gather the fallen. It is for men to do the fighting and writers to do the writing. It was something his father had said.

Later, as a new night fell upon the Chapeltown Rifles, clots of soldiers gathered about their fires to eat from pots full of stew and drink their rations of rum. There were no shells in the air that night. There was extra meat, a hoard of it captured from the fleeing troops, and not all of it was gristle and fat. The men were grateful. Riders came in from the stations outside Ypres and Poperinghe, bearing the thanks of the generals to their men in the ground. The men received it without response, and if any of them were filled with pride at the new land they had conquered, none of them said a word. Then, slowly, they drifted back into the earth and began the long process of dredging the trenches of the dead.

Midnight. Second watch. A new rag of men drifted into the trench with shovels and picks, ready to shore up the captured parados and build them into new parapets. From his stand in the wire, Samuel saw the new captain come. His name was Rice. Samuel had seen him before. He was one of the sergeants in the Lancashire Fusiliers, spent his time presiding over that ragtag of cowards and girls. On the crumbled parapet, looking out over a fresh no man's land of wood and wire, Samuel and Jacob watched him tramp past. It would not be a good thing, said Jacob, when the boys of the Rifles heard about this. How could good lads from the streets of Leeds submit to Lancastrian rule?

As the reinforcements tramped past, gravitating to the men about the border fires, Samuel got to thinking of Captain Arnold. He drifted a little further into the dirt, and Jacob called for him to come back. He imagined the man, again, flailing out there in the mud before the ropes could get to him. He imagined how it might have been if their fingers had met, and somehow Samuel had hauled him out of the earth. Perhaps they would be standing alongside each other now, still solemn but with hope for the future. Perhaps anything might have been possible, if the captain had survived.

It might have been that he had been staring too long into darkness, then, but he thought he saw the earth rippling and shift. It might only have been the way the gusts of rain still played upon the sod, but he thought he saw shapes forming, unseen hands crafting a vision for him alone. At first it was like the pictures of a child's storybook, the horrible, gnarled visage of a face leering from a forest wall. That was all it was. Just a trick of the light. But he saw it in detail, now, the familiar face rising, the familiar consoling eyes. The figure unfolded before him and hung in the air for only a moment. Then it was dispelled, whatever unknown force it was that held it together quickly unravelling and casting it back into the land.

Samuel pushed past Jacob and kicked through the filth at the parapet, unearthing, at last, two lengths of broken rail.

There was wire here, too, and he heaved it from the mud in which it was buried. The barbs tore into his palms, but Samuel did not care. Blood, thick and black, mingled with the dirt of his hands

He had been the only man who knew all that Samuel had done – the good and the bad, and all that fell between. He had been the only man who knew it and didn't care. Samuel took the two lengths of rail and wire to the rear of the conquered lines. He passed through a column of boys who each sat, alone together, in the new dugouts. One of them was shivering, as if racked by fever. On the furthest reach of the line, he ascended to the old parapet and looked out on the stretch of land for which Captain Arnold had died. It was a pathetic thing. He could have yelled to a boy in the old trench and heard the reply. He could have pitched a stone that far.

He drove one of the rails into the earth and bound the other to it with wire, so that a lopsided cross might mark the place where the captain had fallen. There was no body here. No mound. Nothing else to mark the man who was gone. There never would be. Perhaps there would be a name inscribed onto a plaque. Perhaps – if this thing was ever to end – somebody might make a speech. Perhaps it would be Samuel. He would tell them what the man had done. He would tell them that the man had made him proud to have fought.

He looked down at his cross and saw that it was already sinking, half-disappeared into the mire.

He had thought he might feel different once it was finished, but standing here with the night deepening around him, he could not understand why he had ever tolerated such thoughts. He picked a stone from the clinging mud and weighed it in his hand. It was heavy and it was true. Drawing his arm back, he pitched it far into the murk. He did not hear it land. Yes, he understood it now. There were some things that could not change. He was taken by the thought. Even with Lucy's letter folded and stashed against his breast, he could not shake the feeling.

He sensed Jacob behind him, on his shoulder like some angel or some devil.

'Samuel?' he said.

Samuel turned around.

'You got a smoke?'

'No.'

'I'd admire a good smoke.'

'I never did take it up,' said Samuel.

'You wouldn't mind if I had one?'

'You've never had the habit before.'

'I've been thinking about taking it up.'

Samuel glowered.

'I'll go get 'em.'

Jacob clambered back over the mounds and into the dugout. Samuel did not watch him go. He looked, instead, to the tendrils of smoke that rose along the line and the specks of light that were their new border fires. He thought he had never seen a more wretched sight. Thin mist was settling now, and the air was wet. The mud rose about his heels.

He looked back at the barricades, but still Jacob was gone below. Samuel fancied he could hear him sharing a can with the others to whom sleep would not come. Perhaps they were playing cards. He did not begrudge it to the little boy, no matter whose company he now kept. Perhaps even he would have found some common ground with those bastards if things had been different. He had heard it said, long ago, that battles brought men together. It was a thing of stories, and he supposed he himself was part of a story now. He only wished that he could tell what role there was left to play: the hero, or the villain? The victim or the perpetrator? He had been playing

175

the fool for too long. He did not mean to go on like this. And yet he did not mean to submit either. Because that was what it would be, if he joined the boys and fell in line and did everything a good soldier was asked to do: a submission, an acceptance that what was done was done and that the world had moved on. Well, Samuel did not mean to let the world move on. Not yet. Not until he had made things right. Not until he was a good man and had done good things. Not until he had made up for what he was. So he would not go among them and pretend that nothing had happened. He would not be a part of the tribe of Leeds, facing down the guns together month after month, one for all and all for one. It would not have been right. What he had done on the Moor could not be dispelled so easily. It could not be unwritten by the boys in the brigade. He did not know if there was anybody who could dispel it. Not his mother, and not his father. Not Matthias with his eye for an eye and tooth for a tooth. Maybe not even William.

Samuel drifted from his post and dropped through the broken ledges into the channel. In the dugout where they were hiding, it was at least dry. Samuel stopped before he got there, stealing softly around the portal of light. He hovered there, on the cusp of going in, and listened to the gang of friends. There had been a fire, and there had been food. Jacob was among them. His voice rose and fell in the conversation, softer and more frightened than the rest. There was some shred of decency in Jacob that would never be wiped out, no matter how many times the boy was forced to kill.

'Do you think they'll send us home? Back down the line for rest?' somebody asked.

'Which part of the line?'

'Somewhere in France. Anywhere other than here.'

'No,' Matthias interjected. 'There isn't anywhere other than here. It's the same from one ocean to the next.'

'It's getting worse?'

'It's reaching the end.'

'The end of the fighting?'

That was Jacob. Samuel smarted when he heard it, though he knew he had no right.

'No,' said Matthias. 'Not that end.'

There was a lull in the whispering, then. Samuel might have taken the chance to steal into the circle, but instead he remained without. He had made up his mind already, though perhaps he still wanted to be tempted to break his promise. Perhaps there was some part of him that did want to go in.

'He's still up on the parapets,' began Alexander.

'Jacob,' Matthias said. 'Go and get him. Tell him to come back. Tell him to come back down.'

Samuel flattened himself to the wall of earth. The thick sludge was about his shins, and with a great effort he drew back his boots and braced himself against the duckboards.

'Why?' asked Jacob. 'So he can sit in here and you can all take his hand?' He paused. 'Why would you want that, now?' he demanded.

Samuel spluttered a smile. Jacob might have been slight, but he was still stronger than the rest of those boys. He heard one of the men crying. He thought it might have been David, but he could not be sure. He tried to summon another smile at that, and was chagrined to find that it would not come. It was a strange thing, to find that he could no longer take any petty pleasure in listening to those boys cry.

They would take him back in, if that was what he wanted. It could be over, if only he would let it. And perhaps there was some way he could draw strength from that. Perhaps if he was one of them he might be able to bear more days like today, when boys were felled around him and his captain was dragged screaming into the earth. There could be a gang, and he would be among them, not merely tolerated by his brother and his brother's friends, but wanted and needed as well. Jacob needed him. That much was true. And perhaps there was something in Matthias and Alexander and David that needed him as well.

Samuel stopped. No, he could not stoop that low. He would not let them forgive him and heal him when it was not their right. He listened to their chatter, how Jacob's voice rose in the choir, and he knew that he would never walk among them. Not knowing what he was. Not knowing what they had done. He wanted to stride in there and take Jacob by the hand and lead him from them, and though more than once he was on the brink of venturing forward, in the end he did not move. Jacob would need those boys, after it was done. Samuel did not like the idea of him being alone. He breathed deeply. Today the English boys had been victorious, but he could carry none of that victory in his heart.

Climbing back to the parapets, Samuel did not care that he would be alone. He pushed as close to the new snarls of wire as he could, and at last the sounds of boys talking in the trenches disappeared. He was thankful for that. There was a world out there, and he had seen it – a world that was not this Hades of boys trapped in caverns, feasting on filth, riding out against other boys who might, in another world, have been their friends. There were lands like the land at Le Bizet, with all the little things of life that he had grown to hold so dear: grasses and wildflowers and girls who saw some goodness in him that all else refused to find. That was the way he would go. He would find a land like that, and he would make it his own. He would not have to conquer it. There would not be guns and blades and campaigns waged against a bloodthirsty foe. He would go from one end of the world to the next if he had to, looking for the people and the places that he could call his own. Somewhere, in the vastness of creation, there had to exist a place where he could grow and change and truly make up for all that had gone before. A place without the weight of the past.

It was late, perhaps an hour before the dawn. There would be work to do in the morning – men to map the reclaimed trenches; others to build back the parapets and wheel the gargantuan guns into place. There would be raids as well, bands of them dispatched to drive back any little skirmishing parties that the Boche had sent out. It would be an arduous few days as they fortified the new line, but Samuel thought nothing of it. It was no longer any of his concern. He thought about stealing back into the dugouts, ferreting around in the greatcoats of fallen soldiers for trinkets that might have been of some use – but he did nothing. He did not need to wish the place farewell. He had never been one for that kind of sentiment. He had his rifle and he had his boots, and for now that was enough.

Samuel took up his gun, and vanished.

Part Three

THE HARROWING

I

The transport passed through a checkpoint and gradually gathered speed. It seemed to move sluggishly beneath its burden: a dozen or more recuperated invalids, and twice as many young bucks with their unstained uniforms and first issue gas masks. William slumped at the back of the ranks, his cap pulled low before his eyes. Above the guttural groan of the engine, he could dimly perceive the bragging of some lieutenant who claimed he had been part of the Black Watch at Loos. The men around him were silent, as over and again he proclaimed the names of his friends who had fallen: Oakley and Baden, Anderson and Bowes, Oakley and Baden, Anderson and Bowes. He slurred his words, preaching of how he had carried his captain for a night and a day until they reached the tents at Boulogne, where they fed and deloused him and sent him back to face the gas. The men around him sat, rapt, and steeled themselves at what was to come when, at last, they made their stations. William merely sat, and watched through furrowed eyes the pastures that flickered past.

There was still fighting at Verdun, where for long months the French boys had been bloodied, but across the Belgian vales there had been stillness for weeks. Those were the rumours that William heard. That was the idle chatter of the soldiers with whom he was slumped. Flanders fields were silent. At the encampments and the waiting stations, William had heard tell of a vast conflagration at Ypres, where the land had been laced with mines. From the back of the transport, he watched it all roll by – the greens and the greys – and he wondered how long it would be before the whole land was consumed. He could see a vast observation balloon hovering above the green, like some falcon hunting for prey. He hoped that his brother was crouching in the earth somewhere, looking at that same balloon.

There'll be a goodness that comes out of your brother. That is what Mr Finlay had said, when William appeared on the doorstep in the smallest watch of the night, the battered knapsack over his shoulder, the fire fervent in his chest. He isn't rotten yet. But perhaps he'll walk to his death out there. Perhaps he'll march to his end not knowing that goodness is sitting on his shoulder. So yes, I'll make up the papers. Yes, I'll help. But find him, William, and bring him back, and leave your mother and your father to me – and then, let's not go on as it was before. Let's find a new path. Let's find a new world. The fighting can end and something right can come from this. But find him. Find him before the bullets do.

The transports took them to a makeshift station in a stretch of unending grey. William had seen the way the land changed around them as they travelled. It happened in stages, so that he could not tell, at first, how different the land was becoming. He had watched as the trees banking the sides of the road lost their branches and their leaves, becoming skeletons with blackened bark. He had seen the grasses sapped of their colour, brown bayonets that pierced the crust of the land. He had seen towns abandoned and farms lying barren, peopled only by the cats and crows and beasts of burden the fleeing people had left behind. Even the sky above this place was a mirror of what went on below. A pall of smoke hung on the horizon. He could smell it on the wind.

The transports left them at a farmhouse long since deserted, where runners from the Chapeltown Rifles were waiting to welcome them to the land. There was a wind – and, though summer was dawning, they were vicious gusts that swiped at the assembled men. The men marched. William fell into line, his rifle drawn as was his order. They had been drilled in marching at the barracks back home, but it was not until now that William knew he had absorbed every one of those drills. They came through a stretch of grey monoliths, the struts of buildings where once men had lived and worked. Then, slowly, they descended into the earth.

They were led along reserve trenches, where once battles had been fought. William supposed that, in a time not long past, these channels had been closest to the wire, the channels where the real war was waged. There were still bodies piled in one of the dugouts, heaped upon each other, freshly slain and freshly rotting. A man stood like a thief in the shadows, observing them and the flies that swarmed their wounds. William supposed that the boys piled within were his kindred and his friends.

There had been battle, then. It had been scarce days since the bugles called. Grimly, William observed that that was why he was here, that boys must have fallen in their conquest of the dirt and that more were needed to don their boots and take up their rifles and ride out when the horns next blew. He heard, from some of the boys, of the great raids that had been mounted all along the length of the river Somme, of the great furnace that was Flanders and how, from there, the devastation had spread. The Chapeltown Rifles had been spared the worst of the battle. It was a strange thing to think that being here, in the ravaged lands that bordered Belgium, was itself a kind of blessing. The Rifles numbered no more than half the men they had numbered before – but it was said that some of the battalions that had risen to battle were finished now, disappeared completely, dragged to the depths below by groping claws of mud. William was fortunate, they all said, to have been summoned so late.

He spent his first hours in orientation, being led from one end of the furrows to another so that he might know which way to run if the bugles flared. As he went, listening to a sergeant's monotone orders, he was searching for faces that he knew in the murk. There were some, here, that he thought he might have seen, once upon a time, roaming the terraces of Burley and Hyde Park. But certainly, they were different boys now – and if any of them recognised him, they did not deign to crawl out of the dugouts and take his hand. There were other battalions here too, the dregs of regiments obliterated by battle and then cobbled together, so that Cornish men sat beside Scots, and lads from Yorkshire beside boys from the other side of the Pennines. William understood, as he walked those channels, that a great deal of blood had been shed in the conquering of these lands.

Nowhere in the earth was there a sign of his brother.

He had been told, by the sergeants who led them from the transports, in which stretches the officers lay. He set out there now, coming through a part of the catacomb where the dead were only now being interred. Some of the gravediggers craned their heads at him as he came past, as if admonishing him for daring to still live, but he paid them no heed. If he had told them his story, perhaps they would have looked at him differently.

He climbed from the mausoleums and turned into a network of fresh excavations, where boys were still at work, laying new duckboards upon the dirt. Pushing between them, he came slowly to one of the dugouts, where a canvas awning

186

shielded the occupant from the stench that rose without. William did not announce his arrival. He fumbled with the canvas and sloped silently inside.

The man was sitting there, behind a desk of cobbled crates where reams of paper were held in place by stones. Carved into the earth at his feet there was a plan of trenches and fields and roads, marked by shards of flint and pebbles and bone. William stepped forward, and the canvas rippled behind him. The man was peering at him now, bemused at the intrusion. He shifted his papers a little, and William came further into the den. Lanterns hung on metal shafts against the furthest walls, spilling orange light onto the earth.

'Yes?' the man crowed.

'My name is William Redmond,' William began. 'I'm one of your soldiers.'

The man introduced himself as Captain Rice. He was new to these stretches himself, a sergeant of the Lancashire Fusiliers elevated by battle, and he extended a hand in what might have been a warm reception. William took it in his own, and they held the tableau for a strange, sullen moment. When the captain withdrew his hand, it was William who spoke first.

'There's another boy in the battalion,' he began. 'Name of Redmond. I thought there might be some news.'

'Family, is he?'

He knows, thought William. He's taken one look at me, and already he knows.

'He's family,' he replied.

'And he's this side of the line?'

'He's the Chapeltown Rifles, sir. I requested it myself.'

The captain stood. He was a squat hog of a man, his irises so dark that they might have been black. Thin wire spectacles sat on the bridge of a nose swollen from too much whisky, while his white hair was scraped back with grease that might have been put to better use above the fires that burned in the channels without.

'Name of Redmond,' he repeated.

'Samuel Redmond,' William breathed. But you know that already, he thought. It was a poisonous thought, and he let it blossom. You know why I'm here. You know what I'm here to ask. It's written on you, just like it's written on me. How much longer do we have to dance?

'You here to protect him?'

'I'm here to fight,' William lied.

'I don't think you can protect him now.'

William shifted. His feet were already wet, and his toes felt swollen in their socks.

'Your brother ran,' the captain said. 'He was on last watch in the night and, come sun-up, he was gone.' He stopped, then. 'You know what they do to runners, boy?'

William nodded. He was watching Captain Rice move from one end of the chamber to the other, and not once did he look away.

'You'll have to catch him first,' he said.

'They'll get him.' The captain's mouth opened in a tooth-some grin.

'You can't catch a coward. A coward won't make mistakes like a brave man makes. He'll hide in the hay for three days and three nights. He won't ride out and make a stand. Someone will take pity on him and take him in.'

'It's happened before,' the captain conceded.

'It could happen again.'

'It's nothing personal,' the captain lied, 'but men like your brother, they're the reason we'll lose this land. They're the reason we'll fall. We can't let them ride off.' He stopped, then. He studied William like a carrion crow might study a stagger-

188

ing ass. 'They'll put a man on him,' he breathed. 'They train them for it. Rangers. To bring boys like your brother in. He'll ride out on his trail.'

William felt the cold air flurry at his back. He stopped in the archway of dirt that opened onto the earthen pastures. Somewhere, men stood along a rifle range, loosing volley after volley at an imaginary foe.

'Send me after him,' he said.

The captain shifted his eyes.

'You aim to go after your own brother?' he asked, lips curled.

'I'll bring him in.'

'The hell you will.'

'He'll talk to me.'

'This has gone far beyond talking, boy. Don't you know what it is he has done? I see boys like him groping in the mire every day. Scarlet fountains pumping from their chests. Don't you know what he did when he ran?'

'I know it,' said William, 'but there's only me between him and your guns.'

'It isn't the done thing.'

The captain was piling his papers now. He pushed them together as if they mattered, as if here was some way out of these fields, and fastened them with a clip. William watched studiously. He saw, again, the markers of stone that lined the highways between this camp and the next, and turned as if to leave.

'Son,' the captain began as William walked into the dirt, 'I know how it goes: he's your brother, you got blood to think about, you're sworn to protect him. But we're all somebody's brother, boy. Brother or husband or cousin or son. It's all the same. We're all sworn on each other out here, and Samuel, he's thrown his two crooked fingers at all that, wouldn't you say?'

* * *

The man was crouched in the dugout when William turned the tooth in the trench. For a long while, he stood there, framed in the cavern's jaws, considering the man who dwelt within. There were figures shifting at his back, soldiers tramping past on their duties, but William paid them no heed. There arose the dull sound of firing from further down the line. William had heard the singing of shells many times before – the whole land was consumed by it as the transports wound their way across the country – but never had it been this close. He started to picture the boys upon whom the bombs bore down – but quickly he pushed the image aside. He could not waste his thoughts on the plights of other boys. That was not why he was here.

'You're the ranger?' William began.

The man stopped sifting through his packs, and cast William a furrowed glance. When he looked up, William thought he had never seen a man look more feral, like an animal hammered into a human mould. His face was sunken, and pitted by the scars of his youth: measles, and pox, and teenage boils. William thought he might have had a hare lip, but in truth it was just the way his upper lip curled when he spoke. He supposed it was the attitude of his trade.

'My name's Flynn,' he replied. William was surprised to hear it was a soft, lilting brogue, like some of the lads he had heard in the dugout: Irish lads, they were, come up together from the farms of County Wicklow, fighting here alongside the English and the Canadians and the blacks.

'They put you on my brother,' William said.

'Is that right?'

William nodded.

'It isn't right,' he insisted.

The man named Flynn turned back to his pouches. He was piling shells into a saddle-bag now, and draining the dregs from a leather canteen. William saw a Lee-Enfield propped against the wall of the dugout, its barrel broken back. The man had a small jack-knife secreted in his boot and an empty holster slung across his shoulder. There were small packs of rations about his feet, and a quarter-bottle of rum.

'Has there been word of him?'

Flynn looked up. 'There's always word of them,' he softly said. 'Your brother, and others like him. There's always word.'

'How will you find him?'

The ranger stood, hoisting a pack onto his shoulders. He did not look at William as he pushed past. He only muttered words into the ground, as if that was the place to which they were directed.

'Somebody will sell him out. They always do.'

'And if not?'

In the opening of the cavern, Flynn stopped and looked back. William was still watching him as he bowed into the light. 'I'm sorry for your loss,' was all that he said – and then he was gone.

William was still for a long while after Flynn departed. Then, slowly, he turned and he dropped to rifle through the oddments the ranger had left behind. There was little of any use – a new blade for his dagger, a roll of twine fraying at the ends – and he tossed each useless thing aside with little hisses of disgust. He did not know what he had expected to find. Perhaps there ought to have been a sign, some map etched into the earth that would lead him to the hole where his brother was hiding. It was a foolish thought, and quickly he cast it aside.

Samuel had fled. That was the only thing he needed to know. Was it because he was a coward? William delved into a leather pouch left lying in the dirt, and found within it a rusted dagger. He pushed it into his belt. No, it was not because he was a coward. Why, then, had he taken flight? Might it have been that, somehow, he knew? Might he have received word from the streets of Leeds? Might it have been Lucy?

Samuel was not running from war. Samuel was running from his brother. It seemed so clear to William, now. Samuel was running from his blood.

That was what William was thinking of as the shadow cast itself upon him. He thought little of it at first, that some soldier was idling in the mouth of the cavern, that Flynn had returned to collect the oddments he had left behind. But, for too long, the shadow lingered. William did not mean to let whoever it was know that he was concerned. He remained, crouched there among the rags that Flynn had abandoned, and slowly he craned his neck around.

There was a boy standing in the maw of the dugout, a scrawny little creature who might have been no more than five feet tall. Their eyes met, and each studied the other. William decided that he would not be the one to break the silence.

'You even look like him,' the ragged boy said. He moved a little further into the dugout and held himself there, hands braced against the support beams. He was a slight weasel of a man with one shoulder a little hunched and an ear that had been torn and healed and torn again. There was fur on his face, but it could not be called a beard. His brow was furrowed and William could see the way dirt collected in the creases of his skin.

The boy said that his name was Jacob. He was from Leeds himself, born and dragged up on the streets of Sheepscar, and drafted into the Chapeltown Rifles as soon as he came of age. That had been at the end of 1914, and though he had been home since, this was not an Englishman that William saw. This was some creature born of the dirt, some troglodyte birthed here in Flanders fields.

The boy trembled there, in the opening of the dugout, with the fires flickering behind him and the new recruits tramping past in strict formation.

'What do you mean to do?' asked Jacob. He was a weak little thing, and his voice quivered as he spoke. William thought he could almost picture him lurking on one of the street corners in Leeds, begging for food along the canal or in the crevices of the viaduct on Kirkstall Lane.

'I mean to go after him.'

Jacob pitched forward into the chamber. Though he was but small, he blotted out the light of the trench. He reared above William and his face was wrenched into a horrible mockery of anger. His cheeks were bunched and his neck strained.

'What will you do when you find him?' he growled. The way he bore down upon him, the boy put William in mind of a street dog driven to viciousness by years spent living between its den on the scrubland and its hunting grounds in the alleys and yards.

'It's OK, Jacob,' said William, coming slowly to his feet. 'I'm here to take him home.'

'You wouldn't lie?'

'I might, but I'm not.'

'You really do look like him.'

William smiled at the simple observation, and rifled inside his packs. He had decided, already, that he would do it tonight. There were a dozen or more new men in the Rifles tonight, and perhaps he might buy himself some time if none grew too accustomed to his features up and down the line.

'How will you find him?'

'I haven't thought about it.'

'I heard from a ranger that the men who run, they don't run far. They don't know where they're running. It's just the running itself. And then . . .'

William quelled the boy.

'If my brother ran, he'll run a long way. He's my brother. He isn't stupid.'

Jacob rocked a little on his heels. 'He isn't a coward either.'

William looked back at the boy. He was standing now, in the opening of the dugout, listening to the whirring and the screaming of shellfire further down the line. William had not been here for long enough to fully understand the differences between the voices in that unearthly chorus, the way they swooped and sailed among each other, but perhaps it would not take long. He imagined it as a series of shrill war cries, a battalion from the other side bearing down upon a different part of the line.

'I didn't say he was a coward,' answered William.

'You should have been there on the day of the gas. Then you wouldn't think that.'

William did not reply to that. He pushed a little into the open trench, and heard again the roar of shells. It was distant, but still the earth around him throbbed. He ducked back into the dugout.

'Have you seen the rest?' Jacob asked. 'Matthias and Alexander and the others from your streets?'

William considered it. He had not thought of them. He had known, of course, to which battalion all boys from his streets had been posted, but it had not occurred to him, until he heard the names, that he would see them as well. It had not occurred to him that they would have seen Samuel, some-where out here, on the line.

'I haven't seen them,' was all that he said.

'You don't mean to?'

'I don't mean to.'

Jacob paused, then. He moved a little closer to William, so that he might drop his voice, and shield his eyes.

'But don't you know what they did to him?' he breathed.

William stood at the head of the trench, where steps carved into the earth climbed to the dells above. It was late, and he could hear – in one of the warrens below – the familiar voice as it lit upon the familiar tale. He could picture Matthias holding court, self-appointed Lord of the Dirt, his lips parting to form the words with which he always began this particular tale. The fable of Isaac. The slaughter on the mountain.

He took the steps, one at a time, and descended like some otherworld hero into the earth.

There was a little fire in the dugout. It trailed thin smoke into the night. Matthias and Alexander were there, sur-rounded by a dozen other boys who might have come from the streets of Leeds or from any one of the little towns and hamlets that punctured the countryside thereabouts. William could hear, through the insistent chatter, the way the boys responded to Matthias' tale. He stooped low to enter the dugout, and once there he blended effortlessly with the boys. Some of them sat, enraptured, as Matthias' words rang out. Others exchanged knowing smiles with one another – but, always, they kept their silence.

William sat there, just another boy with his face daubed in dirt. It seemed an interminable time before any among them knew he was there. Some of the boys beside him slowly under-stood that he was here, and perhaps they understood as well whose brother he was, and why he had waded among them. But still Matthias' story plunged on.

The Lord had spoken. The knife was drawn. The son scrab-bled on the stone slab.

Their eyes met across the dugout.

'William?'

Matthias mouthed the word with a certain bewilderment.

William lifted his collar, and straightened his greatcoat. He did not respond. There were a dozen faces peering into his now, and he considered each one in turn, before at last he turned to Matthias. The others were here, David and Alexander and the rest he had shared drinks with that day after he woke; only Jonah was not among them. Matthias was peering at him with a brow pointedly furrowed, as if to express concern. William had seen the look before.

'I didn't think they'd send you to a place like this,' said Matthias. 'Not after what happened.'

'I didn't have to come.'

Matthias considered it carefully. Then he nodded his head. It was a worldly movement that he made, but William let it pass by.

'My brother is gone,' said William.

There was a silence. Some of the boys shifted, as if readying to leave the party. Matthias, however, still sat. He paused before he replied.

'That's what they say,' he answered. His voice was feathery and low. 'He was on watch in the night and then, come sun-up, he was gone. There was some that said he must have been sniped while he stood guard, that he used to stray too far from the sandbags whenever he was on watch, that there must have been Bavarian boys left who fled and weren't cut down. But we looked for a body and, William, there wasn't a body. Samuel ran.'

William stopped.

'I'd like to play a hand,' he said, gesturing at the cards that lay strewn across the crates.

'We don't play. We're not gamblers here.'

'Indulge me, Matthias.'

William gathered the cards together and, without looking down, he started to shuffle the pack. He could tell already that it wasn't complete, but that did not matter. The cards were damp, and they were ragged. He dealt two hands and the boys about him shifted a little away, as if sensing that this was not their game.

'Sixes and Sevens,' said William.

'I don't know it.'

'You'll learn.'

They started to play. In truth, William did not know the game well. He remembered it only vaguely, one of the few things he had learned from his grandfather before the old man passed on. He found that he was making it up as they played – although, of course, Matthias would never understand. He aped William pathetically as they played, studying his cards as if trying to read patterns in the numbers there, nodding sagely as if the rules were becoming apparent. That was how boys like him worked, thought William. Because William was making up new rules now, creating them to suit his own whims, and still Matthias pretended to understand, absorbing every one.

'You've seen battle?'

Matthias nodded. 'We took this part of the line ourselves. It was a bloody thing. Our captain fell. Dozens of others.'

'And you killed men?'

Matthias nodded, gravely. It seemed to William that he might as well have been acting.

'Maybe that's why my brother ran. Maybe he didn't have it in him to kill men.'

William saw the way Matthias' face changed. When next he spoke, it was a viper's tongue that lashed out the words.

'Your brother is a traitor, William.' Matthias clenched his hand, and the cards crumpled in his fist. 'I thought that it was cowardice. But I saw him in the deeps. And I saw him when he tumbled into the trench. And he wasn't a coward, William. There was wildness in him, but it wasn't because he was scared.' He stopped. 'And then it was done, and we were gathered in the dens – and then he was gone.' The other boys looked at the ground. They did not dare risk William's gaze. 'He was a traitor before he came to war, and he was a traitor when the day came for battle. That's why he ran. That's just him, William. That's just your brother. Even when we thought it was different, that's the way it went. He was born that way, and that's the way he'll die.'

William lifted a card. He cut the pack.

'Was he a coward when you went after him with a stone?'

He turned the pack and thrust it back at the soldier's hands. Matthias accepted it, but did not look down.

'A coward when you chased him through the streets? A coward when five of you cornered him in a hole in the earth?'

William paused. He bristled. He drew himself tall, and heard for the first time the banshee's wail of cannon fire overhead. 'Did you think it was God's work? As if this . . .' – he gestured wildly at the earthen walls and the duckboards and the rot – '. . . wasn't punishment enough?'

William's fist flew. Perhaps he had not intended to throw that punch when he descended into the dugout, or perhaps it had been simmering there, in the back of his head, all along. All the same, his blow sent Matthias sprawling into his friends. They crowded him now, tending to him, lifting him limply back to his feet. There had been nobody to lift William up, that day when he fell upon the Moor. He had lain there for an endless time. But Matthias was standing again, already, flanked by his companions, bolstered by the words they whispered in his ear.

'You're turning into Samuel, William!' Matthias hissed. 'He tainted you, that day on the Moor!'

William strode from the dugout. There was steady drizzle

now, warm rain unlike any he had known in England, and most of the men had retreated into the earth. It seemed that only Jacob was left, lingering there on the other side of the trench, his hair already matted to his brow.

'What did you do?' he began, as William came past.

William walked on. The little boy was scurrying at his side, eyes opened eagerly.

'They used to live on our streets,' said William. 'Of course, I was very young, and I thought that we were friends, then.'

'I know it,' nodded Jacob. 'I know all about friends.'

They went on in silence a little.

'There's a little town we went to once,' said Jacob, struggling to keep pace with William as he strode along the teeth of the trench. 'Name of Le Bizet. We took one of the freighters and we went there to get drunk and get girls. He'll go that way. If I was Samuel, that's the way I'd go.'

William stopped at an intersection in the trench as a group of men tramped past, laden with packs.

'Thank you, Jacob,' he said.

He waited for the men to pass, and then he hurried on. It was not yet nightfall, but there were things he had to do. He had not planned on it being like this. He had not understood the lengths to which Samuel would go in his quest to disappear. He followed one of the channels until he found an abandoned stretch, and there he turned to the ragged little boy who had been tottering in his wake. His face was screwed in what might have been a smile, and he squinted up at William in a kind of reverie.

'Jacob,' William said. 'Jacob, they'll come and ask questions. Did you like my brother, Jacob?'

Jacob nodded. 'He was a good man,' he said.

'Then you didn't see me,' said William, and lay a hand on his shoulder before he disappeared into the dirt.

II

William had not been numbered with the Chapeltown Rifles three nights when he set out from the line. It had been an easy thing to rise from the trench and bow his head down low as he set out across the glade. It had been a simple thing to climb aboard a wagon of one of the obliterated farms and lie there, in the straw, as the grey monoliths and the shell-ploughed earth disappeared on the horizon. He supposed that it would not long go unnoticed, but he did not dwell on it as he crossed the grasses and wildflowers and turned his back on the grey. He was thinking of other things, then. He was thinking that he was walking in his brother's footprints. He searched, idly, for their impressions on the ground.

He had ideas. That was all that he had – but maybe it was enough. He knew the paths that Flynn was set to follow, and he knew from Jacob of the little town in which he and Samuel had spent that idyllic day, long before the call to arms. It would take him so far, and after that he would trust to his instincts. He knew his brother well. William knew little French – only the few phrases and filthy words that the boys in the barracks had used to taunt each other – but he did not mean to let that stand in his way. He would bend the world to his own will in pursuit of his brother.

He set out, that first night, with the idea that he might reach Le Bizet and find there some rumour or clue that would lead him into the lands where Samuel was hunted. There were stragglers on the road, and through those first days he took up with a small legion of farmers and homesteaders whose land had been razed. They had a wagon and they had rations, and they were pleased to share what little they had with William. One of the travellers there, an elderly man who had spent his life tilling these fields, spoke a broken kind of English, picked up he said from the company of soldiers in some war now long forgotten. He told William how the scorched pastures that they crossed had once been verdant plains, how he and his kind had tended to their flocks here and harvested barleys and wheat and other sorts of grain. It was with a grim regret that the man shared those stories. These lands, he said, were not for his sons. They would not grow grain again. The fields that they loved had been upturned for men to make war, the old farmlands scorched so that, for generations to come, the only things that would grow would be thistles and weeds. His family would not return to their home. A line was being drawn under history and there were some things, he said, that changed the world for ever. It was a terrible thing that the man was explaining, and it stayed with William through every night after that, as he sat up late, staring at stars and thinking of his brother: a line is being drawn under history, and there are some things that change the world for ever.

William did not know at what point he passed through the Belgian borderlands and came into France. He knew a little of the world's geography – he and Samuel had often unfurled their father's charts and dreamt of the things explorers might yet find in the planet's distant realms – but of the vagaries of the Old World he was not sure. The fields of Picardy were lush compared to the lands in which he had roamed, but even here William could feel the conflict's encroaching fingers. The lands that he crossed were not being tilled. Barges did not move upon the brooklets and canals. Drovers did not herd their livestock up and down the trails. In the evenings he could see convoys of military transports smoking out along the roads, while through the days rags of soldiers marched from one outpost to the next. On the occasions he took the high roads, he would look down upon fields carved into devastation like the fields south of Ploegsteert, bordered like country estates with ribbons of trees still in leaf. It seemed that the frontier rippled out there, a constantly shifting shore, bulging and then sinking, swelling and then shrinking as the fighting went on. William stood on the headlands at night and watched the flaring of the border fires in the pastures below. Unable to distinguish the English from the German, it seemed to him that the world was made of a thousand different warring tribes, all vying for the same territory and unwilling to relinquish even an acre of their own. He was only dimly aware of what his tribe claimed to be fighting for, and knew then that the soldiers scattered across that land were fighting only for the few shillings to be won for their children and their wives. Every man who battled in these fields was a mercenary, whether he claimed it as his title or not.

When William came, at last, to the edges of Le Bizet, it was a shattered town that he saw, sitting there on the hillside. A pall of smoke hung above the devastation. Walls still stood, but the houses had been opened by shells, lives and livelihoods spilled there on the stone. The town had been set upon only weeks – maybe days – before. William could tell, for the animal stench of panic was still strong in the air. He crossed the crumbled town wall and wondered that it had ever been as Jacob described: a perfect little hamlet of rose gardens and cottages, and eager French girls lurking on every corner to catch the eye of any passing English soldier.

He wandered, alone, through the ruin. It did not take long to reach the furthest borders of the town, and when he did, he turned back to retrace his steps. This had been a home. This had been the entire world for a hundred or more families, stretching from the markets in the south to the crumbled chapel in the north. Now it was nothing. Overrun. He did not wonder where the people had gone, for he did not want to know. He entertained the idea that they had fled before the shells rained upon them, but it was a lie that he could not stomach for long.

He came along a narrow thoroughfare, and into a square where, somehow, a fountain still spurted from the cobbles. On the other side of the expanse a donkey lounged in the sun. It lifted its head when William's footsteps sounded on the stones, before rising awkwardly onto its hoofs and disappearing under the eaves of a shattered shop-front. It was a wild thing, now, but still it clung to the territories of men.

William thought he could hear something – a voice, a muted whimper from somewhere on the other side of the buildings – but he could not discern from which of the many alleyways the sound came. He pushed along another narrow lane, where the walls still stood, and came upon another square, smaller than the last, where black birds eyed him mordantly from the stones.

He wandered on until he heard the whimpering again, and knew for certain then that he was not the only man who stalked these streets. He searched for the voice in the remnants of the streets, but the town was crumbled now, and it was hard to pick a path through the rubble. When he came, at last, into the broad square where the fountains still trickled water into the debris, he stalled. The buildings that bordered the square were tumbled against each other, and although walls still stood in the semblance of buildings, he felt instead as if he was walking through one of the great slagheaps where Leeds sprawled into Bradford. Pillars of stone rose on either side of him, and as he came between them he heard the whimpering again. It was soft, but something in it was animal as well – a grating undertone of fear, like a baited bear. He climbed to the peak of a mound of fallen stones, and from there he surveyed the square.

The girl was beyond the fallen fountains, slumped there like a ragman in a rack of makeshift stocks. Sometimes her feet scrabbled, and the body righted itself – and it was only this that made William certain she was not already dead. William circled her at a distance, slowly moving towards her like a hunter to his kill. She hissed when she knew that he was there, though she did not open her eyes to see what kind of fiend approached. William dared not imagine what ideas were stampeding through her thoughts. He waited, for a moment, on the cobbles at the edge of the square, and he tried to picture what it had been like for her, when men last walked the streets of Le Bizet. In his head, he heard the slow fading of the footsteps that retreated from her the final time. Then, there was only the gaping silence. He did not linger long on the thought of what she might have done to deserve her punishment. Little things like that did not matter. He went to her slowly, and he whispered soft words.

Although she kicked and spat when he came close, a guttural sound coming from deep in her throat, she did not protest for long. William lay his hands on the stocks, and he made certain his hands did not glance across her body. It was not difficult to open the contraption. There were clasps and there was a latch – but that was all. It was not locked. It seemed such a cruel thing, that the girl was not held here by bolts and by chains, but only by a rusted clasp. William lifted the block, and retreated to the cobbles while the girl lifted herself from the wood.

It took her longer than he had thought, but finally the girl righted herself and teetered as she came away from the stocks.

William saw that her eyes were still closed, and she staggered in circles so that she did not fall. Then, slowly, she dared to peer out. At first the sunlight must have frightened her, for she seemed to shrink inside herself again. Then, bracing herself against the rack that had been her prison, she looked out upon the devastated square.

At once, William knew that the land had been ruined around her, that the soldiers had dragged her to those stocks and she had been locked there as the shells rained down and the guns moved through and the infantry poured over the rubble. She had closed her eyes to her home and opened them again to this harrowed valley. Perhaps that had been why her eyes were screwed so tight. William wanted to go to her, but whenever he took a step in her direction she hissed and spat, and whirled out her arms. It was a long time before she did not look at him like he was the soldier responsible for what had been done to her and her town. Alone, he sat on the edge of the square and left her to her own devices, as slowly she became accustomed to the new world.

She started to circle him, curious as a dog snouting around a new vagrant in its pack. William did not move. He did not beckon her onward or drive her away. The sun was beating high above the wreckage of Le Bizet, and he sat there and tried not to study her as her circles grew tighter, and she drew herself slowly into the shadow of the old shop-front. Even as she slumped to the stones beside him, he did not look around. He may have grunted a little, as if to acknowledge her, and perhaps she too had grunted back. Then, for a long while, there was only the silence.

At last, William dared to look around. The girl was half-asleep, her back braced against the stone and her head lolling forward. Intermittently her neck snapped round and her eyelids parted so that she could squint into the sunlight of the

205

square. She had black hair and blue eyes, and her skin was dark and caked in dust. There was a butterfly etched onto her shoulder, the crude tattoo that a childhood lover had carved into her on some stolen night. It was scarred all around, but the picture was indelible. Some thing of the past always remained. William reached into his packs and slung her his canteen. She fumbled with it weakly, and he took it back to lift back the cap. Most of the water spilled down her breast, but some of it touched her lips. She drank slowly at first, but with increasing greed. She drank like a starving dog.

She could not speak a word of English. William had thought, at first, that she was simply petrified – but when she started to speak, it was a foreign tongue that moved in her mouth. Quickly, she understood that William did not understand, and she sank back into that horrible, scarred silence. She seemed grateful for the water, and when she returned the canteen to William she dared to let her hand linger on his, as if in thanks. He told her she was welcome, though he knew she would not comprehend – and, in that way, there arose a little understanding between them.

The girl teetered as she set out across the square. Her head hung low, she reeled with each step that she took, as if trying to fix bearings in the rubble that had once been her town. At the furthest edge of the square, where a shop-front gaped horribly from the wreckage like the mouth of some anchorite's cavern, she stopped and turned back at William. He was still standing on the opposite side of the square, and for a moment they looked at each other across the fountain that still frothed. She gestured to him, then. He lingered a little while longer, as if to prove to the world in general that he was not like the other soldiers, that he alone meant her no harm. Dusk had already fallen, but still the sky was clear: a velveteen shroud pitted with comets and constellations. William was a boy of the streets, and he had never learned to read the stars like the voyagers in storybooks did. He wondered if stars were the same in every corner of the world, and whether or not Samuel was staring at the same constellations, even now. He nodded at the girl, then, and, at a distance he was certain would not frighten her, he took up her trail.

They came between two racks of ruined buildings and along a narrow thoroughfare where the cobbles had been torn from the earth. At the end of the row, one of the houses was still intact, though its windows were shattered and the wrought-iron balconies had been torn from the stone. The girl led him to it and stood at the bottom, looking reverentially up at the shell. Then, when she was certain William would follow, she reached out for him and together they stole within.

It was the girl's home. William knew it without having to be told. He saw the way her fingers traced the edge of each surface, how she stooped to pluck a pillow from the wreckage and held it tightly to her breast. She murmured something in that foreign tongue, and looked to William with eyes that begged to be understood. Instinctively, William nodded. He could not know to what he had agreed, but suddenly the girl was calmed. She placed the pillow gently in the rubble and set about clearing a space.

They rested. At last, when the girl was finished rearranging the rubble, she was able to sleep, and William sat peacefully at her bedstead, watching over her as she slumbered. It must have been that he slept too, for intermittently he opened his eyes to find that the darkness was thicker over Le Bizet. He had not realised how weary he was, and he shifted uncomfortably in the seat he had been given. He drew his greatcoat close and lifted his collar. Somewhere without, the wind played upon the fallen buildings, rasping through the empty shells.

Something startled William and, again, he woke. Was it just the wind again, or was there something else, tramping through the crumbled streets? William turned instinctively to the fallen walls and tried to fight his imagination. He had been dreaming of English infantry combing the smokestacks, marching through the town in vast grey columns. It struck him, then, that it was the English he was afraid of, and not the Boche.

When he looked back at the girl, she too was awake. It must have been his panic that had roused her, for she was looking at him with unease. There was more colour in her cheeks now, and even in the gloom William could vividly see her eyes.

'Are you well?' he asked, gesturing with his hands as if he might be able to describe the words.

The girl said nothing.

'What is your name?' He tried to say it in French as well, but the words sounded malformed even to him, and quickly he accepted defeat. 'William,' he went on, indicating himself. 'William,' he repeated, placing a hand on his breast.

The girl looked up at him, as if there came upon her a sudden understanding, some dim recollection of the world before the bombing.

'William?' she questioned. The word sounded alien on her lips.

William nodded, and shifted to the pillars of stone.

Outside, the darkness had settled. The ruin lay before him, seemingly as ancient as any of those prehistoric forts that lined the dales back home. Would it soon be dawn? William had no way of knowing. It occurred to him, then, that he had come to this town knowing along which roads his brother had fled, but that he would leave here without direction. It was not even the same town that Samuel had known. Not really. The guns had come since then, and now the land was changed for ever.

William tried to picture it as it had been, that bounteous little place that Jacob had described, but such a flight of the imagination was beyond him. He wondered if it had been like this when Samuel last came through. He began to picture his brother, trekking south through Picardy and the other foreign fields, turning the land to grey, leaving this destruction in his wake.

William looked back, at the girl who lurked there, unseen, in the recesses of the building. She was reshaping her nest now, building walls from the rubble, spreading out salvaged bedspreads – and perhaps she was crafting a nest for William, too. They would sleep – but that, he knew, was where it had to end. A girl like this could not help him in the pursuit of his brother.

He went to her side. She nodded at William, and he gave a weak half-smile. He was going to hate himself for this.

'It's OK,' he said, though he knew she would not understand. He watched her sink into her nest. 'It's all right. Go to sleep,' he said. 'It's only me.' He looked into the girl's searing blue eyes. 'I'll be here in the morning,' he lied. 'I promise.'

III

The darkest watch of night, and William stood on the edges of Le Bizet, the devastation a silhouette on his shoulder. Had the girl wanted to travel with him? William did not know. He did not like to ask himself the question. He had left her in the gut of the building, where she slept, curled like a question, in the rags and fallen leaves. It had not been hard – though he knew that, one day, he would waste hours thinking upon what had become of her after he left. But now it was simple. He had made sure that she still breathed, emptied what few rations he had onto the stones around her – and then he had sloped into the night. He had not looked back as he walked the street between the charcoal shells. If he had looked back, he would have gone to her. He was not a monster. He did not take delight in the thought of her waking to find herself alone. But he looked at the buildings – the struts and structures sunken to the ground, the walls and pillars that still remained – and he knew, without hesitation, that there was something greater at stake. He was sorry for the girl, but that was all.

It was a summer night. July had turned into August. This William knew as fact. He kept track of the days with a religious fervour, lest one of them escape him. He found that he was thinking, with the passing of each hour, of what was happening in Leeds, and the world of redbricks and chimneystacks he had left behind. He knew that morning came later to the people of his home, and it seemed that that small thing opened a chasm between them. He did not wonder what his mother and his father had made of his disappearance. He wondered, instead, how it had been for his uncle when word reached him on the other side of the terraces: both of his nephews, gone to the guns.

He had taken the small roads out of town. He was travelling south. He knew it only because the constant rumbling of the hurricane was on his left. When the land lay low, he could even see the arcing flares and shells. He kept a watch on it as he went. It seemed that it bulged more towards him the further south he came. It seemed that the Boche had advanced. The roads were empty now – though he could see that the fields were pitted with the lights of habitation – and he was glad to be alone. He had never felt so happy to be on his own before; he had always enjoyed the company of friends, but now he felt differently. Other people, they would only hold him back.

The wind rose. He thought, at first, that there was rain carried on those gusts, but the sky was clear – every constellation was shining – and he put his fingers to his face to discover that it was ash that whirled on the wind. Did it really stretch this far? The trail dipped a little, so that he could no longer see the ribbons of colour, and above him the wind ghosted over. It was still in this little depression, and he stopped to gather his bearings. From this dell he could no longer see Le Bizet, and for that too he was thankful. He did not like the thought of the way it had crumbled, how everything Samuel touched was turning to dust.

Samuel. He looked up, saw the flecks of ash that the wind carried. They turned like tendrils, twisting as they flew. He thought he heard his brother's name, whispered and warped by the wind. 'Samuel!' it cried. 'Samuel!' it seemed to be sobbing. He was tired. He sat on the bank and he hung his head low, but still the wind, whipping over the depression of land, seemed to carry his brother's name. It was a ghostly voice that came flurrying around him so that it seemed to come from every direction, stirring a miniature maelstrom. He concentrated hard, tried to shut it out. He thought it was Lucy's voice, crying out for her lover. He thought that if he did not find Samuel soon, if he did not pick up the trail, all this would be for nothing. The land might as well be consumed. He thought he heard the name again, a flock of birds crowing the name. He thought it was the scars that he wore, shrieking it out.

He climbed from the depression of land and he forced himself forth.

He came through a copse of blackened trees, shorn of their branches; a crater in the ground where some skirmish had been fought or some mine exploded. When the darkness was too thick, he gathered the kindling for a fire from ditches on the banks of the road, and settled high on a camp that looked over the lands he had conquered, every rotten vale and blasted heath. Although he cupped the lit match in his hand, he did not immediately put it to the pyre. He pushed a little along the trail instead, scouting out every path that might have led to his hideout, and only when he was sure of the paths he might take if he was discovered did he stir a cauldron of small flames. He crouched there for a while, eating the scraps he had left, and as he curled beneath his greatcoat he thought he heard it again – the wind pushing and moulding words out of the air. He closed his eyes and willed sleep to come, but each time he was on the edge of sinking under, the words of the wind dragged him back.

William. It was William that the words were calling. It was not Samuel. It was not the name of his brother.

He remembered it being much the same as when he lay in that infirmary bed, when the wound at the back of his head was fresh and still weeping through the heavy doctor's thread. He had heard people calling out to him then – his mother, his father, his uncle – and somehow the words had reached him, even through the veil of his sleep. Back then, the words had grown stronger with each new calling. It was the same here, now. As if the predator was circling. Still huddled beneath the greatcoat, William gingerly opened his eyes.

'William!' the wind called. 'William!' it begged.

William's head snapped back. He tore the greatcoat away, opened his eyes wide to the night. He had not been dreaming it this time. It was not some trick of the wind. It was his name, bawled out at him, just as Samuel's had been bawled.

He turned, stared across the remnants of his fire – and there, lit in the orange glow, there stood the girl.

She was just standing there, frail in the night. She was wearing the same dress that he had left her in, and that was all. She was not even wrapped in the rags in which she had slept. William went to her. She was shivering on the edge of the camp, where entangled thorns hid him from the roads beyond, and his first thought was not for the girl. His first thought was only that he had been discovered, that if somebody as unpractised as the girl could hunt him down, then surely some ranger of the military police would find him soon. He could not let that happen. He would never find Samuel if he was to be locked in some earthen oubliette or shot.

On the horizon from which he had come, he could still see the jagged outline that was the ruins of Le Bizet. The girl had come a long way, through scorched woods and blasted heaths. She was still before him, hunched and cowed like some wandering penitent, and she looked to him with her dark eyes open wide. She had trailed him, then. Tracked him like some wolf. William wrapped her in his greatcoat. He had not meant for her to be so cold. She squirmed a little, retreating from his arms – and when she turned back to him, there was a leaf of paper folded in her hands.

William stoked the fire and, in its light, he read the word. The flames danced a vicious fandango, torn at by the wind that clawed through the thorns, but he shielded the paper with his body hunched, studying it over and again. It was nothing, really. Just a word. But William had seen that word scrawled a hundred times or more. He knew each loop of each letter, each depression and indentation made by the point of the pencil. 'Samuel,' it read, in his brother's own hand. From across the camp-fire, the French girl looked at him with pleading eyes. This, then, was why she had come.

Had he been good to her? How long ago had it been? Had they been friends? William knew that he might never find out. There was only one certainty in all this chaos: that his brother had once come through Le Bizet; that this truly was his brother's trail. Again, he lifted the paper to the light and watched, through the leaf, the patterns cast by the light. The word stood out in stark, black symbols: Samuel, ringed in fire.

She must have recognised him. That was all William could surmise. It heartened him to think that there was still something in his countenance that could remember his brother to a girl he did not know. They were not so different, then. Neither could have changed beyond all recognition. They were still brothers.

'You must be hungry,' he said.

The girl lifted her eyes to his.

'I don't have any more food.'

She widened her eyes.

'I have water,' he went on.

'Samuel?' She mouthed the word.

'Samuel,' answered William.

He held her through the night, until her shivering subsided – and, after that, he lay her in his greatcoat, a pillow of rolled sacking at her head. He waited until dawn, stoking the fire, and then he woke her. He had thought, as he prepared to rouse her, that he meant to tell her he was leaving – that again she was to be on her own – but as she stirred and her eyes met his, he knew that it could not be. He had promised himself he would be low and he would be dirty and he would lie and he would cheat – but some vestige of his past self must have remained. Some piece that was good. He could not leave her to the ruins. He brought her water from a brooklet that ran close by, and as he took it to her he found that he was cursing himself. How was he ever to find his brother if he did not think as his brother thought? How was he ever to take him home if such a little thing as a girl could waylay him? Did his brother mean so little to him that he would not cast this girl aside and set out on his trail? Did he really love his brother that little?

They travelled together. By fall of the next night the ruin of Le Bizet was gone from the horizon, and the fields rose green about them. Perhaps it was a remedy of some sort, to no longer see the ghost of her home town, but a change came upon the girl. She seemed stronger. She no longer started at the flickering of each shadow. She drew her back straight and she walked tall, and for the first time William saw that she was more human than she was beast.

They came along trails banked in wild grass. They travelled east and they travelled south. This even William could tell, for he followed the arc of the sun as it sailed overhead. He tried not to think that he was wandering without direction. He studied forks in the track and told himself that he was walking in Samuel's shoes, that of all people on this planet only he might have that instinctive feeling of which fork his brother had chosen. There were times when he thought himself useless, when he stood on headlands and surveyed the endless pastures of France, and thought that his endeavour was pathetic, a little boy's dream of digging in his garden and unearthing buried treasure. A man could disappear in so vast a land if that was what he wanted. William supposed it was a heartening thought as well, for if he could not find Samuel, what chance had Flynn?

Flynn. The man was never far from William's thoughts. He wished he could have spoken to the girl about it, asked her if there had been a man drift through Le Bizet some time before the guns rained, asking questions, ferreting in the secrets of people's lives, demanding to know if his brother had passed through. Fleetingly, he imagined that that was why she had been trapped in the stocks: a punishment for the way she had defended his brother, tortured until she might yield.

On the second day, they strayed into the outskirts of Béthune, and the girl ventured forth to bring back food and drink. William waited for her, crouched in a thicket on the edges of the pastures, and did not doubt that she would return. He saw, from the way the land was ruptured and scattered with debris, that the town was already housing a battalion marched back from the line. He lurked in the thicket and watched three of them stealing along the lane. He had thought that they might have looked grateful for their time away from the guns, but their faces were drawn and their skin still smeared in dirt, and the eldest walked with a strange gait as if, in one of the skirmishes, bullets had raked his leg. They sat together, for a little while, on a mound at the side of the road, and together they smoked. William watched them through the branches that concealed him, and marvelled that those creatures had ever been Englishmen. Deliberately, he checked himself from thinking about what monstrous thing Samuel had become.

After the men moved out, the girl appeared around a bend in the track. William could see, from a distance, that she was not bearing any goods from the town. She was moving towards him swiftly, running for a stretch and then slowing to walk, and as she drew near he noted that there was fire in her stride. Slowly, William came from the thicket to meet her. She stopped dead, a hundred yards along the track, and reached out an arm that he might come to her side. Above them, the sky was a vivid blue, marked only by scattered clouds over the town. It sat there, behind her, crisp against the endless fields. Quickly, William started to walk.

She wanted him to follow. Even before he had come to her side, she wanted him to go after her.

They came into Béthune by one of the small drovers' roads, where the first houses were farmsteads, and then the outhouses where farmhands had once bunked. Then, around them, the village rose. Perhaps it had once been a pleasant town where farmers came to market, but that age had long passed; like most of the towns he had seen squatting on the pastures, there had been skirmishing here. They did not cut through the squares where the soldiers thronged, but followed the dead streets instead, until they came at last to the south-ernmost reaches of the town. The fields were scattered with refuse here, but they followed the trail and came, again, to greener pastures. He looked after the girl as she scouted the trail, and was drawn forward like an obedient dog when she looked back to urge him on. There was a new life in her now, and she walked eagerly, head rolling as if to survey the grass-land. The grasses rippled and a swarm of insects played upon the flowers that blossomed between the blades.

He trailed after her a little way, through a stretch of road banked in sweet chestnuts. There, the road forked. It must have been a road the girl knew well. There was a new flickering in her eyes, and she was pushing along the bank, where the wildflowers were blossoming. Every time she took a few paces, she turned back and squinted at William, who trudged wearily in her wake. The sun was riding high, and the few clouds left were scattered and thin.

In the shadow of the chestnuts, they came to a small pasture bordered by yet more trees. It had been a paddock for horses, but there were no longer any beasts kept here, every one of them requisitioned to ride out against the guns. The grass had grown long, and thick clover was sprouting between the blades. Through the furthest line of trees, William saw that a ragtag of tents had arisen. There were covered wagons there, traps with harnesses for horses that must have been set to tether in a pasture further beyond. The girl set off across the grass at a run. Half-way to the trees, she was calling out, hallo-ing the encampment. William did not follow. He saw that there were men gathered beyond the branches. The girl was nearly upon them. He called for her, and she turned. There was a quizzical expression on her face. 'William!' she cried. The sun momentarily obscured her face, so that all that William could see was a fleshy orb curtained in black. He hurried to her side. He felt suddenly alone in the middle of that expanse, as if at any moment he might be set upon by wild beasts. He heard his name called again.

A cry. The report of a weapon. William instinctively turned his shoulder, unsure from which directions the gunshots came. There were other voices now, people barking out commands – but William did not understand a word. It was French that they spoke, and he cowered from it as if the words themselves were a shower of bullets. The girl was edging from him, and he clawed out at her to rein her back in. Another flurry of gunfire rent the air about his head, and somehow the girl scrambled from his grasp. She was running, but it took

William a moment to understand that she was running to and not from the voices. His arms raised high to form a useless shield around his face, he sank to the ground and felt the rushes surging at his knees.

Men stampeded around him. He saw them rampaging through the sliver of light between his arms. He turned, uselessly, in the grass – but they were on all points of him now, and advancing with their weapons raised. They were ancient weapons that the men bore – muskets and shotguns from some century past – but William could still smell the shots that had already been fired. Grey vapour rose from the barrels of those guns. The men bawled at him in that foreign tongue, and instinctively he called out. When the men understood what he was, their voices softened. One of them came closer to William and pressed a foot against his back, so that he sprawled in the grass. His cap must have tumbled from his head, then, for at once he felt the blast of cold air against the scars at the back of his head. They screamed. Perhaps the men saw them, too, for now they were speaking in low whispers. One of them crouched at William's side and snatched the rifle from his shoulder, feverishly checking in every pocket and lining for any other weapon the boy had secreted away. Only when they were certain he was unarmed did they haul him back to his feet.

William was looking into a bank of men – aged Frenchmen bearing their fathers' arms. They were not soldiers. They wore the rags of farmers and tradesmen, and each of them was old enough to have lost sons in the ruptured fields. Beyond them, half-hidden beyond a line of trees, there sat a little caravan of horses and traps, where other figures were hidden from the skirmish in the field. The girl was disappearing into the wagons already, shepherded there by two other men. William wanted to cry out to her, but he did not know her name.

219

One of the men barked out a question. William could not reply. He edged a little forward, and the men tensed their rifles. One of them hissed a question at another, but the oldest man shook his head. William reeled. His vision was blurring now, the men and the trees and the field swimming in and out of focus. He spoke the little French he could recall – stupid, broken words, a plea for help, his name repeated again and again as if it might save him. Then there was a holler. Some of the gunmen turned to see an even older man emerging from the bank of trees, hobbling forward with a staff in each hand. William saw him approach, framed by the men who bore muskets. He grappled forward, plunged back to his knees. The world was whining now. It started to shriek. He felt ripples move up and down his arms, steadied himself just in time to see the older man come among them – and then the shrieking rose to a hideous crescendo, some fell wail that started to smother him. Foolishly, he gulped at the air. One gulp, then two, then a third – and still none of the air rushed into his lungs.

There was blackness: cold and comforting.

William awoke with the girl at his side. He knew it even before his eyes had opened, for he could smell the soap with which she had scoured herself clean. He felt strangely safe, then, and he turned in his blankets to see her. As his eyes righted themselves, the first thing to emerge from the blur was the crude butterfly tattoo that marked her arm. She dropped a hand to his brow and lightly she fingered his hair. It was still short, and softly her fingers whispered through it until they danced upon the edge of his scar. They did not light upon the wounds themselves, but simply hovered there gently, as if refusing to intrude.

'William,' she said. It was not a question. She only wanted to whisper his name.

'Where am I?' he asked.

The girl shook her head sadly, as if to indicate that she did not understand. In response, William rocked back on his pillows, and stared at the ceiling. He was lying in a vast canvas tent. It was a military tent, but it was not of this century. William supposed that it must have been salvaged decades before, taken back to Le Bizet by one of the men who lived there. He was lying on a mattress of straw, and the sheets in which he was wrapped were the best cotton that the people had to offer. He looked up at the girl.

'William?'

He did not know how long he had been asleep, but perhaps it had been for days. There was a hunger in his gut, and his body felt light and weak. He cursed himself. He cursed the pathetic wound that had felled him all over again.

She spoke again, feathery words that he did not catch, and then she turned to the opening of the tent. There was another figure there, and it responded in the same tongue as the girl. It was a man. It was the old man that William had seen, advancing towards him when the blackness first came. There was a certain resemblance between them, and William knew, then, that he was the girl's grandfather. It was in the eyes. There was always some feature that betrayed your blood. He heard figures shifting outside the tent, saw the shadows that they cast on the canvas, and understood that he was among the families who had fled Le Bizet.

The girl whispered to him in French, and it pained him that he did not understand. She was stroking the side of his face, and somehow he knew that her words were full of unease.

'She says you need your sleep,' the old man began, still standing in the corner of the tent. It was English, and for that William was thankful. 'She says: where did you get the wound at the back of your head?'

William's neck craned at the girl. 'Samuel . . .' he wanted to say. 'Samuel . . .' he wanted her to hear. But instead he said nothing. He peered back, through the gloom, at her grandfather, and tried to prop himself up in bed. 'She knew my brother. Ask her if she knew my brother.'

'She did,' breathed the old man. 'For a little while,' he added.

'When?'

'It was May. A month or more before the bombs.'

William wrenched himself so that he was sitting. He must have shown how much it strained him, for the girl's hands fell to his shoulder in support.

'I want to know where he is. Can you ask her?' he breathed.

'It was a long time gone.'

'Ask her!' William seethed.

The girl's grandfather came forward.

'She saw him only once,' he uttered, coming close so that William could see the features of his face. His eyes, vivid blue and young like the girl's, were strangely out of place, flanked there on his pockmarked face by thick crow's feet. 'The land changed since then. She doesn't know a thing.'

William doubted that the old man was lying, but still it reared within him, a desire to leap at him and drive him down and know for certain that he was speaking the truth. It was something base inside him, something he had not felt before, and he was not sure that he wanted to bury it. He thought suddenly of Samuel, that day up on the Moor.

'The land changed?' he hissed, his jaw set tight.

'There was fighting.'

'Fighting?' William scoffed.

'Your brother's regiment were fortunate not to be there. Stupid luck that they held some other part of the line. Men came out of holes up and down the river. The length and breadth of the Somme swirled in their blood. There was a fortress at Thiepval, and they set their sights on it. But within hours the dead were smoking in stacks. The land just couldn't bear to take them. You could smell that ash from here to the Pyrenees. The hills themselves must have wept. That was when Le Bizet fell. We thought we might escape it. There was talk of a surrender – but I'm an old man; I've seen the towns that surrendered. We ran instead.'

William choked. The girl was looking at him, her face furrowed in concern for her patient, but he did not dare catch her eyes. Stark images came upon him as he imagined the horror of that morning. He had seen what it was like at Ploegsteert, and now he pictured it in those fields that bordered the Somme: the river that raged at their backs, the sound of silence as the shelling came to an end, the rows and rows of boys plunging to the earth as their fellows stumbled blindly behind them. He breathed hard, and struggled to stand. A whisper of wind fluttered through the flaps of canvas, spilling daylight within.

'But my brother?' William demanded. 'He didn't fall. He came through it.'

The old man did not reply.

'And then he ran.'

The old man nodded again. 'The Lord moves in mysterious ways,' he quoted, and then turned to leave William alone with the girl.

It was days later that William began to feel well. They had moved from the first camp while he was still recovering, leaving the fields of Picardy to drift south, along trails that led into the Ardennes, and now they moved by night through a level countryside of farms and grassy plains. There were still some farmers herding beasts here, though other farmsteads had been put to the torch and now simply sat there, smouldering over the land. A wandering doctor came among them to check for ailments and cleanse them of lice, and when he chanced upon William he asked him what battalion he was from, and how he had strayed so far from his post. It was an ungainly English that the doctor spoke, a southern dialect that William might not have understood even if it was the man's first tongue, and at first he refused to answer. Some of the other men were looking at him now, as if sensing that here there was trouble brewing. But at last William spoke. He was of the Chapeltown Rifles, he said. His unit had been scattered, he lied. Divided by guns and cowardly captains. He was on his way to his rendezvous when he found the girl of Le Bizet. He had broken rank to bring her here, and he had fallen ill. He would reach the rendezvous soon.

The people of Le Bizet stood by William. They were good people, and they were pleased to carry him with them and feed him and thank him for bringing back the girl. More than that, they were concerned. The girl's grandfather relayed it to him, and he heard snatches of it from the women and the men. They had seen the wound. While he was asleep, they had washed and dressed it, and wondered what horror he had seen on the front to sustain such an injury. They had heard the stories, of course, of how soldiers met their end. A generation of Le Bizet's young men were, even now, interred in the grounds of Verdun. But there was something different about William's wound, something strange, that demanded a story. More than once, they asked him. More than once, William demurred. He told them, instead, that he had seen combat, somewhere at the northernmost stretch of the front. He told them he had been felled out there, in the storm, but that somehow the stretcher-bearers had reached him. That was all he would say – and though the Frenchmen knew he lied, he did not care.

As he drifted with them, he came to know the girl a little. She had once had a sister, he learned. She had been pretty, with red hair and green eyes. The people of the village had teased her on account of her hair. They said she had the blood of ancient Gaul in her. It was her sister for whom the girl had strayed back into Le Bizet. She had been taken by the shells. Not a piece of her remained. She had not been the only one to vanish like that. There had been others too, turned to vapour, with nothing left to bury or mourn. The girl's family set out from Le Bizet the following dusk, hoping to make the rendezvous with the others of the village at Béthune, but something – the memory of her obliterated sister, a deep and inscrutable hope that some vestige might have remained – drew the girl back. By then, the place was overrun. Soldiers had poured into the ruin to pillage all they could find. They had cornered the girl in one of the gutted halls. It had been dark, but still she had seen those shadow men moving towards her. It had lasted until the morning. Then, her humiliation complete, and so that they might not bear the guilt for her murder, they had left her to die in the stocks.

After William heard that, he did not think it fair to ask her of Samuel. He hated himself for being so weak, but something in him stopped him from demanding answers. Samuel would not have been so sentimental. Samuel would have had the strength to go on. He resolved to wait a little, to find the right time, but time was short. He did not have long. It might have been that Flynn was closing in on Samuel, even now. It might have been that Samuel was in shackles, being led back to his battalion. He went to see the girl's grandfather.

They were camped, now, outside the town of Bray, and making preparations to venture within. William had heard that here the people would find the sanctuary of families and friends. The exodus was coming to an end. He was sad for that, but heartened as well. Too long had he been idle. Too long had he been waylaid.

He walked the periphery of the camp with the girl's grand-father, and they talked of all manner of things. William was thankful for the conversation. It was a strange thing to be isolated by language, and it gave him some kind of succour to hear his mother tongue, no matter how unknown the accent. It was a long time into that conversation when he confessed why he had stumbled through the shell of Le Bizet. He told the old man everything that he could bear to tell. His brother, too young to bear arms, had run away to war. William was charged with bringing him back. He mentioned nothing of the Moor, or of his mother and his father. He let the old man believe that Samuel was a brave lad with faith in his country, that he had come out here to serve his king but had been overcome by the killing fields so that something in him had snapped. He told the old man that he cared for his brother more than for his country, that he knew he too would be hunted now, but that none of it mattered, so long as he could send his brother back to England. He was thankful that he had found the girl. In a peculiar way, it made him feel that his brother still existed, that he had not been completely lost to this Hell.

At last, he asked of Flynn.

Flynn, too, had come through Le Bizet. It was after the shells, and only the most stubborn habitants of Le Bizet remained. He had appeared on his ass, trotting untouched through the devastation, cornering the people who ran and rasping out his demands. Their world was crumbled now, and they had greater burdens to bear than the aiding of some insidious English soldier. The girl's grandfather had been lurking on the edges of the square, that day. To him, Flynn had first been a smudge on the horizon, a rider formed out of the settling dust.

Then, the questions had begun. He sloped among the people of Le Bizet, speaking his chipped French, its every nuance and inflection butchered by his English tongue. People had spoken to him, because that was what he expected. Men like Flynn had a way of bending people to his will. He heard stories of the soldiers who came up from the reserve lines and the occupied lands thereabouts. He heard of the inns where people played cards and drank wine. He heard about the two lowly soldiers who had hovered there, on the edge of the throng, not knowing if they would be permitted to wander in.

'That was when he came to me,' said the girl's grandfather. 'I'd known about it, of course. But I'm a grandfather, not a father, so of course I let it happen. She told me about it, afterwards. How your brother had been in her chamber. How he'd run from her like he was a frightened child. How she listened to his footfalls as he fled and somehow it had warmed her to him.' He stopped. William was considering the old man carefully. Something bristled there. Behind them, Bray crouched like an ogre. A ribbon of men was moving into it along one of the roads. 'There was another boy with him,' the girl's grandfather went on. 'An ugly sort. The kind they breed on your island.' He grinned, knowingly. 'Flynn asked about it all. He knew it already. You could see the fable forming. It was in the way he spoke. He was crafting it out of every little image he was given. He was stitching the pieces together.'

The old man shifted. He spoke of the paths that each of them travelled. The pine forests and the hills and the verdant farms. They were not the safe green lands that they looked. That was the message of the girl's grandfather. Perhaps the land here was not ravaged as it was at Ploegsteert and Verdun and Le Bizet – but there were things in this world more dangerous than gases and guns. Green lands like this could ensnare wayfarers such as William. If they had not already ensnared his brother, it was only a matter of time before he grew comfortable and confident and made a mistake. The lanes of these lands were travelled by rags of men who had run from their stations, gangs of boys from the other side trapped behind lines and desperate not to be found, hunters and rangers and men robbed of their homes and eager to betray any soldier in revenge. It was dusk already, a low wind stirring about the caravan, and William understood that he could not stay with them for ever.

'You've been good to my girl,' he said. 'You both have, in your way. William and Samuel, she says. I hadn't dreamt that there might have been good English boys.' He smiled at that last remark, and William returned the expression. 'You must love your brother very much, to be searching for him in the middle of all this.' He shrugged, and held a hand to his head. 'Love him or hate him. Which is it? Why are you hunting him?'

At first, William did not respond. Then, slowly, he looked away, across the undulating field.

'Because there was nothing else I could do,' he admitted.

The girl's grandfather understood. He said he understood it well. He did not have a brother, he said, but he had had sons and he had had grandsons as well. He knew well how it went when there was blood to think about.

'I heard rumours,' he began. 'Stories of a boy at one of the farms in the lower Ardennes. The hills are alive with stories, William. It may yet be a myth. But there is a farm in the glades south of here, and they say there is a boy there, an English boy like yourself, hiding there through the days, venturing out only at night, waiting for this thing to finish and the hunters to be called off. A boy, they say, who does not dream of England.'

William did not say a word. He studied the old man's face. No, the old man was not a liar. The old man would not deceive. An English boy like yourself. A boy, they say, who does not dream of England.

'They say he has a countenance much like your own,' the girl's grandfather went on.

'Which roads would I travel?' William breathed.

The old man stooped to scratch a line in the dirt. It was a crude map that he drew, but still William understood. It would not take long. The pastures were only a few days hence. He understood that he could be there by the time the new moon was high.

'But, William,' the girl's grandfather went on. 'William, if the rumour is right, if the word I heard is true – then I won't be the only one to have heard it. And these lands are full of traitors, William. People with everything to gain by selling your brother out. William, if it is your brother, he won't have long.'

IV

The night was not yet deep enough to hold William back. He made his adieux to the girl's grandfather, and then he went in search of the girl. Behind the wagons she was already asleep, peaceful there in her nest, and he decided, then, that he would not wake her. He watched her for a moment, and then he stole away. He hoped it was over for her. He hoped that it was done. But if it was not, if this thing enveloped her again, it was not his cross to bear. He had a bigger burden. Some place else he had to be. The girl and her family would find their own way – and he would find his brother.

They gave him food, and they filled his canteen, and though few of them could breathe a word of his language, each of them said farewells in their own way. He decided that he would not venture through Bray, and followed instead the trails that ran around the town walls. He had gone a long way before he turned back, to see the line of wagons and horses and cauldrons of fire that had been his makeshift battalion. Even then, he did not turn back for long.

He came to the banks of the great river the following morning, when the sun's first light was spilling onto the vale. There were ferrymen to take him across it. He had no coins with which to pay them, so instead they took his knapsack and the oddments that he kept within. He bartered with them and managed to keep his canteen, but in truth he was glad to be rid of the rest. He did not need to be encumbered. The ferrymen rested on the southern bank as he left them, whispering lowly as they divided their spoils, and William allowed himself a fleeting smile at their expense. Charon would not have been bought so easily.

The land south of the Somme was not in itself different. It was as fresh and green as the land he had left behind, broken by the same tributaries and canals where the river's wild waters were tamed, but still there was something different about this domain. The soldiers that shifted in the towns and the farms were not English boys, but French instead. They had about them a different look, as if a man's mother country stained him with a certain expression. William ventured among them, and when they hollered out for his attention, he did not hear a word that they said. There was a certain holiness in being alone like this, distinct somehow from the shifting throng. He found, soon, that without a language to share, it was as if he was invisible. He faded into the hillsides and the masonry. He disappeared against walls of stones and banks of trees as yet untouched by the shells. If, at times, he stood stock still, it might have been that he did not exist at all. He hoped that, wherever he roamed, Samuel was the same. He flitted, a shadow man, through dance halls and squares where soldiers lounged, and began to think, at last, that he was becoming his brother, that if only he followed these paths a little further he might learn the secret things his brother had always thought when, silently, he flitted through the gangs of Leeds. There was something lonesome and yet exalted about the sensation. He wondered if this, too, was what Samuel had felt, as he traipsed after William through the terraces. When he was not filled with spite, did his lonesomeness lift him above the rest? Would it have been such a terrible thing to find some comfort in the rejection? At last, William thought that he understood. He stood, one twilight, on the corner of a square where the cathedral was crumbled and a statue of the Madonna clung precariously to the ruin, and as he watched the French soldiers tramping past, visions of men crafted out of mist, he thought he could see the world in exactly the same shades as his brother. And he was happy, then. Happy that he had come this far. Happy, at last, that the mystery had been revealed to him. Because he had promised himself it would be this way, that he would do anything that Samuel would do, that he would think as his brother thought, see all his brother saw, walk in his brother's shoes – anything and everything, so long as, before their seasons were through, they might walk together again.

He slept, at night, in the hollows of the city walls, or in houses long abandoned to the guns. There was always food to be found in these towns. There were halls where the soldiers were fed and deloused, and if William was sly enough, he was able to slope among them, to take his share of the gruel and scour himself from time to time in the cold-water showers. He came, on the seventh day, through Reims, where not a man spoke a word of his own tongue. He sensed that he was close to the chaos now, for the sky throbbed with sound, and the streets were thronged with soldiers – French battalions, and not an Englishman in sight. He found food in a small, ill-lit banqueting hall at the dirty end of town, where most of the houses were obliterated and all the families had fled. Soldiers only rarely came here, and scarcely a dozen of them lay slumped upon the tables, some asleep where they had fallen. William weaved his way between them. He had hoped that it might have been the same here, that the old spell of invisibility might be invoked, but one of the men in the corner of the room kept his eyes fixed upon him throughout. William tried not to notice. He shovelled food into his craw and he tried to think of prettier things – of meadow grasses on the Moor, of Joshua and Samuel when they had been but small – but always the man's gaze bored into him. William had long since torn the emblems of his battalion from his greatcoat, but still he wondered if somehow the soldier knew, if somehow this stranger had singled him out as a boy of the Chapeltown Rifles.

The man was not English, but neither was he French. William heard him murmuring, lowly, into his wine, and it was a fully different tongue that came from his lips – English words drawled differently, as if misshapen and mispronounced. An American boy. William knew that scores of them had come across the water to join the Legion in France, but he had not happened upon them before. The boy might have been no older than himself, and he lazed indifferently in his seat, his dishes lying empty before him. William found that his eyes kept drifting back to the face. It was clean and shaven, unmarked by the scars of any battle. The boy raised his cap, as if in salute, and cautiously, William did the same. As he did so, cold air whipped through the room, tearing at the scar he still wore. It sang a little, but quickly the sensation passed.

On the other side of the room, the soldier stood, as if readying to leave. William did not turn to watch as the American boy bustled past him, tossing crumpled coins onto a table. Something in him did not want to see. But then the room was still again, silent but for the coins still spinning on the woodwork, and William felt the familiar cloak fall gently over him. He glanced quickly around, knew that not a man here cared or even knew that he was among them. It was only the American boy who had seen. He was a ghost again. If he existed at all, it was only as an echo. It was only the boy who had brushed past him who had seen the scar at the back of his head.

It was after dusk when William knew for certain that he was being followed. He had sloped out of Reims before the streetlights were snuffed and the men came to patrol the boundary walls, and alone he followed the small roads into a thicket of hazels and beech. He had planned on making camp there, stoking a small fire and roasting whatever he could forage from the roots of the trees, but some vague instinct made him drift further on, through the trees, along the ridge of a hillside where ferns grew thickly and a small freshwater brook burst from the rocks.

A ribbon of shadow men moved along one of the distant ridges, heads bowed as they disappeared into the horizon's dark smear. Some of them were brandishing torches, orbs of orange that seemed to hover, unearthly, above their heads as they marched. Like penitents, they moved into the storm and disappeared. They were only spectres. He heard howitzers wail, and stumbled, then, onto a stretch of land that had once been a farm. There was an expanse of untamed grassland between him and the next line of trees, and for a moment he retreated into the safety of the branches. Cocooned there, he sheltered from the world.

A man was crossing the prairie. At first, it was only an indistinct shadow that loped out of the gloom and set off. Then, slowly, William watched it become a man. He recognised the American boy almost at once. He was coming through the undulating waves with the same gait that William had seen in Reims, shoulders only slightly hunched against the wind. At first, William thought that he was approaching him, that they had picked each other out in the darkness – but then the soldier turned on his heel, and made for the lone pine that stood sentry over the plain. Too late, William saw that there was another figure standing there, a lean man in an oversized greatcoat, tending to his ass beneath the curtain of rain. The American boy lifted a hand as they met, and slowly the man turned around.

William waited. He wished he could have picked out the

words that they were whispering, but the noises of night were thick around him, and all he could see were the gestures they made. They were not together for long, the American boy and the stranger, and they did not depart alongside each other, shuffling off instead in different directions over the plain. William's eyes darted from one to the other, until they were almost lost in the night. Then, he let the American boy go. He was beginning to understand what had been said, out there in the pasture. The words of the girl's grandfather were circling like carrion crows in his head. *These lands are full of traitors, William. People with everything to gain by selling your brother out.*

William found that, without knowing it, he had been fondling his gun. He had not fired it yet. It was still cold. Not since the chaos of training and drills had he lifted a rifle to his shoulder and taken aim. He drew back his hand, and when he looked again into the night, the American boy was already gone.

It was a hard thing to locate the stranger and his ass again, but William surveyed the darkness and saw them trampling a trail towards the furthest flourish of trees. William wondered who had followed whom to this pasture. Men like Flynn were practised at these arts. He watched until the ranger and the ass were almost at the line of the trees – and only then did he venture forth. Even after that, he might have turned back, something instinctive imploring him to flee and find sanctuary in the thicket, but he fought the sensation and forced himself to go on. Through the stygian gloom, he thought he saw Flynn turn to leer, knowingly, over his shoulder. There was only one way that William could react to that expression. It did not matter that he was being lured. It did not matter how much Flynn puppeteered with his life. They were after the same thing, really. They were both set on finding his brother.

To walk in each other's footsteps – that was a blessing, and not a curse.

William looked upwards, saw a trail of stars appear through the clouds, and imagined Samuel, on the other side of the forest, looking up at the same constellations. Lifting his collar, as if to salute Flynn, he marched across the plain.

The way was dark, the causeway narrow. Through banks of entangled trees – hazels and beech and pine, all wrestling for control of this ground – he walked in the ranger's footsteps. The rain fell more heavily through the branches now, cascading from the drooping leaves. Along the trail, the pines bowed towards him, so that it seemed he was entering some overgrown archway, treading into a new catacomb of brambles and bark. The air was heavy with scent; dark shapes flitted in the shadows.

He did not pretend to know which way he was travelling. He was not like the boys in stories, who could crouch low to the earth and pick out footprints and patterns and secret markings. He knew, only, that this was the way Flynn had travelled. He walked deeper into the groves, and with each step it seemed that the sounds of the world beyond the thicket were dampening. He fancied that the war itself was fading from existence, that he was following the trail into some netherworld in which the fighting was yet to come. In the branches above him, birds moved restlessly in their roosts. He began to think that they were following him along the causeway, just as he was following Flynn, a cacophony of murderous voices sitting on his shoulder as he came along the path.

At last, he saw light through the branches. It was only fleeting at first, but he clawed forward through entangled briar to see the orange glow in the clearing beyond. For a moment, he stalled, listening to the birds above him as they too came to a rest. Then, cautiously, he moved on, burying himself in the undergrowth so that he might spy on the camp-site beyond. The bracken here was razor sharp and beaded with rain, the earth a carpet of moist needles beneath his feet. Some of the birds that had flocked after him were chittering, already singing out a dirge for his death.

William reached out and parted the ferns. He nestled there, a creature lying in wait, and studied the way that the man had constructed his camp. There was a fire that smouldered low in a circle of stones, and above it a small mess tin that simmered with bully beef and water. On a line between the trees he had hung his greatcoat and a huge pair of drawers that looked as if they had been worn for many long months. It was a comical thing, really. There was nothing else to be seen.

Where was the ranger gone? William could not tell. The fire was still smouldering and the food was not yet eaten, so he knew he had not gone far. Men would not dare abandon such a bounty for any length of time – not if these glades really did swarm with stragglers and deserters and hunters and the homeless. He pushed a little closer, so that he was surrounded by ferns on all sides, crouched in the middle like the stamen of some monstrous flower. He waited. He remembered the last time he had seen Flynn, that first day in the dugout. Both men had known, then, that it was not the last time they would meet. It had been written on the sneer Flynn had worn as he ducked to drift from the dugout. William was almost aggrieved that he would make the man's prophecy come true.

With the night thickening around him, he lay in wait. More than once, he found his head lolling forward, sleep stealing upon him, but each time he forced himself to stay awake, riding the waves of exhaustion until they passed. The wind rose about him that night, shrieking through the canopy of the treetops and setting the birds that roosted there into panicked flight. Above William they cawed, black starlings

237

tossed on the wind, a hundred shards of darkness flung from the branches and into the gale.

The fire died. William saw it ebb in increments. Each time he woke from the slumber that kept coming to smother him, he saw that the flames did not dart as viciously, that the stones did not glow with an urgency as bright. Perhaps it was the only way he could measure the hours. He heard, in one of the valleys not far from this, the relentless sounding of guns, an ever-present bass beneath the wind. He began to wonder how many other boys there were, hidden in thickets like this, waiting for morning, praying for a lull in the storm.

He woke. He muttered an oath that he had let himself succumb to sleep – and saw before him, then, that the flames were dancing higher, that somehow they were revived. They spat and spiralled now, crafting strange shapes that he could not name, hissing out a warning. It seemed that a voice might have been trying to reach him from the heart of that fire, like the muffled voices tumbling from a broken gramophone. William twisted a little, saw that an ass was tethered in the ferns beyond the flames. Through the leaves, it turned its eye upon him, lifting back its lips in a crude mockery of a smile. Even the ass, then. Even the ass was scorning him.

There was a shadow upon him. William breathed deeply. He stopped himself from wrenching instinctively around, and looked one final time at the beast beyond the fire. Then, slowly, he turned. The silhouette was so close that, at first, he did not know it was a man. He reeled backwards, ferns slashing at his face, and when he looked again the black outline was clear. He stood there, towering above William, a rifle slung across his shoulder, the collars of his greatcoat turned up against the cold and the wind.

The figure bent low, and William scrabbled backwards. He was shrinking from the silhouette now, but already a cold hand was clasping his chin, and all he could feel was his skin as it whitened beneath the apparition's touch.

'Yes,' said Flynn, coming at last into the light and forcing William to look into his eyes. 'Yes, I remember you.'

The fire burned low between them that night. Intermittently it hissed, and little flames danced higher into the darkness. They were measly little things and, without more kindling, they would soon be gone. A thin column of smoke rose and disappeared on the wind.

Bound in lengths of twine twisted into cold, hard knots, William studied his captor. He supposed that he could have put up a fight, that it might have come down to a brawl through the thicket – but that was not why he was here. Knowing what he was set to find, he would have walked willingly into Flynn's arms.

Through the trees, the stutter of guns. It was a distant sound, snatched from the valleys and whirled their way on the wind, but to William it seemed horribly close. This was not just the wailing of ghosts. He fancied he could see the faces of the boys who had screamed, picked out by the wind in particles of earth and motes of dust. In the undergrowth, Flynn's ass too must have sensed it, for suddenly it turned in startled circles, worrying hard at its tether. Flynn stood to console the beast, and disappeared momentarily into the wall of ferns on the other side of the clearing. William tensed. He knew, already, that he did not mean to run – but, alone now, there was something petrifying in the way the forest surged about him. He felt, for a second, that he was tumbling from a precipice, arms flailing wildly for something onto which he could cling, every last ounce of air forced from his lungs. Then, Flynn was back, re-emerged from the undergrowth, eyes narrowed at the boy who sat beyond his fire.

239

'I can help you, you understand,' he murmured.

William did not dignify it with a response. He was not here to be lulled into a false sense of security. He was not here to be befriended or seduced.

'How did you come this far?'

William allowed himself a fleeting smile. It seemed to injure Flynn.

'There was a man, yes? The girl from Le Bizet. Her family. Isn't that so?'

'Then I really am on his trail?' William began, the challenge rising at the back of his throat.

'They'll have men trailing you by now,' Flynn went on, prowling the ground in the clearing like a circus bear. 'Your name, whispered from station to station along with your brother's.' He stopped, and he turned. 'The two of you, acting like what happens out here is a game, playing your pathetic cat and mouse, while boys are dying out there on your account.'

William bristled.

'You understand it, then? You understand why you shouldn't have run?'

Flynn was lit in the gloaming light, like some spirit of the forest. In the corner of the camp, he crouched alongside one of his traps, a small cage of wicker and string beneath which an old hare scrabbled. Occasionally it turned in panicked circles, but the cage was too tight, and more often than not it snared itself in the wicker bars. Flynn was studying it now, and whispering to it. It seemed to subdue the animal. Its eyes were dimmed.

He killed it in the French way – he lifted it high, the thing dangled before him, the flat of his hand came across it like a girl might slap her lover – and he set to skinning it against a rock. He broke each of its legs in turn, and then disrobed it

240

with only a modicum of mess. It was an art, William decided, that he would never master – and, for that, he was grateful.

'You'll be hungry by now,' said Flynn, tearing the carcass apart and placing the severed pieces into the stones.

William had not thought upon it, but he had to admit that he was. He nodded, with mock good grace, and Flynn smiled.

'I wouldn't let you starve,' the ranger said.

'You'd rather see me shot.'

'A war is a curious beast,' said Flynn, in that soft, lilting way that was his. 'Men commit evils, but they commit them without evil in their hearts. It can ruin men. I'm not hunting your brother because there's something rotten in me. I'm hunting him because it has to be done.' He paused, then. 'Why are you hunting your brother, William?'

William did not mean to give him an answer. He was thinking about the war as well, how men took up guns and knives and grenades, and all of it in the cause of good. He was picturing Matthias as he thought of that, seeing again that image of Matthias and his followers prowling the streets of Leeds in search of Samuel. But Flynn was wrong. Out there in the dirt, boys tore each other down because, if they did not, they themselves would be torn apart. When boys streamed over the sandbags and met in the deeps they were not thinking of right and wrong and the just causes of their battle; they were thinking only of how to get to the other side. Flynn was separate from all that. Flynn did what he did without the fear of a bullet in his back or a knife in his side.

'I've seen your brother,' said Flynn.

'The hell you have.'

'I've seen your brother, lurking in the rocks like some caveman in a bearskin. Foraging for scraps in the blown-out towns. Three times I've seen him, and three times he's stolen past. Each time a little bit different to the last. Each time a little more savage. A little more wild.' The smirk was flourishing further on Flynn's face with each word that he spoke. 'You've seen wolves, of course.'

William had not. He was a boy of the streets. He had seen stray dogs and he had seen foxes.

'I have,' whispered Flynn. 'I've seen the wolves that wander into villages and farms. And I've seen the wolves in their heart-lands, up there in the peaks.' He gestured, expansively, as if all about were crags and ravines. The rain was a little heavier now. It hissed upon the fire. 'That's what your brother is like. Less and less like one of those docile dogs of the street. More and more like the things up there, baring his teeth, turning a snarl upon every flicker in the shadows. That's your brother.'

William would not give Flynn the pleasure of the image. He thought about Samuel, up and down the streets of Hyde Park and Burley. That was the thing he would keep in his head. That was his brother.

'You still haven't captured him,' said William.

Flynn had to concede that he had not.

'He's clever,' he said. 'There aren't many clever boys wearing the uniform. It isn't a trade for boys who read books.'

'You underestimated him.'

'I knew he was a coward. That's what I knew. They're all cowards who set out like that.' Flynn stopped. 'All apart from you,' he said. He advanced a little then, craning over the circle of stones so that, for a second, the fire was cast into shadow and all about was black. He bent low and leered at William, and William did not flinch. 'What's so different about you that you can run away out of courage?' he asked.

It wasn't so courageous, thought William. It wasn't a brave thing he had done. He shifted a little, the earth growing wet underneath him, and waited for Flynn to retreat, as surely he did.

242

'He'll come to me,' said the ranger, cutting back across the fire. His voice was flat, and without emotion. 'How could he not, when you're here on his account? He'll come to me this time.'

William grinned.

'You don't know my brother,' he said.

They came, that next day, to the border of the pines, where gullies climbed to escarpments high above and fields of untended grain fell into the pastures below. Together they rode, William shackled like an oaf on the back of Flynn's ass, Flynn leading the brute by a rope, refusing to look back at his charge. They kept to the small roads, skirting the townships and farms that still clung to the land, half-empty now and half-driven into the earth. As the light waned in the evening, and they came again to the shelter of the pines, William saw a line of wearied horsemen crossing the dells under a long pall of grey cloud. Some of the troops were crafting camps where they might spend the night. Bonfires rose upon the plains to ward off the gathering dark. Like the warning pyres put to flame to spread the message of warfare across some prehistoric land, the fires picked out a path from one horizon to the next. Battle, at last, was coming to these fields. In weeks, thought William, they would be torn asunder like the lands from which he and Samuel had fled.

He did not know which paths they had taken during the day. It seemed that Flynn had walked these roads before, as if these were his streets and his feet could instinctively pick the way. They were travelling south. William knew it, for he had learnt a little of the stars, and always he followed the arc of the sun. They had not ventured far from the fields of wire, for still the soldiers marched, and still the air hummed with the sounds of war. As if drums were beating. And it seemed to

William, as he followed Flynn through those killing fields, that the drums were beating in his own head as well. It had been a soft sound once, an insistent tapping as of a dog pawing at a door – but now it was pounding. Now, it was thundering more fiercely with every step he took towards his brother.

Dusk was upon them before either stooped to say a word. Flynn turned to him, at last, as they bent low to go back into the forest, and in mock good grace he nodded. They had not spoken during the day. The only conversation had been a string of muted snorts and grunts, as if there was a language that came between them as well. But there, in the darkness, he whispered a word. It was nothing really, but William heard it as distinctly as he heard the cawing of birds settling in the branches above. 'Nearly,' the ranger said, and gestured for William to climb from the back of the ass.

There was a trail beaten already through the firs, and they followed it until they were walking through a thick darkness swirling with scent. Behind William, Flynn whistled some half-familiar marching tune. Like a nursery rhyme, vague and out of tune, it swelled to fill William's thoughts. He groped on, gripped by that insidious melody, and at last he became dimly aware of the thinning of the trees. The trail broadened here, and light spilled into a clearing from the vaults above. The clouds were parting, and stars glimmered against the blackness.

The camp-site had been constructed some days before. Ashes sat in a circle of stones, and racks of branches hung above the remnants of a long-dead fire. Against the trees a small shelter of ferns and felled saplings had been woven, big enough for only one man, while a wicker trap of the kind William had seen sprung the night before was propped, without bait, in one of the darkest hollows.

The camp had belonged to Flynn. William supposed that

these dens were littering the hillsides hereabouts, waiting patiently for their master's return. He was throwing his packs, now, into the roots of one of the firs; stooping, then, to water his ass. Though the beast was grateful for the respite, it kept its black eyes fixed on William throughout, never flinching, even as William returned the glare. He was becoming accustomed to the gloom now, and in the darkness he saw that Flynn was gathering the kindling with which he would stoke a fire. A match hissed, an orange light flared, and then the familiar crackling began. Oranges and reds danced in the basin of stones. Thin plumes of smoke spiralled into the air.

'You can sit down,' Flynn murmured.

'I mean to,' answered William.

'It doesn't make you a brave man to resist everything I say,' Flynn quipped.

'It doesn't?'

The ranger grinned, then, his smile caught suddenly in an upsurge of flame.

'Do you know where we're going?'

William did not reply. Awkwardly, he dropped to the carpet of pines. The earth was cold where he sat, and he braced himself against a tree. His wrists, still shackled, wore sores where the ropes had worked against his skin.

'I thought it was you leading me,' William finally said.

Flynn shrugged, idly. He sank, himself, into the pines and lay there, staring at William through the haze of the fire. From his packs he produced a mess tin, and hung it to bubble over the flames.

'I'll know it if you try and run,' he began.

'Where in hell would I be running to?' William answered.

'There are yet places in the world a boy might want to go.'

William lay against the stump of a pine and, through the flames, he saw Flynn close his eyes. No, William would not run. Not yet. There might have been places in the world a boy would want to go – but not a boy like William. For a boy like William, it was not the place that was seared into his thoughts. No matter how much he bore the stains of the streets where he had been dredged up, it was not the redbricks and chimneystacks and suet pudding that made him what he was.

Softly, he began to whistle. It was the same lilting tune that Flynn had trilled as they came through the firs, and instantly the ranger's eyes snapped upon him. Then, as if in hysteria, he too began to sing. The ugly chorus rose and swelled, each voice vying with the other, the distant roar of guns a deep and sonorous baritone to underpin the melody. Perhaps it frightened the ravens – or perhaps they wished to join the unearthly choir – for soon they too were cawing, adding their murderous voices to the din.

Then, as quickly as the song had arisen, the silence returned.

'You know the next verse?' muttered Flynn.

In the corner of the camp, the ass brayed in discontent.

Break of day. A cockerel, long abandoned, could be heard crowing in one of the nearby farms. William woke, and William was alone. He thought it might have been a dream at first, some pathetic trick he was playing on himself, but he came from sleep to find that his arms were no longer bound and his ankles no longer shackled. It was still the semi-darkness of dawn, and the embers of last night's fire glowed in the circle of rocks. There was a mess tin by the fire, filled with the gruel from the night before. William came curiously out of his blankets, and lifted the tin to his nose. It still smelt good. He wondered that the rats and other creatures of these forests had not already lit upon it.

Flynn was nowhere to be found. His packs were still

246

tethered to the tree, his tent still erect and hidden by the underbrush, but of the man himself there was no sign. William was not stupid enough to think it a lucky break, and for a little while he simply sat by the sinking flames, waiting for the ranger's return. The forest stirred around him, new sunlight filtering down through the pines, and even after an hour had passed there was no sign of his captor coming from the trees. Where, then, had he gone? William was certain it was not only to set and spring traps. Had there been a struggle? He paced the circumference of their camp, crouching with each step with the vague idea that he might read, in the way the pines had fallen and the undergrowth rustled, the path that Flynn had taken. But there was no sign. No trampled ferns. No bootprints left in the mulch of the forest floor. Such things, William realised, did not happen outside of stories.

William turned. There, at the edges of the dying fire, lay Flynn's packs. The haversack rested, drawstrings pulled back, against an outcrop of rock, while various oddments were littered across the earth. It seemed that Flynn had left in a hurry. Cautious, William approached the scattered packs. A sudden wind ghosted through the pines, and for a moment the air was alive with midges and moths.

There was a chart, pinned down by stones at the side of Flynn's knapsack. William knelt at its side. Then, bewildered, he scanned the shadows between the trees. He thought he might see something there, some scornful face shaped in needles and bark, but instead there was nothing. He called out once, and then twice, Flynn's name rising into the forest and then fading from him. No holler returned his own.

He turned to the map. It was a chart drawn by Flynn's own hand, a crude thing of charcoals and watercolours where rivers were marked and cities and glades. He recognised the shape of the northern coast, and the stark black line that marked the

English encampments. Here was Picardy, and here the Ardennes – and here, south of a salient in the line, was where he now camped.

There was a cross marked in one of the glades only inches away.

William's body wrenched. Was that Flynn's ploy? He allowed his fingers to trace that little mark and, feverish, he angled the map so that he might be facing in its direction. He thought he should bow down to it, like a heathen. He scrambled at the map and decided it was only a day's trek away. A day and he could be there.

But how had Flynn known? How certain was he that this was the hideout of his brother? William tore the haversack apart and unearthed a stash of little notebooks secreted in the bottom. They were old and bound in dogskin, and the pages were crammed with words that William could not read – not French and not English, but some strange cipher of Flynn's own concoction. William tossed the books aside and turned back to the map. It did not matter. William had faith. He had faith in Samuel but, most of all, he had faith in Flynn. He pressed his fingers to the cross.

This was like some adventure of childhood now: the knight setting out to rescue his beloved squire. It was as if he had unearthed some buried treasure, family heirlooms locked into a chest and buried six feet under the sod. There were place-names inscribed on the parchment, and as he stared at them, slowly he began to learn a little of the land in which he walked: the great river Somme that divided the country, the mighty Ancre that flowed from that river and north, into the German lines. There were towns here that he had heard soldiers speak of – the fortresses at Albert, the reserve billets further south at Corbie and Le Quesnel – and for the first time he saw how many leagues he had travelled from the trenches to which he had been posted. It did not stagger him, for he knew that Samuel had travelled this far, too. Whatever Samuel could do, William could do better. Hadn't that been the beginning of this thing?

William folded the map and stashed it inside his packs. He supposed that the theft meant little, that Flynn was not a man stupid enough to entrust his enterprise entirely to atlases and charts, but still he took some little pride in the deception. He salvaged other things as well. He found strings of bullets, a pair of Mills bombs that Flynn must have kept hidden since his own days as a soldier. There was a canteen less battered than William's own and a pair of boots exactly the same as his. There was even a compass. William had only seen a compass once before – a thing his father kept in a cabinet, and only produced when feeling his most nostalgic. He rested it on the palm of his hand and smiled to see that the needle aligned itself exactly as he had expected. Perhaps he could yet learn the ancient arts of navigation.

He stopped only briefly on the outskirts of the camp. He supposed that Flynn must have been watching him. He supposed that the ranger and his ass were lurking on one of the ridges thereabouts, telescope held high, smug grin plastered across each of their faces. He supposed, in spite of this façade, that he was doing exactly what was expected. That was what Samuel had taught William. That was the true meaning of the Moor. The world had a way of twisting things and funnelling you down a path that was not your choice. For Samuel it had ended with a stone in his hand – and for William? William did not yet know how his path would end. He knew only that he was walking willingly into the trap, that he would be trailed from here to the pasture where Samuel lay, that Flynn would be waiting for William to lead his brother out. William did not blame Flynn for it. Some things just happened. They just had to be. That was another of Samuel's lessons. But if there was a way William could rail against it, if there was a way it could be subverted, surely he would find it out there. Surely, when he was at Samuel's side, he could change the whole course of history.

William bowed his head and walked into the pines.

V

Thirty days and thirty nights. That was how Samuel remembered it. He was certain he had not lost a day. He had noted the falling and rise of each sun, and he knew he had made no mistake. What he was counting down to, he did not want to admit. The thought came upon him sometimes – that he was not running from anything, that he was running towards it instead – but he knew that they were the thoughts of a man who had for too long kept only his own company. More than once, he had caught himself speaking out loud, holding court, as he pushed along the trails, with a thousand different versions of himself. He had come to believe that he might even have been happy, as he pressed on through the vales of the Ardennes, alone against all the world. A boy like Samuel had to trust in somebody, even if that somebody was only his ghost.

It must have been nearing summer now, for the trees along the trail were starting to bud and the smell of pines in the forests was growing sweet. Summers had never been like this at home – those old English summers of refuse rotting in the yards and tar glowing black on the gutters of the terrace – but, still, these were unmistakably the signs of a season on the turn. You did not have to be a boy from the hills to know that. Some things were ancestral knowledge – even to a boy birthed on the streets. Samuel found that it even touched him as he travelled – that the smell of new leaves and dew on the grass was infecting him. He felt lighter than he could remember. He did not walk with the hunch that he had worn when he lived in the ground. He walked tall, and he brushed his fingers through the foliage – and he felt it, cool and wet upon his skin, the touch of new life. The summer of 1916. Samuel decided that, whether they found him in a month or whether they did not hunt him down until he was an old, decrepit man, he would forever remember these months of summer. It was to be a new beginning. It was to be a new life.

It was on the thirtieth day that he had found the girl. He had broken, that morning, from the shadow of the trees, and the glade that stretched before him was undulating with grasses grown wild. The sun was low. It lit the rippling ears of grain. Perhaps these pastures had been farmland once, the personal fiefdom of some foreign peasant, but now the land was being reclaimed. Samuel stood on the edge of the pines, and he saw, in that land, the entire story: the long years of peace, the babies birthed in the farmsteads, the children who were raised to work and sire and die on these lands. And now: the silence. The young men marshalled by the riders sent from farm to farm. The boys sent back from the fronts to face families that no longer knew how to look into their eyes. The fathers robbed of their sons and their grandsons. Dynasties and ancestries scoured from history by strafing guns and silent gas. The land forgotten and wild.

It had been a long journey, but here it would end. Samuel had sensed that, even before he took his first step onto the pastures, even before he had seen the farmhouse and the barn, and the girl that lived within. It had been a long month since he left Jacob to the boys of his streets and set out from the conquered ditches. He had come through the wire first, tracing the paths of the battle back, back across the craters of the earth, back through the trenches from which they had poured, back through the catacombs and up into the fields:

the torn remnants of the shadow woods; the grey monoliths that still stood along the roads at Armentières and beyond. There were other stragglers here, men driven mad and out of their homes, and it was not hard to lose himself among them. A tinker with a cart ferried him through the night, and when morning came the greyness was almost gone from the horizon and the green, unsullied lands were opening before him.

Samuel had come through Le Bizet before the shells transformed that land for ever, though even then he had seen the wagons loaded and the trails of men setting out from their home. He had wasted precious hours looking for the sisters with whom he and Jacob had spent that idyllic day, but it was to no avail. The girls and their families were already gone by the time he walked those streets. He stood on the cobbles, looking up at the house in which he had almost betrayed Lucy, and it was a long time before he could tear himself away. He ferreted in the shells of those homes for anything useful he might stow in his pack, and then he set out once more, into the night.

He spent his nights in ditches by the side of the road, or sheltered in whatever little caverns he could find, sharing his dens with dogs and rats and whichever lonesome wayfarer was travelling his way. There were more men than Samuel had hoped for, following these roads. Some of them were Frenchmen, retreating in the face of the advancing hordes, their homesteads put to the torch behind them – but there were Englishmen too, roaming these pastures alone, wary of any other drifter that chanced across their path. Once, Samuel stumbled across one of them, a grizzled veteran from one of the Black Country battalions, and they passed each other guardedly, hackles risen like fighting dogs. After that, he learnt to follow the wildest trails, to seek the paths that the fewest men travelled, to keep his head down and not look a stranger in the eye. He learnt to forage for his foods in the bleakest of the bombed towns, and sleep only in caverns that other men might have shunned. He learnt, in those weeks, to be alone.

It was in one of those caverns that the pack of men found him. He had been sleeping, and it was only when he awoke that he understood he had chanced upon their hideout, that they had come back from their forays and found him lying there like some golden-haired girl plucked from a fable. For a long while there was silence in the cavern, and it was only by studying the ragged emblems still stitched into the men's clothing that Samuel knew that they were English soldiers, runaways like himself. He saw that only two of them wore the same insignia – the white stripes of a Lincolnshire battalion – while the five others came from regiments marshalled from the island's most distant provinces: the fenlands of Norfolk and the forests of Northumberland; the Cornish cliffs where it was said that, on a clear day, you could hear the screaming of battle, borne by vicious winds over the waters. It seemed, then, that they had not run away together – that they had found each other on the trails, stumbled upon each other in whatever little grottoes they were hiding away, and somehow formed this new battalion of deserters. Samuel pictured them as a company of thieves, or perhaps some party of medieval adventurers – a warrior, a thief, a bard – setting out along the highways to find and slay beasts. Recumbent on the ground, he looked from one to another and wondered what horrors they had seen to make them flee.

The men gathered in the opening of the cavern, their heads bowed in whispered conversation, like penitents at prayer. For a long while, Samuel watched them. He tried to read the words on their lips, but it was dark in the cavern and he was not practised at that particular form of deception. In silence, he

254

waited. He tried not to dwell on what they were deliberating. He did not want to know. But the thoughts wormed into him like parasites. Did they think he was sent here to find them? Were they plotting to kill him? The idea smashed Samuel in the back of the head. It stove in his skull. It must have occurred to them. He was certain of that. These men were not marked for no reason. They were soldiers, and they had it in them to kill. They were deserters, and they had it in them to turn on their own kin. Why, then, would they risk letting the boy live?

They were older than Samuel. He supposed that some of them might even have been too old to fight in these wars, that perhaps they too had lied about their age when they went to the boards. Their uniforms had disintegrated about them, and their skin was hard and caked in dirt. Samuel did not know how long they had been running, but it seemed to him that they had been running for ever, living like some prehistoric tribe of men, moving with the seasons and the fluctuating fronts from one realm to the next.

Slowly, their gathering came apart, and the oldest of them approached the earth where Samuel lay. Samuel peered up, then, into big black eyes. The man seemed to tower above him, an ogre or a giant or worse. Behind him, the other soldiers were crowded together, obscuring all light from the mouth of the cavern, shrouding the party in shadow. One of them brandished his rifle; another a small steel blade.

Samuel did not know what happened next. He only knew that the callused hand was closing about his.

'Boy,' the soldier said, 'you've got yourself in a whole lot of trouble.'

The men helped him to his feet. They dusted him down, and they considered him closely, as if they were farmers inspecting a beast at market, and then they came to his side. The men did not speak each other's names, and Samuel quickly understood that each of them had shed that marker now, lest they were one day betrayed by the men with whom they travelled. They asked him who he was and from whence he had come. Samuel was going to introduce himself, then, but one of the men motioned that he should be silent, that he should not give up his own name. They found bread and water for him, and gratefully he accepted the gesture. He was beginning to understand that he was a blight on these men – another mouth to feed, another man to conceal – but that he was a blight that none of them would shun. It had once been said that there was a strange kind of honour in the groves of sinners. The words rebounded in Samuel's head.

They formed a ring around him, then, and demanded to know the way he had come and the things he had seen. Samuel supposed that what they were really asking was if he had led any huntsmen to their hideout. He decided, for the first time, that he was bound to tell them the truth – but, when he told them of the paths he had followed, each of them looked at him with reproach. Had he really wandered the pastures that stretched between Picardy and the Belgian lines? Did he have any idea of the shifting of the fronts, the clawing and pushing of one line of soldiers against the next? Did the boy even know in which realm he now trod? Samuel admitted he did not. He tried to tell them of the city he was from, how it was all he had ever known, how once this world beyond the terraces had been nothing but a flight of the imagination – but the men there looked at him as if they might have been looking at a savant. Some of them grinned. It was a wonder he had lasted so long, one of them began. Had he thought about where he might find a sanctuary? Had he plotted and planned? Samuel cringed at the idea. No, he had not plotted and planned. He had not planned on any of this, and nor would he now. He wanted to be free of everything that had flown: thinking and conniving and trying to look for reasons *why*.

And that was how he took up with the men. They welcomed him as one of their own, and in the gloaming they embarked together, another rag of runaways sloping out along the roads. Before night, he came with them over the great river Somme, whose murky waters must have hidden the blood of a thousand English boys like himself. They were ferried across the murk by strangers in little rowing boats and, for a while, as they spiralled with the current on those waters, Samuel could picture the land as it had been in centuries past: the river, as ancient as the hills from which it ran, bearing upon it the longboats of conquerors and kings, setting out for an England that would soon belong to them.

He had not planned on staying with that group of stragglers for longer than a night – but somehow, one night turned into two, and then two into three. He felt safe when he was among them, almost invisible, and for a time he even stopped thinking about the rangers who he knew had been sent to track him down. Not one of them mentioned the fact that they were hunted, marked men. They kept watches in the night and searched for camp-sites that would shield them from the world, but it was an unspoken thing between them, the thing they had done. Samuel supposed that each of them must have had friends in their trenches, boys they left behind out of cowardice and fear. He supposed that each of them had their Jacob. It was a wretched thing that each of them had done, but somehow being there, alongside others who had done the same thing, seemed to quell something that had festered for so long inside him. Samuel felt as if he had found his clan.

It was from those men that he picked up his first fragments of French. It was a tongue he would have to master, they told him, if he was to last long on the trails. It did not come naturally to him – it was fey and it was feathery, and rolled differently on the lips to the language he had always known. But slowly, he learnt to form words – and, from those words, crude sentences sprang. It was a grand thing when he asked his first question in French and heard the answer, no longer incomprehensible, come back from one of the men.

On the seventh evening, they asked him to share with them his story. Some of them were eager to hear it. They were camped together in the bottom of a valley, a fenland that bordered the great river, and the waters rose and swelled beside them. They did not build fires – the men had long ago learnt how quickly their fires would betray them – and instead they shared what meagre rations they had between them, a banquet of biscuits and breads and freshly plundered eggs. They were hidden from the fields here, bordered on three sides by steep banks of scrub, and for as far as the eye could see not a light wavered upon the water.

Samuel sat among them, and though he could still see, in stark silhouette, the images of everything that had happened, he did not know if this was a tale that any of them could bear to hear. They were all of them cowards, but there was something in the tale that not even they could understand. Neither did he know if it was a story he was willing to tell. Somehow, he knew that it was not a story that William would ever tell either. He did not know if that irked him or not. If what Lucy had said was true, William might even be here now, crouching in his own little corner of the earth with his own battalion of boys around him. Samuel knew that William would have covered his wound, and told nobody of what had happened. William would protect the secret just as fervently as had Samuel. There seemed an injustice in that, something secretive and dirty. It was not an injustice to which Samuel was a stranger.

258

He started slowly. He told the men a little about himself, though still he kept his name a secret: that he came from the city of Leeds, that his battalion was the Chapeltown Rifles, that he had been numbered with them since the first days of this year, and seen his first battle in a raid on the lands that bordered Ploegsteert in Flanders. He told them that he was only a boy, but as the words fell from his tongue, he realised that even that was a lie. His birthday was in the first days of May, and that day had surely passed, unnoticed and unnumbered like all the rest. He wondered if his fine and noble parents had held a banquet in honour of the occasion.

And so it was that Samuel spun for them a story. He had always been a liar, and now, he decided, he would trade in even bigger lies. He would craft for them a yarn that each of them would recognise, and it would be laced with so many shards of the truth that, before long, not even he would be able to perceive where facts ended and fiction began. He would tell them of a great battle at the Ridge, and how he had seen his friends slain, and how he was the last of his battalion to come from the dirt, the only one alive in that blasted land. And then he would recount how he found a boy, half-mired there in the earth, and with his last words how he had begged Samuel to carry word back to the English shores – that he loved his girl, and he loved his family, and he had died an honourable death so that they might go on. Samuel would tell them how he had drifted for days, searching for the remnants of his regiment, and only when he was certain they had been completely overrun, did he take up his gun and vanish into the mist.

He had it planned, each and every word. He would spin it like some raconteur of old. Samuel had often dreamt about being one of those travellers, a minstrel or a bard, rolling from town to town and earning his supper with a tale or song – but he knew, before he had spoken one word, that there was only one tale he was bound to tell. It was not an easy thing, but he could not hide it any longer. He had to tell it. If he did not, it would fester forever within him. There had to be some way of driving the daemon out. But where did it begin? Surely it did not begin that day, up on top of the Moor? Surely that was not where life had unravelled? A stone in a hand. Surely it was bigger than that?

'I have a brother,' Samuel began. It was as good a start as any. It was the truth. He did have a brother. His brother was not dead. His brother was set on finding him. His whole heart was bent on it. 'He's older than me. Two years and more.'

Samuel looked at the men. He was aware, then, that he was shaking. It rippled through him, like the first waves of a fever. He kneaded his fingers against the heels of his hand. It seemed that the river was roaring, fit to burst its banks.

'He was older than me, and he looked after me when I was young, and he led me from street to street and . . .' Samuel stopped. And what? And I followed him? Was that what he meant to say? He looked after me and I followed him and when, fifteen years later, I was following him still, I led him to the Moor on which we were forbidden to walk, and I lifted a stone and I smashed it into his skull. Was Samuel really such a monster?

He said nothing further. It was finished. He had stalled. The words drifted from him. They hung, unformed and unsaid, in the air between the soldiers. Samuel knew that the men were expecting something dreadful, for they looked at him in silence and did not say a word. Their faces were eager, but it was not an ugly kind of zeal. They were not scorning him like the boys in the trench.

Sheepishly, Samuel looked away. The only sound around them was the swelling and flowing of the great river. The oldest soldier, the Cornish man who was surely too old to ply this trade, looked at him kindly, then. He clapped a hand on Samuel's shoulder and told him that he should sleep. Samuel nodded, though he knew that sleep would not come to him that night. The men about him were silent, but slowly, fragment by fragment, conversation came back to the circle. There was whispered singing, off-key but no less beautiful for that – and then, from somewhere, a canteen where the dregs of a ration of rum had been mixed with water from the river. The canteen went round, and it did not miss Samuel.

There is a strange kind of honour in the groves of sinners. Samuel remembered those words vividly. They were his uncle's words. He had not thought of his uncle for such a long time that, for the briefest moment, it was a ridiculous thought that Joshua was still alive, that there were still terraces and streets, that the old man had spent his entire life spurned and set aside by Samuel's mother and father. He doubted, as he watched the river's flow and the way it reflected the stars, that he would ever see his uncle again. It was the first time he had considered a life that went on, beyond this running. It filled him with vigour that, at last, he could picture himself growing into manhood and growing old, and not just falling for ever in these foreign fields. There is a strange kind of honour in the groves of sinners, but Samuel would not be a sinner for long.

That night, while the men around him slept, he climbed the banks of the river and he vanished.

He had chanced across the girl's pasture only nights later, when the air was heavy with the scent of pines and the sky, in the distance, was streaked with the trailing lights of flares. Samuel did not know how to read the stars, and he had long since abandoned all hope of keeping track of the direction he travelled, but he supposed the war was clawing further into the untouched lands now, that somewhere battles had been won and battles had been lost – that new forests were being felled and new fields upturned. As he came from the pines and saw the glades, their grasses grown long and already gone to seed, he got to thinking that it would not be long before even these lands were devoured.

He had seen the farmhouse from the other side of the pasture – and, though he could see the smoke trailing from its chimney, he knew from a distance that the land had long since stopped being a farm. There were cows clustered about a barn at the bottom of the dell, but they were half-wild and had not been milked in many months. The fields around him were full and untamed – and it was not barley that grew there, nor wheat, but reeds and grass and thistles as well. He strode, defiantly, into those banks of nettles and thorn – and though the prickles ran up and down his legs, it was not pain that he felt, but a sort of triumph instead. The land here was untouched by people. The wilderness was calling its children back. Boys did not have to live on streets and terraces and scrubs. It had not been that way once. There were not always cities. It did not have to be that way again. Perhaps Samuel could be a boy of the country, and learn about the land and the stars and the patterns that could be read in the clouds. There was purity in that, he decided. Perhaps Samuel could be pure.

He stole across the pasture and into the barn, where cows – those dumb creatures of habit – still basked in the hay. They shifted only slightly when he came between them, rolling their ignorant heads at him as he passed. It was a big barn, with rafters above where bales had once been kept, now disintegrated into huge mounds of hay, and ladders that stretched to the levels above. It had seemed perfect to Samuel: a lone outpost on the fringes of any civilisation, a half-way house between the world of men and the world of the wild. There was water here, and if he was clever, he was certain there would be food as well. This, he had decided as he climbed into the mountains of hay, was where his new life would begin.

And that was where he had met the girl. She had found him on the third day, nestled there in the hay, and at first she had been stricken with terror. Samuel had seen the way her face contorted. But then he had seen the way her throat constricted to swallow the shriek that he had thought would surely come. She had advanced, warily at first, pitchfork wielded like some demon's trident or medieval pike, until she had reached the earth beneath him. He had stood there, waist-deep in the hay, and slowly he had inched down the ladder to meet her.

'You wouldn't send out word on a man who doesn't want a part in it, would you?' he had asked, nervously extending his hand.

'No,' the girl had replied. 'I don't sit at the king's table.'

Her name was Elisa. She spoke a little English and he a little French, and in that way there had been conversation between them. It was tentative at first, clumsy speeches and hands thrown wildly about as if to describe words in the air, but as one day bled into the next, there arose between them a kind of understanding. At first, Samuel had insisted upon sleeping in the hay. It was not only a thing of manners. It was a thing of honour, too. Elisa had seemed to understand, and for three days she had brought him food and drink, and soap so that he might scrub himself clean in the troughs she still kept for the beasts. It was an awkward thing, to bathe in that trough, and it was Elisa laughing at him from the doors of the barn that had made Samuel finally acquiesce. That evening, he had followed her into the farm.

It was a spare little building. Samuel could tell, from the photographs that adorned the walls, that it had once been the home of a great family, with grandmothers and grandfathers and cousins and uncles all living under one roof. Now, however, the rooms lay silent. Elisa was the only one left. She made no mention of where they had gone, and Samuel did not ask. Some things, he finally understood, were meant to remain unsaid. As he followed her through the hallways, he was plagued by the thought of soldiers tramping through these lands to marshal a battalion of farmhands who would wield pitchforks and shovels in battle. He wondered how long Elisa had been waiting for her brothers and her uncles and her father to return.

There was a chamber at the back of the room where she had made up a cot, and there were foodstuffs enough in the cellar to last for the summer and the winter, and most likely for the seasons that followed. All that the little farmstead needed was a drawbridge and moat, and then perhaps Elisa could have lived here safely for the rest of her days.

In one of the rooms, a range was glowing. Elisa took Samuel to its side, and there he warmed his hands. After he was finished, she fed him and watered him, attentive as only a woman robbed of her family could be, and then led him to one of the smaller chambers, where they sat together in small woven chairs. The windows here were overgrown with grasses and scrub, so that it seemed as if they sat in a cocoon, protected from the outside world and the killing that went on in those distant fields. Apart from the spitting of the fire in the grate, the only sound was of the branches scratching at the glass. Samuel and Elisa spoke only rarely that night, but that did not matter. Together, they were hidden from the world.

Elisa knew nothing of Samuel. She must have known that he soldiered, that his trade was in making war, but above that, she knew nothing at all. It occurred to Samuel, as he sat there on that first night, that he could have been anything. He could have been a hero. He could have been a killer. He supposed, then, that somehow he had become both of those things. She was sitting there with him, adding new kindling to the fire, and she did not know about the gas and she did not know about the German lad with the dagger in his breast. And she did not know about William. She did not and she could not and she would not ever know what he had done up on the Moor.

Did he want to tell her? As the darkness thickened and the music of war rose dimly in the distant fields, did Samuel want to tell her it all? Perhaps it would not have mattered. Elisa did not have the look of a stupid girl. She would have speared him with her pitchfork if she had thought he meant her any harm. Certainly, she would not have taken him in. There must have been something in his countenance that convinced her. There must have been something in his eyes. Something honest and good that not even Samuel could see when he peered into a looking glass. It was an instinct she had had to trust in him. He had never known that instinct before – not in his mother, and not in his father. It was a little thing, but the difference it made was great. Already, he could feel the effects of that incantation.

He slept, that first night, in the cot she had made up. Later, he was to sleep in the same bed as her – though not once did he wrap his arms around her, or run his fingers through her hair, or take her hand in his. By the fourth morning they were rising and retiring together. It seemed the most natural thing in the world – and neither one pored over what it might have meant. That was the beautiful thing about being here, locked away from everything he had known, with Elisa: he was not condemned to think. He could live from hour to hour, without dwelling on what had gone before. He did not have to search the recesses of his mind for the meaning implicit in every little action he made, or look he gave. He did not have to ask himself what was good and what was bad. Slowly, she unburdened him of the voices that once whispered to him at night.

They spent their days in idleness. They rose late, and they stoked fires, and in the evenings – when Samuel was certain that no traitors passing in the woodlands might see – they took long walks along the pathways of the farm. She showed him all its secret haunts: the outcrops of rocks beyond the line of the barns; the ruins of a farmhouse more ancient still, where prehistoric men had no doubt tended their beasts; a verdant dell hidden just within the reach of the forest. To Samuel, it was like being taken on a tour of the girl's most beloved memories. Vaguely, he thought of his own haunts, the nooks in the terraces and the snickets between the yards that he knew so well, but he could not remember them as fondly as those remembered by the girl. They were not his haunts. He had known it all along, he supposed, but never before had it been so clear. They were not his secrets, but secrets that William had stooped to share. He did not have a history of his own – but soon, perhaps, he would make one.

Piece by piece, he learnt of Elisa's history. She was seventeen, a year and more older than Samuel – though to Samuel she looked as grown a woman as he had ever known. The farm and the fields were the only land she had ever lived upon. Indeed, she had been birthed here, in the same room in which she and Samuel now slept. Her father, who himself had been born and reared in these glades, was a man much older than might have been thought – and yet, he was the first of them to answer the summons, riding out to find a battalion even before the officers started trawling from farm to farm. Then, slowly, it was her brothers who were taken: first the eldest, and then the second, and then the third – younger than her and petrified as they led him to the back of the wagon and took him away. She had seen none of them since. She told him all this on one still, cool evening, when together they followed the line of a brook that separated one wild field from the next. Her youngest brother, who she could still remember as a crawling child, gone to the fight and never to return.

After that, Samuel understood why she had taken him in. He started to understand why she would lead him to her bed at night and expect nothing of him. He started to see why she was not the same as Lucy, nor the same as the girl at Le Bizet. And yet, none of it aggrieved him. He knew that she took some small pleasure in tending to him – in bathing the cuts that now riddled his arms, in finding him a new pair of boots from the chests that had once been her brothers', in dressing him in her brothers' shirts while she stitched together the rags of his own – and he, in turn, took pleasure in her company. Was there something about her that made him feel like this? Or was it some change in himself? He found that watching her do the smallest things brought him small flutters of joy. Even the way she draped his greatcoat across the chairs before the hearth made him think that there could still be a life, away from everything that had gone before: the city and the trenches and the boys who had harried him from one to the other. She spread preserved fruits upon the bread that she baked, and it was a revelation to him that something so simple could be so good. A jam sandwich. It was an absurd thing that he thought.

And that was how it was with Elisa. It was nice. Samuel could think of no other word for it. He woke up, on the fifteenth day, and it was long into the afternoon before his thoughts had flickered to trenches and holes in the ground and boys bearing guns and boys bearing rocks. By some strange mercy, he was starting to forget.

They sat together, in the evening, sated by another meal of

salted pork and eggs and the fruits that they collected from the furthest reach of what had once been the farm. They had been together through the day and now, as twilight returned, they were together still. There was not enough wood to fuel any fire in the grate, and with mock ill-grace Samuel agreed that he would venture out and collect some more. Elisa was happy with that, and promised him a roaring range upon his return. It was not an offer that a ragman like Samuel was likely to refuse.

Together they stood at the window, watching the sun dip behind the contour of the pines. It flared for a moment, rich and golden, and then it was gone.

'Isn't it beautiful?' she said. It was here again, that way that she had of finding joy in the little things that Samuel could not understand. Her elbows were poised on the ledge and, together, they looked out on the hills untouched by men in uniform.

'Sometimes you miss the ugly things more,' smiled Samuel.

She wrapped her arms around him. It was the first time he had kissed her. Indeed, it was the first time he had kissed anyone who was not Lucy. And he did not feel guilt and he did not feel pain, and he did not feel that familiar twisting in his gut. There was no shadow on him tonight, not here in these pastures; there was no mark. He was not walking in William's footsteps. The world was not watching. He was nothing he had been before, and nothing he had ever been told to be. He drew his lips back from hers, and when he opened his eyes he realised that she had never closed hers. Again, he kissed her – and, this time, they held each other's gaze.

Though summer had surely come, the evening brought with it a certain chill. Samuel lifted his collar as he set out through the reeds and long grass. The smell of the pines at the head of the glade was carried on the breeze. It was soft and it was sweet. It was hard to believe that those were the same entangled woodlands from which he had emerged, scant weeks ago. Back then, they had seemed a nightmarish world of shadows and spirits waiting in the trees. Now, they seemed to shield him from whatever horrors still rose and fell in the lands on the other side. He looked over the land, and dared to think that this was a kingdom he could live in for ever, that this land might one day bear his imprint, just as the streets had imprinted their mark upon everyone back home.

The doors of the barn were open, and as Samuel stepped within he heard the lowing of the cows that lay beyond the bales of hay. They had been creatures of the farm, once, but Samuel supposed that they were no longer bound to any farmer or any butcher's hand. They paid him little heed as he came among them and lifted an axe to the chopping block. Slung across his shoulder, his rifle swung rhythmically each time he brought the blade down to sever the logs. One of the cows snorted, but he fancied that there was some sense of humour in that snort. At least the axe was for the wood and not the beast.

It might have been that the snorting lasted too long, or that it changed in pitch – but Samuel became suddenly aware that something was wrong. He slowed in the arc he was cutting to the block, and allowed the axe to tumble from his hand. Where it landed in the hay, there was nothing but a dull thud. He listened for the beasts that lay about him. He heard them breathing. Was he imagining it, or was there a new voice in that chorus? It forked across the back of his eyes, that day in the Reservoir when he had seen Jacques for the first time – humbled and shackled, and dragged along the trench. Was this it? Was this how it happened? Did it have to come so soon?

He turned. He saw William. He reached for his rifle.

VI

They wheeled around each other, like swordsmen at duel. William could feel his own rifle hanging at his back, but he did not reach for it. He was looking at his brother now, and trying not to look at the barrel that stared at him with its deep, black eye. It had not occurred to William that his brother would not be the same boy that last he saw, walking on Woodhouse Moor. He was different now. His hair had grown, and it hung in thick coils around his shoulder, shrouding half of his face. He was thinner than William had ever seen, and his face had the same ghoulish look that William had seen on some of the men outside Ploegsteert. His cheeks were sunken and his cheekbones crested through the skin, like some horrible phantom plucked from fable. Although he still wore the great-coat he had been issued, it was torn and dirtied beyond recognition. The trousers and the boots that he wore were not those of the Chapeltown Rifles. He had, then, had some help in his escape. William was thankful for that.

William stepped to his left, and Samuel mirrored the motion to his right. It was a strange thing, looking down the barrel of a gun at a vision of his brother. In those weeks since his flight Samuel had often thought upon this meeting, but not once had he pictured it taking place on a night such as this, with the sounds of shells still wailing in the distance. It was true, what Lucy had written. There was something different in William. It was not only that his hair had been shorn – that was to be expected – but that he stood differently, still willowy and tall, but with a new surefootedness that made Samuel think, at first, that this was surely some doppelganger sent to try him. He moved forward a little, gesturing with the rifle for he knew not what reason. William did as he was bid, and shifted further into the barn.

For a long time, neither one of them spoke.

'Samuel . . .' William breathed.

Samuel jerked. It was an instinctive thing, something animal inside him. He snatched the gun into his shoulder, his eyes flitting nervously from one corner of the room to another. Had William come alone? Was that it? Or were there others, lurking in the corners of that building, crouched there with weapons already loaded? Samuel wrenched. He imagined Matthias and Alexander and David, each of them kneeling in his secret station, each of them ready to pounce.

'There's no need to put a gun on me,' William said.

'I'll be the judge of that.'

'You've never put a gun on me before.'

It seemed such a ridiculous thing to say. Samuel imagined himself parading Kirkstall Lane with a rifle on his back. It would have been a laughable sight.

'I've never had a need to.'

'I didn't come out here to kill you.'

Samuel snorted.

'That's what you think, isn't it? Well, it isn't so, Samuel.'

Samuel circled, again. Though he still brandished the gun, he held it a little lower, his hands a little softer around its butt.

'You're wearing a uniform,' Samuel began.

He said it with a strange incredulousness, as if the idea was too peculiar to comprehend. He cast his eyes slowly over William, from his boots caked in earth to his collar stained with dirt, and read there, in the stitching, the name of his battalion.

271

'The Chapeltown Rifles?' he asked.

'Where else?' answered William.

'And Mother? And Father? Do they know you're here?'

It was such a childish question to ask, and both of them knew it. William spread his arms wide and, as if in supplication, he sank into the hay. He said nothing. He was staring at Samuel, and Samuel was staring back, and both were trying to see the same thing in the other: what was it that made him my brother? What was this thing that made us kin? It seemed, then, that they did not even look the same: one with his hair shorn short, the other dishevelled and wild; one still with life in his cheeks, the other pitted and sallow.

'They didn't send me,' William stated.

'No,' breathed Samuel. 'They sent me. It's me they sent out here, not you. They tried to keep you from it. Remember that, William? Visits to the board and to Finlay and the rest . . . Strange to think it was me who kept you from it in the end.'

William stole a glance beyond Samuel, at the farmhouse that stood there, framed by pines.

'Somebody took you in,' he said.

'What of it?'

'A girl?'

Samuel nodded. 'It isn't like you're thinking,' he said. 'It isn't a bad thing, William. You're looking at me like it's something wrong, but it isn't. I found her. She found me. That's the world, isn't it? I'm a part of it now, William.' He stopped. Slowly, he lowered the gun. 'How is Lucy?' he breathed.

'She's still there,' answered William.

'She sent me letters.'

'Why shouldn't she send you letters?'

'Nobody else did. Not a soul.' Samuel wavered, then. His voice trailed off. 'Not my mother. Not my father. Not a Christian soul stooped to scratch three words on a card.'

Again, he stopped. Was he challenging William, then? It seemed such a laughable thing, that he had been troubled that William did not write. 'How did you find me?' he demanded.

'There was a girl. Another girl.'

'I know what you're saying, William. But it just isn't so. It was never about the girl.'

It was such a stupid thing, that they should be talking about girls in this blasted land of ghosts and men.

'She was in a place named Le Bizet. She had a scrap of paper. Did you give it to her, Samuel? It bore your name. That was how I knew which roads you'd taken.' He paused. 'And there was a boy. His name was Jacob . . .'

William noted the way the name stirred Samuel. He tensed a little, his whole body wrenching, each time he heard the name.

'He still lives?' Samuel started. His words were whispered.

'He's a fierce little bastard.'

'He's my friend,' Samuel spat. He was going to go on, then. The memories of that final night were scudding through his thoughts: the bugles sounding as they rose to stream over the wire; the horse braying in daemonic fury as he lifted his gun to end its life; the daggers drawn and boys fumbling awkwardly in the enemy trench, the mud about their shins marbled with dark black blood.

'Still, you left him behind.'

Samuel did not respond. He straightened the rifle.

'Have you killed a man?' William ventured.

Samuel did not like to think about it. It played again, across the backs of his eyes: the German boy, his face streaked in dirt; the terrible grating of his blade as it pushed between the boy's ribs; the way he had slumped forward, arms and legs flailing; how difficult it had been to draw back his blade.

'I'm a soldier. Of course I've killed men.'

William trembled.

'I didn't want you to have killed men.'

'I suppose that means you're still pure, does it?'

'I didn't say a thing about being pure.' William was thinking, then, of the soldier in the Royal Park, and how he had bawled out those words for all to hear. Dark, ugly things, they had been. He tried not to think of his brother with a bayonet in his hands.

'You've always tried to protect me, William. Well, I never once asked for protecting. I never once asked for you to pick me up when I fell in the streets, or carry me home, or make excuses to our parents on my account. And . . .' He stopped, the words choking in his throat. 'Why couldn't you just leave it, William? You could have stayed. With that thing on your head, they'd never have made you leave Leeds. Why in hell did you come?'

William did not reply. He had heard it before – that things were as they were, that he could not change things now, that he should not interfere with what had been accomplished while he slept – but he had not expected to hear it from Samuel himself. His brother was shaking.

'You want to be a fucking hero. That's all it is. That's the story they taught us since we were in the crib, isn't it? William the Captain and Samuel the Private, from now until the end of all things.'

They were the words William had spoken upon the Moor, scant moments before the stone found its mark upon his head. He had not recalled such things before, and yet, here they were, emblazoned upon him. He wanted to cry out, to tell his brother it was not what he had meant, that he did not want to be a saviour, that he wanted only for none of this to have been. He did not care about heroes and heroism and the looks of adulation they received. He understood that people had told him to let it be, but it wasn't a simple thing, it just wouldn't

274

work out that way, there were greater things to think of. There were stars in the sky above them. He could see them through holes in the rafters. They shone.

'I want you to come home.'

'Why is it always about what you want?' Samuel returned. He looked into his brother's eyes for the first time, and though instinctively his face wrenched away, somehow he held the gaze. 'You want me to come home? Well, I don't want to go, William. I don't want to go back to streets and terraces and chimneystacks and suet pudding. To people looking at me out of the corners of their eyes. To being William's brother and nothing else. I want to be out here.'

William stood. 'You don't want to be here!' he sniped. 'Isn't that why you ran?'

'I didn't run back home,' Samuel spat. 'I'm still here, aren't I?'

'They got you labelled a deserter. They put a man on you.'

Samuel stirred. His fingers curled around the butt of his weapon, and his eyes swept the room. Again, he raised the rifle.

'I know how it goes.'

'Well?'

'You're that man, aren't you?' he demanded.

'Don't say that.'

'They put you on me. They think you can bring me in. Because of what you are. Because you're my brother. Because of blood.'

William was silent.

'It isn't like that,' he breathed. 'Samuel, why won't you listen? I came to warn you about him. I followed him out of the trench. A man named Flynn. They'll have me listed now. I came to get you because I want you to come home.'

Samuel grunted an incredulous snort.

'Why the fuck would you want that?'

'Don't talk like that . . .'

'Why not?' Samuel broke. 'Why wouldn't I ask?'

'Samuel . . .'

'You won't even say it. Look at you, standing there . . . and you won't even say it.'

William said nothing. He stepped forward, and then he stepped back again. A gust of wind tore at the sides of the barn. He felt it claw through the cracks in the wood. He faced Samuel, and each edged away from the other.

'I'll say it,' sneered William. He did not mean to say it so, but his lips curled as the words came to his tongue, and his head pitched forward and he felt full of spite. 'I'll say it, if that's what you want. You nearly killed me, Samuel. You tried and you failed. I'm still here. I'm still alive.'

Involuntarily, Samuel shivered. 'Well, well done, William. You came back even from death, didn't you? Some greater good was looking out for you, even then.' Samuel backed, awkwardly, towards the doors of the barn. From the hay, a lone cow released a low moan, discomforted as a dying man. 'I'll shoot you if you try and follow,' he said.

'I know you will,' William said.

Samuel was in the doorway now. Outside, it was beautiful in the dark. Blossoms from the trees turned in patterns through the air, whipped by a low wind. At the farmhouse at the top of the trail, a single lantern burned.

'What do you mean by that?' he snapped.

'What happened on the Moor doesn't have to change the world,' William whispered. 'You think it does, but life doesn't work that way. Life isn't a storybook. I don't care what you did, Samuel.'

'Maybe I wanted to change the world,' Samuel swore as he turned into the night.

* * *

276

William watched him go. It was a dreadful thing, but he stood there in the doors of the barn and, with the cow lowing behind him, he watched the shadow of his brother as it retreated over the hill. In the distance, the guns throbbed. William recalled the sight of those enormous weapons, the howitzers, as they were wheeled into place like some ancient engines of war. He wondered if it had already begun, for those boys out there.

He had nowhere to go. He shifted a little, back into the barn, and then he turned again to look at the farmstead in which Samuel had found sanctuary. It was finished, then. It had been finished so easily that he still did not understand. He tried to imagine what it would be like when he returned to England, and stepped off the train in Leeds to see his mother and his father standing there. He kicked, wildly, at the bales of hay. For a moment, the cow ceased its incessant groaning and looked at him with mild reproach.

A look. That was all it had taken to end things for ever. An almost incidental thing. The flicker of an eye. William cursed that it could have gone that way. He slumped, for a while, in the hay – and the thoughts of what he might do now scrabbled through his head like a thousand tumbling rats. He could not go back. That much was certain. He was not a soldier any longer; he was a coward, and cowards did not bear arms. He could not return to his post. The only thing, then, was to run. Was there a way he could reach England? Or was he condemned forever to wander these foreign lands?

William shouldered his rifle and drifted through the doors of the barn. He knew that Samuel would be within, now, falling into the arms of whatever girl it was who had taken him in. He tramped a little along the path towards the building, and then he turned back to the pines that covered the glade. He could still hear the distant drumming of guns. He could still see the arcs of light the shells left in their wake as they roared over the ruin. There were other boys dying out there. But they were not his brother. He stole one last look at the farmhouse, and set off for the trees.

It was an almost imperceptible thing that he saw, then: a tiny flaring of orange light, as of a man drawing at a cigarette. For an instant it burned, and then just as swiftly it was gone. But it was all that William needed. It was all that William feared. He hurried to the cover of a lone pine, and furrowed his eyes that he might discern the shapes in those shadows. And there it was, hidden in the firs: the silhouette of a man.

Samuel closed the door as he came into the farmstead, and stood there in the darkness, listening to Elisa shifting on the floorboards above. It was a long time before he realised that he was crying, that perhaps he had been crying as he crossed the grasses surrounding the farm, that perhaps he might even have been crying as he turned from his brother for the final time. The tears streamed unchecked down his cheeks now. He could taste them where they glanced upon his lips.

He had not expected to see his brother. He had not wanted to see him out here, among the guns and the blood and the erupting earth. Was it not enough that he had taken that stone in his fist and brought it down upon William's head? Was that not a sin enough without having lured him to his end out here? Samuel thought of him, sitting alone there in the barn, and he tried to picture everything that William had done to reach him here. The papers. The training. The running of bayonets into hanging sacks of straw and incredulous piglets brought in from market. He wondered how easy it had been for William to disappear from his trench.

Samuel tried to imagine how the city would look, if he walked back there at William's side. A hailstorm of images

278

forced themselves upon him, then, grainy and ugly and unclear. He saw himself trailing William onto the platform at Leeds, following the path that William carved into the waiting crowd. He saw them slowly approaching their parents, who stood there underneath the eaves of the old clock tower, waiting patiently for the horde to part. He saw them open their arms to William, and there beyond them, he saw Lucy. She caught his eye only fleetingly, before she too turned to William and thanked him for returning Samuel to England's shores, for being so brave and so true and so right that he would dare venture into the destruction over the sea. He saw himself trailing William.

Samuel's hand curled gently around the handle of the door, as if he might venture back into the night – and then, just as gently, he drew it away.

In the chamber upstairs, Elisa was waiting. She had been pacing, and she stopped as Samuel stole into the room, moving as lightly as a wraith.

'Samuel?' she began. 'You are well?'

Samuel looked at her. He knew that his gaze must have been withering, for though she did not move, she seemed to retreat inside herself a little. She seemed to become small.

He propped the gun against the wall and dropped to his knees to ferret in the chest at the foot of the bed. There were few things here that would be of any use – only rags and vests and lengths of old lace – but he was a scavenger now, and he would take anything that he could get. He looked back up at Elisa, who watched him from the doorway with the lines deepening on her face.

'I'm sorry,' he said. 'I can't stay.'

He tightened the laces in his boots and shifted to the window. The barns sat in the grasses below, but there was no longer the light of any lantern shining within. Perhaps it had worked, then. Perhaps, for the first time in their lives, his brother had listened.

There was a scrabbling in the chamber below, as of a man fumbling with a latch.

Samuel tensed. He and Elisa stared at one another.

'I'll go,' she said.

Samuel snatched her arm.

'Stay where you are,' he hissed.

He moved, in silence, to the banister rails and then to the top of the stairs. Somebody was in the house. He hissed for Elisa to bring him his rifle, and together they stood there, peering into the darkness below. Down there, the shape of a man moved.

'Who is it?'

Samuel pushed her back into the recesses of the hall.

'Don't say a word,' he breathed.

The figure was at the foot of the stairs. Samuel and Elisa listened to the first footfalls on the steps. First one, and then another; the figure advanced. Samuel hustled Elisa into the shadows. He pressed his hand against her lips so that she knew not to breathe and, mutely, she obeyed. She did not squirm. Her eyes were opened wide.

They hung there, where the light could not reach, as the silhouette came over the top of the stairs. Samuel recognised it at once. A long shadow was cast by the low light of the lantern – his brother's impression thrown upon the wall. He held Elisa tightly so that she would not move. He could feel the warmth of her skin. Her heart pounding in her breast. His brother stole past, oblivious to the watchers in the shadows – and then Samuel pounced.

'William,' he snarled, reaching out to rip at his brother's greatcoat. 'Why do you follow? Why must you always follow?'

William stalled, trapped like a fly in amber in the lantern's orange light. He saw, now, his brother's face banked in stark shadows. Behind him, there stood the girl who had taken him in. She was not unlike the girl of Le Bizet, thought William. There was something in her countenance that brought her back to his mind. He supposed he should not have been surprised. He supposed there must have been a certain kind of girl who took traitors and cowards to her breast.

'Samuel,' he breathed. 'I was going to run. I did mean to run, Samuel. But there's something else. You've got to listen . . .'

William pushed along the hall and into the room. Samuel hissed, then, and wrenched himself to follow. Facing each other across the boards, the two brothers stalled.

'I'm not the only one following you,' William hissed.

'It isn't your concern.'

'Of course it's my concern!'

'You still won't listen.'

William threw the first punch, and it caught Samuel off guard. From the hallway beyond the room, Elisa's shrieking filled the silence. Samuel staggered against the stone, and when he righted himself, he brought his own fist back. Then, deliberately, the fist unclenched. They had not fought since they were boys, scrapping out in the streets, and there was an anger in William's blow that Samuel did not recognise. William had never thrown a punch at him before. He had kicked and he had bitten and he had pushed and he had shoved – but a punch was a man's thing, and William had never fought like a man.

'He's out there,' William began.

Samuel wanted to tear down the lie, but he did not dare. He stared, disconsolate, at his brother.

'The man they sent, the man who's on you,' said William. 'His name is Flynn.' Samuel twitched. It was a little thing, but still William saw it. He had known that gesture since a time he could not remember. 'It means something to you, doesn't it?'

'I've seen him,' Samuel began.

'Well?'

'He brought in a boy, when I was still on the line. They shot him dead.'

'They'll shoot you dead, too.'

'I know,' breathed Samuel. 'That's why, William. That's why I have to keep on running.'

'We can run together.'

Samuel considered it. He shifted, uneasily, from one foot to the next. He seemed to be shuffling, then, though he did not move from where he stood.

'You know we can't do that.'

William burned. 'Shut up, Samuel,' he sniped. 'For once in your life, just shut up.'

He snarled the final words. He was thinking, for the first time, how foolish he had been. It was an ugly thought, but already it was blossoming inside him, and he could not drive it away. He looked at Samuel, and Samuel's face was cast at the ground, the black hair hanging low across his eyes. He was thinking, then, of how foolish he had been to leave the streets where he was safe and come so far for the sake of somebody who did not care. How he had stalked those terraces and delivered blows to his mother and his father and everybody else who stood in his way. How none of it had mattered back then, as long as one day he might see his brother again.

He was thinking that his father was right.

'Look,' said the girl.

William joined her at the drapes. She had drawn them back just a little, so that they might see the forest glade without. There were trees growing, thick and wild, upon the banks, the same pines through which William had travelled. It was hard to believe that, somewhere, on the other side of the green, the chaos reigned.

Flynn was still standing there, propped against one of the pines that skirted the grass, pressed so close to its trunk that he might have been a part of the tree itself. He was camouflaged there, but William could still discern the shape of his face, a different texture in the darkness. He saw the head turn to survey the building and the outhouses that lurked around.

'Is it him?'

'It's him.'

'I'll snuff the lantern,' said Samuel.

'Don't touch that fucking lantern,' hissed William, without turning round.

'What?'

'He'll see,' William went on. 'Don't touch the light.'

They waited in silence a little longer. Out there, Flynn was prowling the edge of the grasses, studying the house like some burglar on the streets of Leeds, considering it methodically for points of weakness and paths of attack. It was possible that he had seen them already. Flynn was not the sort of creature to miss the twitching of a curtain.

'What will we do?' asked Samuel. He pressed his back against the stone and stood there, straight as a sentry.

William looked round. He eased the drapes slowly back into place. Elisa was beside Samuel now, her hand upon his shoulder. Gently, she moved long fingers up and down his arm.

'She'll lead him off,' said William. He was adamant, and he moved for his rifle.

'What?' snapped Samuel.

'She'll take the lantern and she'll go into the trees. He'll trail after her. He'll know what we did, but by then we'll be gone.'

Samuel clenched Elisa's hand, and slowly teased his fingers through hers. Already, William had moved from the room. Samuel left the girl and hurried after.

'He'll kill her,' he whispered.

'No, he won't,' answered William. 'He has honour, remember?'

They stood together, at the top of the staircase, and for a long while they did not speak. Each was studying the other's face. The only light that came to them spilled from the lantern on the other side of the wall. It was a low light, and it lit them in stark, spidery shadows.

'I forgot it could be honourable to kill men,' said Samuel.

William advanced on him.

'I didn't come out here to see you die,' he hissed.

'I didn't ask you to come at all.'

'He won't kill the girl because he's a man and he wasn't tasked with killing the girl. He's tasked with killing you. With taking you back so that they can thrust you into some rat-infested oubliette, and then lead you proudly out of it one morning for the good and glory of all mankind. Well, it isn't going to go that way. He'll see the girl, he'll realise what it is that we did – and maybe he'll beat her, maybe he'll teach her a lesson in how to win wars, but what does that matter to you? Who is this girl?'

'She's just a girl,' breathed Samuel.

'Exactly.'

'She doesn't deserve that.'

'Bad things happen to good people, Samuel. That's life.'

Samuel paused. The light caught William's eyes, and for a moment they glowed a brilliant white. Samuel had never heard such things froth on the lips of his brother. He wondered who it was he was looking at. He wondered what phantom this was in the shape of his kin.

'Go and get the girl,' said William. 'She'll listen to you. Get the lantern and send her out.' He pushed back into the chamber. 'I'll watch Flynn,' he said. 'I'll make sure it's safe.'

Back in the chamber, William sat for a moment with his back braced against the stone, listening to the footfalls of his brother and the girl as they dropped into the chambers below. He held his head, kneaded his wearied eyes with the heels of his hands, and tried not to think. This was not a time for thinking. There had been a time for that – a time that would surely come again – but right now he knew they had to move. This was a time of flight. He had been so set upon finding his brother that he had not thought upon what might happen when finally they met. He knew, now, that Samuel was intent on not returning, that perhaps he was intent on scouring the streets of Leeds for ever from his life. William did not mean to let it happen. How could the old times ever be brought back if Samuel was not alongside him, walking those terraces? It was a battle he was set on waging – but he would have to wage it later. He rose from where he was slumped, and furtively drew back a corner of the drape.

There was Flynn. Still, he stood in the shadow of those trees, shrouded there like a sapling just poking forth from the sod. Had it been Flynn who led William to this glade, or had it been William who led Flynn? William would never know. He heard the snap of a latch through the floorboards, and watched as the girl moved out with the lantern in her hands.

She had moved only yards when Flynn's attention was roused. The ranger moved a little from the cover of the trees and William saw, then, in the silvery light, the familiar features: the craning neck and disappearing hair, the nose that pushed forward like a snout. He was not trailing her yet, but still William saw the head rotate, swaying low like a wolf venturing out of his heartland. He watched a little longer, and then drew slowly back from the curtains.

He paused at the top of the staircase, before taking that first step. He had come this far for Samuel, and he did not intend to stop now. He listened to his brother shifting in the darkness at the bottom of the steps. It felt, for a second, like one of those ancient nights they had spent together when they were small boys, creeping from their bedroom in the smallest hours to embark on some grand endeavour. He wanted it to be like that again: he and Samuel setting out, like warriors of old, to raid the jars in the larder, or sneaking out to take some petty revenge against a spiteful neighbour.

He came down the shadowed staircase and into the little chamber below. The darkness was thick, but he could see the figure crouched at the window. Beyond the glass, he saw the orb of light as it bobbed away, disappearing into the trees. Flynn would be following it by now. He would have shouldered his rifle and set out, along the line of the firs, prowling there like some prehistoric hunter.

The figure at the window flinched, as if to flee.

'Not yet,' whispered William. 'Samuel, wait.'

William hung at the back of the room, and watched over his brother's shoulder. It seemed to take interminably long for the light of the lantern to cross that expanse of grass. He stood flat against the wall and wondered what was going through the girl's head as she bore it aloft. She was just a girl. Those were Samuel's words. That was what he had said to himself. But now he was thinking differently. Now he was thinking that she was Lucy, or any one of the other girls from his streets. He was seeing her face, contorted in fear as she staggered forth through the branches like some fairybook heroine, on the way to see her grandmother. He was picturing the images that might have been thundering through her thoughts, of wolves snarling as they chased her through the scrub, of old men lurking behind trees with their lips curled and their fingers tensed. He had sent her to that end, but he would make her sacrifice worthwhile. She would not feel Flynn's wrath for nothing. Even if he beat her until she screamed and she sobbed, even if he bent low over her and throttled her until she spluttered out every secret in her heart, it would not have been for nothing. William knew, then, as he looked at the shape of his brother, how it would go. Somebody would have to die tonight, and he had sworn he was taking his brother back home.

The light disappeared, reappearing moments later through the branches. From then on it seemed to flash, on and off, like some secret torchbearer alone in the deeps and relaying information to his comrades crouched safely in their trench.

William lifted himself and moved for the door.

'Samuel,' he said. 'It's time. We have to go.'

William was already at the door when he realised that he was not being followed. He turned, and he hissed a command – and then his whole body wrenched. He took a step backward, steadying himself against the wall. Because it was not Samuel that he saw. It was not Samuel who stood there in the room, ready to follow him into the night. It was Elisa who turned to stare at him with her eyes opened wide; Elisa who groped forward with her hands to take hold of his wrist; Elisa whose face was daubed in horror as, behind her, the light of the lantern finally vanished.

'Where is he?' breathed William – but, already, he knew that his brother was gone.

He did not wait. He pushed the girl aside and tore at the latches on the door. The dusk had thickened into night, but the air was balmy, almost warm, and he bolted for the cover of the pines. The smell of blossom was heavy in the air.

'Samuel!' he bawled, staggering forward through the grass. 'Samuel!' he thundered. He did not care that Flynn would hear. He did not care about a thing. He made the line of the trees, and lifted his shoulder as he thundered within. 'Don't run,' he pleaded, softly and under his breath. 'Please don't run again, Samuel.' He flailed on through entangled thorns. 'Samuel?' he called, floundering after the retreating shadows. 'Samuel?' he repeated, the word disappearing into the trees. 'Samuel?'

William took off through the pines. His brother had not had such a start that he would evade him for ever. What trail there was quickly petered out, but still he could see the route that Samuel had taken. It was marked there in trampled ferns and branches snapped back. In a little ditch between the trees the storm lantern sat, snuffed out now and with its casing shattered. And where was Flynn? Was he upon Samuel already? Had another shot rung out to join the distant music of howitzers over the hills? William stopped at a crop of trees that marked the steepening of the bank, and tried to listen for footfalls in the thick carpet of needles. Somewhere, a bird was startled from its roost. Its wings beat furiously, stirring the branches into a fury of motion. He thought he heard boots kicking through the dirt, and again he took off.

Samuel would die out there, if he did not stop running. And then, be it in sixty years time, William too would pass on – and there the story would end. And if he was thinking anything as he pushed down the gully, it was only that: that one day they both would be dead. The day might come tomorrow, or it might come in the months of war that were bound to follow, or if Flynn and the Rifles had finally found them it might come this very night. That much did not matter. As he ran, William knew with a burning clarity the one and only fact of life: that everybody he knew or had known or would ever know would one day be gone. And there would be no reunion in the vaults above. He was certain of that. There would be no lounging on clouds with the music of harps to soothe them into sleep. There would be nothing but a coldness he dared not imagine, and a slow forgetting of everything that had ever been, until nothing was left: no memory, no imprint, no echo. He had been there once. He remembered that now. He clawed through entangled boughs and remembered Joshua's weathered face as he had retold the story, that night in the infirmary. *'Your heart wasn't beating, and your chest was still – and there was snow falling outside, little flakes, thin snow like it is tonight, and it really was a beautiful sight, William. It was still and it was silent.'* There had been such tenderness in his voice that, even after all this time, it brought tears to William's eyes. He loved his uncle. The feeling was towering. He wanted to think the same of his mother and his father, but he could not. He stopped himself. He thought he heard Samuel's footsteps floundering in the woodland above, and urgently he pressed on.

One day, he and his brother would both be gone. But before that happened, they were young, and there was still an England to go back to, with all its terraces and streets and scrublands and parks. There was still Lucy and there was still Joshua and if there was still Matthias and Alexander and David and Jonah, well, that was as it should be, too. There could still be a land where the wildflowers flourished on the grasses of the Moor and they sat there together, all of them, watching clouds coming together and parting in the sky. They could still gather like that, every summer, and list every beautiful thing that there was. But if Samuel died out here, if he ran headlong into that death, then the land would open up and the ravines would widen and the ash would spread so that all that was left was a grey devastation, the same as he had seen at

289

Le Bizet. If Samuel was intent on running, he would never be able to tell him the thing he longed to say: that he loved him above all else.

William broke from the scrub and came, at last, to the head of a glade that fell steeply to the valley below. It was a jagged headland onto which he had emerged, and steep ridges of rock rose all about him. Thorn bushes clung to the slopes. The moon, a phantom, rose through the pines. He walked on a little, surveying the land that stretched before him for sight of his brother – and then he saw, on one of the ridges to his left, a silhouette rise: not Samuel, but Flynn.

He was up there, forging a path along one of the ridges above the glade. William set out along the basin of the valley, tracking the ranger on the escarpment above. The grass was thick and coarse; it swayed about his knees. He wove desperately through an entangled arch of briar and when he emerged, back into the night, Flynn had somehow drawn ahead, moving with an ease he thought unnatural along the rim of the valley. His body was hunched low, and when he reached out to part the snarling branches it looked as if he was an animal born of this terrain. William felt thorns lash him as he flew, and wondered that he was not the same. He came to a steep incline of scree, and flailed his way across.

He was lost in the murk with only the ranger to guide him when he heard the guns firing in one of the nearby pastures. Perhaps they had been sounding for days now, or perhaps these were the first loosening shots that warmed the howitzers and cannons. However long it had been, the din was starting to grow. It was a rumble now, but soon it would be an unstoppable choir. William cast it from his mind. He thundered on through the scrub, the horns sounding to summon soldiers in the distance. It was not his war. It never had been. It was not such a little thing as a war that had brought him to these fields.

He stopped. Flynn was turning now, lifting a glass to his eye as he spied into the pastures below. Below, the trail wound into darkness. His brother was gone, but he would not be gone far enough. Instinctively, he felt for the rifle on his back. The cold steel was in his hand, but he knew the hour was nigh; he was set on slaying a man tonight.

VII

William tore along the trail, shadowed on each side by tall fangs of rock. Above him, Flynn had already found the trail. William was certain of it. He saw the way the ranger stopped at each tree or outcrop of rock, stooping there to sift the dirt through his fingers, or trace the prints of boots in the sod. William hung in the shadows, a murderer stalking his victim, and watched. William was not born of this land – he was a boy sculpted by the streets – but here there was a man who knew the ways of the wild. William would use him, if that was what he had to do.

The horizon was lit now with arcing shells and flares rising in the deeps; coils of smoke turned in the darkness, and William knew that the fighting could not be far. Fevered, he scrambled to the top of the crest, and found there a path that ran parallel to Flynn's. Above them, the moon rode up on high, bathing the land in its light. He thought, then, that he had lost Flynn in the shadows – but no, there he was, appearing again along the line of firs, bracing himself against a wall of sheer stone. William rampaged on a little further, and saw, then, that they were perched at the peak of a great headland, below which a pasture was shielded by steep slopes on all four sides. It was not yet dark enough that William could not see his brother tearing wildly through the scrub down there. Intermittently he appeared from the rocks, arms flailing, greatcoat flying, weaving backwards and forwards between the walls of the chasm like a hare beneath the beating wings of a hawk. William stopped. His brother reared from a sudden depression in the land and, though he was lost momentarily in the ferns that flourished in the valley, he was not lost for long enough. In the dim lights of dusk, William could see the rifle, slung across Samuel's shoulders and swaying there as he ran. He willed his brother to whirl around. He willed him to loose shot after shot blindly into the night.

'Run . . .' William whispered. 'Run!' he wanted to scream. He dared to tear his eyes from his brother and lift them to the ridge above, and there he saw Flynn, palming the round into his weapon and stroking the barrel with the heel of his hand.

William's blood beat black. Flynn was raising his rifle. Flynn was going to shoot. There was going to be an end to all this running. One way or another, Flynn had decided that the time was nigh.

He knew that the rifle was on his back, but was it enough? Could he lay claim to another man's life? William saw his brother hurtling, oblivious, through shadows below. Yes, he thought. Yes, he could kill. If it was in Samuel, it was in William as well. He scrambled a little further down the gorge, and braced himself against an outcrop of rock. He drew his rifle from his back. It was light in his hands. His fingers danced up and down the barrel. He broke it back, and palmed bullets into the shaft. It had not been like this in training. There had been cans against a wall. That had been England. That was what Englishmen did. He looked again into the valley below, where his brother ran, unguarded, into the gloom. He was a fool. He was a fucking fool.

As he broke free from an outcrop of scrub, Samuel turned his head to the vaults above. It was a strange thing, as if he himself was praying to the constellations. William choked. Why did his brother have to pray? What daemons sat on his shoulder and whispered to him their words of hate? What had become of the bundle, sticky and warm, that had been pressed into his arms on that evening that he dreamt about? How had it come to this? How had it come to what had happened that day on the Moor? William knew that there was nothing to which he could point. He knew it was not one thing. It was a thousand little things that flourished and grew and entangled together – and blossomed with a rock in a hand.

Too late, William took to his gun. A lone shot rang out in the darkness – and, in the rushes below, his brother fell.

William tore down the track through the trees. He had nothing any longer: no packs to weigh him down, no gun with which he might drive Flynn back. He had cast it all aside as he charged. And there Samuel lay, head craned back at an unnatural angle, mouth half-open and tongue lolling from lips.

'Shit, Samuel. Shit, Samuel.'

William tried to cross the bare expanse of dirt to reach his brother, but the fallen boy twitched and his head snapped round. He was breathing, each breath long and laboured, and there was something quelling about the way he looked upon William. The bullet had found that stretch of flesh between his breast and his shoulder. William stalled.

'Samuel?'

As he stood there, watching, William became aware for the first time since Béthune of the way the wound at the back of his head burned. It was screaming out, now, bawling with an anger that only William could understand. His eyes locked with Samuel's. Out there, even now, Flynn was thundering through the trees. He pictured him vaulting jagged rocks and fallen boughs in the race to find his quarry. William stepped a little forward, close enough now to hear each breath choking in Samuel's throat.

'Samuel,' he said. 'Samuel, is it bad?'

Samuel heaved.

'You followed me . . .' he breathed.

William moved forward. Then, just as before, again he stalled.

'You keep on following me.'

'Samuel?'

'I thought I told you not to follow.'

William rushed forward. Samuel was writhing there in the grass. His head swayed. He dropped to the earth beside him, lifted him, and saw the tear where the bullet had come through his shoulder and disappeared into the night.

'Samuel.'

'I'm going to die.'

William wrenched.

'You're not going to die.'

Samuel might have laughed, then. William could not be certain.

'Take my gun,' he said.

'Samuel?'

'Take it!' William's brother growled. 'If Flynn comes, if Flynn finds you here . . .'

William looked, plainly, at his brother.

'I'll shoot him down.'

'The hell you will. You don't have it in you.'

He was laughing, then. They were both laughing.

'You'll tell Uncle Joshua?'

William looked at his brother's face. Slowly, it was draining of all colour, a gaunt and pallid face banked in curtains of black hair. He turned, fleetingly, over his shoulder, imagined

295

that Flynn might come careening out of the undergrowth before he dared take another breath.

'I won't have to tell him a fucking thing,' William insisted, sinking to the sod.

'You should never have left Leeds. I didn't mean for you to come after me. They'll hunt you down as well.'

'Oh Christ, Samuel.' William bent low. He scrabbled at his brother's breast, tearing his own shirt free that it might staunch the scarlet spray. 'Every time I walked those streets it was on me. I couldn't walk those streets without you. You're there in every piece of brick and mortar. We both are. I couldn't stay there, knowing where you'd gone.'

'William, please . . .'

'You're my brother,' he said. 'You always were. I didn't stop thinking about it. I dreamt about it, back when I was sleeping. You're my brother, Samuel. Did you think a thing like that was so easy to forget?'

'Don't say that.'

'Did you think I'd leave you out here? Did you really think I'd do that? We were boys together. We were going to be old men. Sitting on a bench. Walking on the Moor. That's what I thought. That's what I think.'

'Like Uncle Joshua and Father?'

'No,' said William. 'Not like them at all.' He hesitated, only for a second, the words lodged in his throat. 'I never said it, Samuel. I never thought you didn't know. And I don't care what you thought about me that day. It doesn't mean a thing. I love you, Samuel.'

William's arms tightened around his brother. He could feel, through their matted uniforms, the fervent beat of Samuel's heart. His hands were red and sticky.

'Oh, William, I wish I could enjoy all the little things of life. The sun on my face in the morning. The dew on the grass.

Waving to strangers in the street. But it isn't . . . It isn't for me. Not after what I've done. Not knowing what I am.' Samuel writhed. He pressed his hands hard to the wound. 'I'm sorry, William. Jesus, I'm sorry. I was sorry before I did it. It's not like Matthias and Alexander think it is . . .'

William's eyes welled. 'Fuck Matthias and Alexander,' he growled, holding tight to his brother. 'And fuck our Mother and fuck our Father.'

'They can go to Hell . . .'

'And we won't go and fetch them . . .'

'I didn't mean it. It just happened. It just was.'

'I know.'

'It wasn't a plan I had.'

'I know that as well.'

'It was just in me. It's been in me since we were boys. And now – now it's out . . .'

'It doesn't mean a thing.'

'Jesus, William, I can't see a thing. I can't hear the shells any more. Fuck, William, it got cold quick. It got cold horrible quickly, William. It got fucking cold.'

William came over the ridge. Samuel hung limp in his arms, lolling there like some childhood doll. The devastation stretched before them. He did not know how far he and Samuel had come in their flight from Flynn, but he saw now that the land was consumed. From high on the crest of that valley he could see them tumbling from their holes in the ground, a thousand boys like he and his brother, daggers in their fists, gas masks slung upon their backs. They swarmed. He could see the other boys too, the guttural boys, the lads from Prussia and Bavaria and everywhere in-between, as they massed on the other side of the greyness. From somewhere, men on horses reared and rode like chargers in some medieval skirmish, while on the other flank a great metal hulk rolled forth on its rutted tracks.

Samuel stirred. William was certain that he stirred, for he heard him moan. It was a beautiful sound, like singing – but he was gone again now, still and silent, and William started to thunder down the slope. He came, at last, to the bottom of the escarpment, where the grasses were perished and the land flayed bare. Mounds had risen here, ugly heaps of earth where men had burrowed into the ground, while the shell of an old farmstead stood, strange and alone, in the vast grey surrounds. William lurched on, and the scar at the back of his head moaned. A horrible thing, it was, like dying. He saw, half-buried in the earth, an old farmer's plough, its harnesses streaming like banners in the wind.

Samuel was light and limp as William came between the mounds, the world opening before him in swathes of brown and black. He dared to look back, up the towering slope, and saw, standing there like some archer on the parapets, the figure of Flynn silhouetted against the clouds. His long hair was blasted by the wind. William could see the way that it flew. He stopped, and felt the earth rise about his boots. He must have looked so insignificant from up there, a mere mark on the churned land below, and yet somehow he knew that Flynn's eyes bored into him and his brother. He breathed deeply, and he turned, as with a great effort he drew his boots from the mire. Onward, and onward, and onward he went. He would not look back. Somewhere, a violent explosion rocked the ravaged fields. No doubt boys fell out there, never to see England again. But not William. William would not fall. Not while there was life still seeping out of his brother.

'Put him down, William.'

Flynn emerged from a crevice between the mounds. His rifle was already drawn, lifted high, and pressed hard against his shoulder. With a black serpent's eye, it stared at William and his sleeping brother.

William dragged himself forward. Flynn mirrored the motion. An arc of shells cut a trail through the vaults above them, carving their craters somewhere on the other side of the mounds. Samuel's body tensed, and for a second it might have been that he was stirring. Then he was limp again, lolling there uselessly, cradled in William's arms.

William knew he could not run. The earth was already rising about his ankles, and it was all he could do to keep himself from sinking.

'And if I put him down?'

'He might live.'

William looked up. The sky was a kaleidoscope. It came apart in fragments, shifting in synchronised patterns, mortars rising, shells descending. There was nothing up there, beyond that veil. He squeezed Samuel tight, hoped that he might feel his brother's hands tighten around him. But, again, there was nothing. The world swelled and tore around them, but here there was only stillness. He rocked his brother. There were no angels watching over him. There never had been. If such a thing existed, they had been watching William for all his life, dragged him back even from death – but, always, Samuel had been alone. William felt sick for him. He heaved himself forward, laid his brother down on the sod. The earth was packed hard at the foot of the mounds, but still its thick fingers began to grope at his body.

William spun, feral, upon Flynn.

'And me?' he hissed.

'They might look kindly on you.' Flynn shifted forward. 'They're not animals. They just make war. They need braves in their battalions. They might yet be swung by a story like yours.'

Flynn's lips were curled as he came forward to look upon Samuel's recumbent form. William saw that smile, and his blood beat black. 'They might yet be swung by a story like yours.' Even here, at the end of everything, the story went on: the good son and the bad; the hero and the coward. Even here, in this chaos of guns, the words that had been spewed by his mother and his father and the men of Hyde Park were being sung. Well, William had never meant it to go that way. William had never held with that. And if the world was to decree that he should live for running and his brother should die for the very same crime, well, he would not hold with that either.

Flynn was still speaking, but in the hurricane William could not hear a word.

'It wouldn't have been this way if he hadn't kept running,' he finally said.

William choked, then. 'Then help me?' he breathed. He gagged on the words. 'Help me with him,' he went on. 'He can't die, Flynn. Not like this. Not here.'

Flynn nodded. There was a flicker of something victorious on his face, but William would not stoop to see it. He stepped back and watched as the ranger advanced, watched as he propped his rifle against the mound and bent low to find Samuel's pulse, to feel the life that even now ebbed out of him. William was staring at the back of Flynn's head. The bastard was pressing two fingers to his brother's neck. He was making a show of it. Some preposterous performance. The sound of shells about them rose to a violent crescendo, and then slowly faded. There was only a second of hush before the wailing started all over again. William shuffled forward, made sure that his boots were not being drawn into the sod. It was a simple thing to lift Flynn's rifle from the mound. It was a simple thing to break back the barrel and make certain it was loaded.

'Will he really die out here?' asked William. He cried out the words, eager to be heard.

'I don't know,' said Flynn.

He turned. He saw the rifle. He froze in the glare of its empty, black eye.

And that was all that William needed. A look. That was all it would take to end things for ever. An almost incidental thing. The flicker of an eye. The ranger shifted, but he would never be fast enough. Could William lay claim to another man's life? It was not a question any longer. He had said it long ago: he would be low down and he would be dirty; he would be everything that Samuel was, if only he could come out here and bring him back. The scar on his head was searing. He stroked the trigger.

There was no sound as he squeezed. Lost in the maelstrom, the bullet made no noise – but, all the same, Flynn toppled into the earth.

There were tents raised on the furthest side of the farmsteads. William saw them as he came between the mounds. Fleetingly, he saw the lines of trenches and everything that lay beyond: banks of rolled wire, craters in the earth, boys smeared there against the ground, never to go home. He dropped again, so that all of that was gone from sight. A trail of men crossed the paths ahead of him, stretcher-bearers ferrying the fallen out of the deep, and William heard horses bray for the first time. He lurched forward. He lost his footing in the deepening mud – and now he was on his knees, still bearing his brother aloft, and now he too was sinking beneath his burden. Like mammoths in a prehistoric tar pit, they were, locked there in a frozen waltz. He wrenched against himself and, somehow, he tore one foot free of the mire. He cried out, but they were not words that gushed from his lips. He tried to find some purchase, to tear his other foot free – but all around there was only the thick mud, and again he could not move. He wanted to pray, but prayer had never ridden to his rescue in the past. And yet he could feel the warmth running down his hands, his brother's life disappearing as together they sank, and if it was prayer that would save him, well, William was not stubborn enough to resist that. He craned his head to look at the churning skies above, and thought for a moment that they were trapped in some vast underworld cavern, in which there was no sky but only a distant roof of rock. No, there was no God up there who would save them. There was no one to whom he could direct those prayers. He knew that, now. He struggled again, and then he cried out.

'Somebody!' he called. 'Anyone!' he wailed. He saw, then, that a nurse shifted on the other side of the tents, and two men tumbled from a field ambulance hidden behind the nearest mound. They came together on the trail and, faces drawn in consternation, they peered down at him, this ugly creature being spewed out by the sod. 'Please!' he cried. 'You've got to help me! There's been . . .' He stopped, then. Already, they were coming towards him. He felt his body shift in the dirt, and he strained to keep Samuel aloft. The sobbing of his scar was rising to join the unholy din, and he knew, then, that he too was fading out of all thought. 'There's been an accident,' he breathed.

Epilogue

It spread out before him, and it was terraces and chimneystacks and redbricks and slates – everything he had started to forget. At the head of the path, he looked back at the brother who trailed in his wake, and waited for him to reach the edge of the trees. They both moved under their separate burdens now. A reef of white cloud turned wearily above them, and as they walked that familiar causeway, the shadows spread and joined and disappeared. The Moor fell away and the redbricks rose.

Summer's end. The final days. Samuel had imagined he was coming back to some land as changed as the fields and farms on the other side of the water, but they walked now through the old haunts of their childhood, a landscape set in stone and time, and he knew that lands such as theirs did not change. Here there were the same spires, and here the same rooftops, and here the same snickets and lanes. He was treading the boards of his past now, but it would not be for long.

Beside him, shouldering packs, William too surveyed the land that he had fled. And if it seemed to Samuel that he was wandering back into a world carved out of granite, immune even to the ravages of time, it seemed to William that he was on virgin territory, unmapped and unexplored. He saw the same sights he had seen since the days before he could walk, the hills and streets that had crafted him, and it was as if he was studying the wilted photographs of someone else's past. William still recalled the prophecy of his father: we can come through this, but we will not be the same men who wandered unknowingly in. In this, at least, his father had spoken the truth. William had let his hair grow long, but underneath that the marks of the Moor still blazed. He wore stubble, too, the thick strands of his first beard coiling along the line of his jaw. It was a different face that blinked back at him whenever he peered into a looking glass, now. But perhaps it had been different from the moment he awoke in that infirmary room, with the ghosts of soldiers shifting about him. He looked back, over his shoulder, and fancied he could see that building's spires in the distance, poking through the tops of the trees. It was smaller than the hospice to which he and Samuel had been ferried, but still it stood there, grimly defiant. In the end, he had not come so very far.

They came between the trees, and though they both must have thought of it, neither paused on the edges of that patch of land in which William had been felled. They were high on the Moor here, and the first familiar terraces could be seen through the scrub. Abreast of each other, they meandered down the hill. There was not a soul to be seen, and for a moment it might have been that they were the only two to survive the carnage over the water. For a while, nothing else existed: Elisa and Jacob and bayonets and battalions; all that was dust.

They followed, instinctively, an old trail of trampled earth, where the grass had long ago learned not to grow. Gorse grew on the banks here, and as it parted they came to see the streets to which they were bound. They did not need to plot a course. They had walked the route a thousand times before, conspiring together to keep it from their father. It had been a secret voyage then and, so they supposed, it was a secret voyage now. The streets would give them up in the end, but for a little while, at least, there would be peace. Joshua would be there and Lucy would be there – and Jacob would be there, too, if somehow he had walked unscathed from the battle. They would meet in that snarl of streets where Woodhouse ran into Little London, there to drink and dance and not be compelled to share the stories of all they had seen and done. For the first time, there would be lights strung in the doorway of Joshua's house. And if, after that, they had to wander back to the old house, there to make up the bed and hang shirts in the wardrobe and put the lead soldier back on its shelf, well, that could wait. There would be another day, and another after that.

'What will we tell them?' asked Samuel.

William gave an idle shrug.

'They won't ask,' he answered.

Those had been good days to get lost. There had been thousands of men left for dead like Samuel and his brother, and perhaps disappearing among them had not been the strangest magic they performed in those months. When they awoke, the guns still sang. They might have been in any of the foreign fields in which war was plied, then – in France or Flanders or Germany or any of the fiefdoms beyond – but it mattered little to them; it mattered only that they were awake. It had been a clearing station of vast proportion, an untamed sea of stretchers and tents through which horses drew traps and nurses of every nationality weaved. In the eye of that storm, Samuel lay beside William, and though his wounds had been dressed and a poultice pressed to his flesh, it was with a death rattle that he spoke, and with sweat streaming unchecked down his cheeks. He had begged William to run. He had been plagued with the thought of what might happen to his brother on his account, and through fevered eyes he had implored William to flee. But William did not flinch. He knelt at his brother's side and he told him that it was done, that Flynn would hunt them no longer.

'I'm sorry,' Samuel had said, knowing for the first time the depths to which he had sent his brother.

'I don't care,' answered William.

For endless nights William, too, lay among the dying men.

And if he did not seem as afflicted as Samuel, his wounds did not go unnoticed by the nurses who looked over their flock. They tended to his scar and they bathed his head, and though it must have seemed to them a strange wound to come out of the battle, they had perhaps seen stranger, more terrifying things in the course of their work. They did not ask William about it, just as they did not ask Samuel. They told him only one thing: that England would look after its sons; that the transports and ships were already wheeling into place.

As they awaited that new dawn, William spent his nights writing letters, carefully composing each sentence, wielding his pen with as much vigour as the boys around him had once wielded their bayonets. He had written to Joshua first, for that had been easy. He tried, at first, to recount everything that had been since he embarked from Leeds: the men who had trained him to wield a bayonet, the transports that took him through the Flanders mud, the night he spent with Flynn, crouched there in the firelight as the shells arced overhead. But soon he discovered that his was not the story to tell. He wrote only one thing, then. 'We are coming home,' he had said, and there the letter had ended, for both of them knew the story that was loaded into those four simple words. He had written to Lucy as well, for although he knew that when last they had spoken, the bitter words had flown, he knew too that she waited for his signal. It would be the dying days of summer when they finally reached home, and perhaps there would yet be a few weeks of sunshine in which the three of them might wander the city from end to end, tracking cats and watching strangers because they had nothing better to do.

William had not written the final letter. He had meant to fold the page in its envelope and scrawl his father's name on the front, but as he was inscribing the first words Samuel had stirred and he had known, at last, that there was no letter to write. There

306

were no reparations to make. There never had been. He had brought Samuel water instead, and asked of him what they should do. The land around them was still in uproar, but every day the transports wheeled through, ferrying the fallen men to the hospices back home. Every day men came and men rose and men died. It would be a simple, silent thing to lose themselves among them.

'Back to England?' William had ventured.

For a long time, Samuel did not answer. A nurse passed and cupped a hand to his face, and then passed on. There was more to think about, now, a life that was not bordered by the railway to the north and the moorland in the south; the world was bigger than the English terrace and stretch of scrub that had once been his sentence. He hardly dared think that it had started on top of the Moor, that it had started years before that, when he was barely a boy. He tried to picture how it would be, and for the first time it was not the redbricks and the smokestacks bearing down upon him that came to his mind. He thought about Lucy and Joshua and, if he thought about the city at all, it was only as a silhouette of townships clinging to the hillsides, not some sprawling monster from fable waiting to ensnare him in its webs. There was a world out here, and perhaps one day it would welcome him back.

'Back to England,' Samuel had breathed.

There was another wanderer on the Moor now. Below them, the figure crossed their path, a girl from the terrace dressed in red pleats and with no shoes on her feet, a beautiful urchin walking there through the summer grass. Samuel thought of Lucy, waiting for him down in that snarl of streets where Woodhouse ran into Little London. He had been imagining seeing her since the ships first brought him back to English shores – and, if he did not mean to linger in these terraces for long, he would at least stay long enough to tell her that she had a permanent piece of his heart, that there were some things of a boy's youth even he did not want to shed.

They came, at last, to the edge of the scrub, the clouds above them shifting and coming apart. Autumnal sunlight dappled the rooftops below: on one side, the rolling slates of Burley; on the other, the ridges of Woodhouse that bled into Sheepscar and the countless rotten burghs beyond. Along the thoroughfare, one of the ancient ragmen turned his head to look at the brothers, and though Samuel lifted his hand in vague recognition, the vagrant did not do the same. Samuel looked closer, and decided he could no longer tell which one of the streets' spectres it was. And did he feel sad, then? Did he know that something was finished for ever? He followed the path of the old man with his eyes, watched him bow low to cup an aged hand around the muzzle of a bedraggled dog come snouting out of its yard. Some vestige of his past self must have remained, for it was a sudden pang that came to his breast. He felt, underneath his clothes, for the dark knot of skin that signalled the path of Flynn's bullet through his flesh, his own mark to carry with him until the end of his days. Above his breast and below his shoulder, sometimes it still burned. He supposed it sang in chorus with the wound that William wore. He supposed he did not want it to fade for ever.

Together, they descended the last stretch of scrub. On the banks at the side of the road, the flowers of summer's end were still in bloom: willow herb and buttercup and dog rose.

'You don't have to,' one boy said to his brother.

'I always had to,' his brother replied.

And neither said a word as they followed that road, the two brothers, living still, side by side, each carrying the other's packs as they walked, one last time, through the city where they were raised.

THE END

Acknowledgements

Thanks to: WD, KCS, PEW, CAM – and Amy.